DAYS LIKE TO

Rachel Ingalls grew up in Cambridge, Massachusetts. She has had various jobs, from theatre dresser and librarian to publisher's reader. She is a confirmed radio and film addict and has lived in London since 1965. She is the author of several novels and collections of short stories.

by the same author

DAYS LIKE TODAY

Rachel Ingalls

faber and faber

First published in Great Britain in 2002
by Faber and Faber Limited
3 Queen Square London WC1N 3AU

Typeset by Faber and Faber Ltd
Printed in Scotland by Omnia Books Limited, Glasgow

A CIP record for this book
is available from the British Library

ISBN 0–571–20590–9

2 4 6 8 10 9 7 5 3 1

Contents

DAYS LIKE TODAY

1 Correspondent

Joan met Max when she was working at the library. She hadn't seen him come in because she was reading a book under the counter but she heard him and, as he approached the desk, she prepared to release her attention from the page.

Every day she read books and magazines, only occasionally looking at a newspaper and then often preferring the less respectable ones that had the scandals and amazing stories and the little snippets of weird fact. At the end of the previous week she'd read that – according to the latest research – four out of five women succeeded in business, whereas three out of five men failed. She'd been wondering about the statistics for most of the morning. Were those numbers just for a few countries? Did they include only particular trades or types of job? One of the other girls at the library had suggested that probably what was meant by business was small businesses started up by a single person who had taken out a loan from a bank: that might make sense, because the women would have to have serious intentions; and the men might just want to raise money to spend on something else.

The best stories, and the one subject that held everyone's attention, found full scope only in the three or four tabloids regularly read by everyone on the staff. Crime was the favorite issue; from the information desk to the archives, crime reports had become an addiction with all the librarians. Whether their need to read about it sprang from fear of becoming the victims of violence or from a suppressed wish to lead a more active, passionate – or even lawless – life, they were so eager to get at the latest installment of murder investigations that often one of them would have to hold the paper and read it out loud to the others.

In recent years there had also been many national and international crises and catastrophes but wartime made the act of killing so lacking in personal detail as to be almost anonymous. That thirty people had died in a mortar attack was horrible but not interesting; that someone had killed someone else was shocking and at the same time fascinating. Everyone had at some point had the wish to murder; most possessed the ability to suppress it. Both the hideousness and the allure were immediately understandable. Murder was a civilian crime and for amateurs. Military matters lacked the personal touch. They were for the professional.

Max's specialty was war. He'd begun on court cases, accidents, political interviews and natural disasters: fire, flood, avalanche, earthquake. Only gradually had he been drawn towards what was to become his chosen field. He'd started with a good ear for languages – that had turned out to be one of his greatest assets: it had allowed him to communicate with all sides in a conflict and then to translate the general sense without being too literal. Experience taught him which people to approach and how to frame questions. And thanks to an ability to speak calmly and clearly while observing turbulent events, his eyewitness accounts sounded real. Most newspaper readers or radio listeners, like Joan, thought that his reports from the front were completely true. What he told them was better than one man's opinion: it was information. After a while it could be considered history – a personal account, but one that didn't twist the facts.

He was at the top now, at the peak of his profession.

Joan, on the other hand, hadn't really started to do anything. She'd just been reading about it.

With her eyes still on the page, she sensed him coming nearer. She picked up her Degas postcard to mark her place in the book. Just at that moment he asked her to find a title for him.

She recognized his voice and she looked up with an expression of delight on her face, but she couldn't place the man in front of her.

As for him, he was so taken with the change in her as her concentration passed from her book to him, that he too felt an agreeable sense of recognition, almost like a sudden appreciation of beauty.

She wasn't beautiful but she was pretty enough to give that impression every once in a while.

He also saw that she liked him and that she was somebody he could talk to.

He spent most of his time talking to people. In war zones and conference centers he talked and listened. And afterwards he'd unwind, also by talking and listening and, sometimes in addition, by making love.

'I know your voice,' she said.

'Do you ever watch the news?'

'Never. I listen. I watched so much TV when I was fifteen that I'll never have to have a set of my own, even if I live to be a hundred. But I do lean on friends every once in a while. Are you on television?'

'Sometimes,' he said, as if it didn't matter.

'By the time I was sixteen, I'd seen every B-feature ever made. It saved my life. Now I go out. Or I do something while I'm listening to the radio. Is this research for a show?'

'Background information. Just to check if my possibly unreliable facts line up with the possibly unreliable history books.'

'My grandfather used to say that history was the great subject. History and law.'

'I think I'd agree with that.'

'I guess most men would.'

'Wouldn't you?'

'Maybe.'

'Why? What do you think the most important subject is?'

'Oh, religion. Not that I've got one, but I've always wished that I'd been brought up in a faith.'

'Why?'

'Well, otherwise everything's just bits and pieces. Nothing to live by.'

'That's a lot better than war. Religious certainties and intolerance can lead to some pretty nasty activity.'

At the mention of war she recognized him: Max Dangerfield, the famous foreign correspondent.

'Oh, my God,' she said, 'that's who you are. Of course.

That recording where you could hear the bombs going off. And then the earthquake. And when you were shot and you kept right on broadcasting. I must be the only person in the world who doesn't know you by sight. How rude of me. I'm really sorry.'

He told her that it was refreshing to meet someone who still listened to the radio. And to find anyone who could remember his work in such precise detail was flattering in the extreme. The trouble with television was that after a certain point audiences tended to think of you as if you were the lead actor in their favorite soap opera or the star who advertised the breakfast cereal. You became part of a pantheon; your appearance on the screen was congenial and reassuring, but nobody really listened to what you were saying.

'Oh, they listen to you,' she said.

He asked her if she'd still be at the desk in another forty minutes or so. He wondered whether she'd come out for a cup of coffee with him.

She told him that she'd have loved to, but she didn't get off work for another two hours.

He repeated the title of his book. There was plenty of reading he could do, he said. Two hours would go by in a flash.

If everything hadn't happened so fast – if there had been a day between his invitation and the evening out – she'd have been too nervous to open her mouth. But while they were talking she'd felt so easy with him that when he reappeared at the desk with the book in his hand, she was elated. She was ready to enjoy herself.

❧

They took a stroll until the buses and subway trains thinned out the rush-hour crowds.

As they walked, their conversation jumped from one topic to another until something he said reminded her of a newspaper report that morning, about a player of loud music and an old couple he'd had killed because they'd asked him to turn the volume down. NOISE THUG KILLER SHOCK VERDICT, the headlines had read. The aggressor himself had received a fairly light sentence: a matter of months. The two boys he'd hired, who had ignited a gasoline trail into the couple's apartment, had each been given a few years. 'That's what I can't figure out,' Joan said. 'Not just that the incredibly painful, terrifying death of two innocent people is only worth a couple of years, but the fact that the really guilty one was the man who hired them and yet he's gotten away with a shorter jail sentence. None of it would have happened if it hadn't been for him.'

'He didn't do the killing.'

'But he started everything. That's the strange thing about the law – it's so unfair.'

'It's merely inexact, like us. It has to cover all kinds of situations and combinations.'

'Subjecting people to that kind of noise – that unrelenting beat – it's a recognized torture technique, a form of assault, a kind of oppression. People who inflict it on someone else think they can do what they like and at the same time diminish everyone else's capacity. It's an abuse of the pow-

ers that freedom should give you. In a free world you ought
to be able to have everything you want without making life
intolerable for the rest of society.'

She laughed a little and felt embarrassed at having talked
so much. 'A completely uninformed view,' she added. It
was then that she realized what had made him ask her out.
It might have been loneliness, but it wasn't. It was desire.
She could have said just about anything and he'd be interested. She wanted to say that without equality there were
no relationships; there was only the oppressor and the
slave, the host and the parasite. Later on she was glad that
she'd shut up for a while. It was his turn to speak. And it
wasn't long before she'd changed her mind about equality,
anyway. Once you were living with somebody, you had to
reorder your ideas.

'The younger generation has always been loud,' he told
her. 'Loud, selfish and careless. I think the only difference
nowadays is that the technology is capable of boosting
sound so high without distortion that most Western kids
are partly deaf. So then, of course, they have to turn the volume up higher and even more of their hearing goes. I think
I'm beginning to suffer some hearing loss myself, from
gunfire and other explosions. But you're right. Noise is
going to become an increasingly unattractive aspect of
modern life unless there's some way of keeping it under
control. In most countries it seems to fall into the category
of environmental pollution rather than simple assault.'

'If you're the one whose walls are pounding with it – like
my friend, Katie – that's juggling with words. Not even

earplugs work against that. She's had to move out twice. The law can't help you against neighbors like that.'

'Of course it can. The law is for people who can't come to an agreement with each other. They need a third party to make a decision that's going to be binding on them both.'

Before she could stop herself, she said, 'And wars are for people who don't want to get along together, no matter what the law says.'

'Is that really what you think?'

'No. It's what I feel. When it's too late, you destroy everything and start again.'

'That's a counsel of desperation. I'd rather have as little as possible destroyed. The big difficulty is getting people to the bargaining table.'

'That's right. After a while, they don't want to talk. They want to rip it all up and walk away.'

'But once you can get them to sit down around a table, you can make them see that there's no need to do that. It's always better to remain friends, even if it's only on paper and you never actually like them.'

'Isn't it harder to make them listen when they're in the same room with each other?'

'On the contrary. You throw a bone to one side and then you slip a tidbit to the others. And if you time it right, pretty soon they're accepting things they don't want, so that they can have what they do want. They'll even give up an advantage in the hope of gaining a different one. No. The difficulty is getting them there in the first place.'

*

before your teenagers drive you crazy, read this!

Battlefield wisdom
for stressed out
parents

Nigel Latta

 HarperCollins*Publishers*

National Library of New Zealand Cataloguing-in-Publication Data

Latta, Nigel, 1967–
Before your teenagers drive you crazy, read this! : battlefield
wisdom for stressed-out parents / Nigel Latta.
ISBN 978-1-86950-713-8
1. Teenagers. 2. Parent and teenager. 3. Parenting. 4. Teenagers
—Family relationships. 5. Adolescent psychology. I. Title.
306.8740835—dc 22

First published 2008
Reprinted 2008 (twice), 2009 (twice), 2010
HarperCollins*Publishers (New Zealand) Limited*
P.O. Box 1, Auckland

ISBN: 978 1 86950 713 8

Cover design by Wide Open Media, www.wideopen.net.au
Cover image courtesy of Masterfile Images
Internal text typesetting by IslandBridge

Printed by Griffin Press, Australia, on 70gsm Classic used
by HarperCollins*Publishers* is a natural, recyclable product
made from wood grown in sustainable forests. The manufacturing
processes conform to the environmental regulations in the
country of origin, Finland.

contents

preface

the rudest 13-year-old girl in the world

She didn't even look up as I walked into the room, instead she picked angrily at a loose thread in the chair. The thread hadn't begun the day that way, but it was certainly loose now. She had a way of convincing the world that her way was the best way, or more accurately, the *only* way. If she decided that the thread should be loose, then loose it would be. And if you were stupid enough to disagree, she'd rip away at you until you came around to her way of thinking.

She'd come to me because she'd been effectively charged with aggravated granny-napping. She'd approached an elderly woman in a supermarket car park and told her to get out of her car. When the woman didn't comply, she'd grabbed her, pulled her out, put her in a headlock, and started to punch her.

Nice.

Oddly, the police summary of facts stated that as all this was going on — the headlocking and the punching — a security guard had walked up and asked the elderly woman if she knew the young lady. In between blows, the woman informed him she didn't know the young lady. Sherlock Holmes he most definitely was not.

So the young lady in question had been arrested and taken first to the cells and then brought down to the local social work office. I worked out of the office a couple of afternoons a week, seeing kids and families, and this little bundle of joy had been placed on my list. When I'd asked the social workers what they wanted me to do with her, they shrugged their shoulders. Fair enough. She was the kind of a kid that could squeeze a shrug out of even the most steadfast shoulders.

So in I walk, and I have to say I'm curious, I'm interested. Kids like her pique my curiosity, because I want to see how they're wired together. I could see right away she was an angry young thing — it wasn't just her deft upholstery work, it was as if there were dark grey storm clouds hovering permanently above her head. This girl was so angry, she was her own weather system. Planes would be warned to fly around her because of the turbulence.

She was dressed in faded, ripped jeans that hung alarmingly low, as was the fashion with kids her age, and a black Adidas hoody. She had bright red sneakers, and for some strange reason I found myself thinking of Krusty the Clown.

I sat down opposite her and she did that thing kids like her do — that 'I don't see you' thing — where we both know she does in fact see me, but she wants me to know I'm not worthy of the retinal activity it would cause to actually look at me. We sat like that for a minute, and I could feel waves of hostility. She was like an angry, buzzing swarm of bees that curiously resembled a 13-year-old girl.

After a few moments of silence — which I let drift on long enough so she knew I didn't mind it at all — I open my mouth to speak: 'So . . .'

And *boom*, up came her eyes, all venom.

In the jungles of South America, there is a small yellow frog called *Phyllobates teribillis*, or the Golden Poison Dart Frog, which has skin secretions so deadly that the slime from a single frog can kill seven people. It is so deadly that children and dogs have died after drinking from a pool of water into which it has maliciously dipped a single webbed toe.

In that moment, her eyes were all frog.

'*Fuck off, man*,' she spat at me. 'I'm not talking to *you*. You're the fucking ugliest man in the whole fucking *world*.'

Hmmm.

Now, because of my advanced psychological training I was able to immediately deduce somethings that civilians (non-psychologists like yourself) may not have realised: This girl did not like me very much. I also knew she expected that this would throw me off my game, that I might run from the room in tears. Actually, I liked her straight away. You just have to like someone who can be that rude before you've even had a chance to speak. Adults might want to be rude from time to time, but we rarely achieve it with this level of gall. If this kid was any more direct she would have been an assault rifle.

Of course, it goes without saying that I was not offended, or indeed even slightly perturbed by her outburst. First off, I have a number of robust frameworks I use to make sense of teenage rudeness that we'll talk more about later. Secondly, I have spent some time perusing the internet and in my travels have discovered that there are at least three people in the world who are uglier than me: a man in Eastern Europe, a very disturbing farmer from Kentucky, and a woman from Bristol who would almost make a blind man grimace. If she'd called me the fourth ugliest person in the world, I might have blinked; but she didn't. She said I was number one, which was her big mistake. She hadn't done her homework.

I've spent the better part of two decades working with all kinds of teenagers, and in that time I've been called everything you could ever imagine. I've been sneered at by the best, and seen eyes roll far enough to circumnavigate the globe. Over that time I've learned a trick or two about how to play this particular game. She was probably the rudest 13-year-old girl I'd ever met, perhaps even the rudest 13-year-old girl in the world, but I'd had plenty of practice with this stuff.

So I didn't cry and run from the room; instead, I leaned forward in my chair and smiled. 'You know,' I said, 'it's funny you say that, because I used to be a stunningly handsome man, but it just wasn't working for me. So I went to a mate of mine who's a plastic surgeon . . .' I leaned forward just a little more, 'and I asked him if he could fuck me up a little. And as you can see,' I said, pointing at my face and smiling oddly, 'he did a fucking outstanding job.'

Two things happened, very quickly.

The first is that she laughed.

And the second is that she then got instantly even more annoyed that she'd just laughed.

Brilliant.

Needless to say, my response was to become even more determined to make her laugh again.

It's hard for a lot of people to understand this, but I love working with obnoxious teenagers. I love their weird politics, their anarchic philosophies, and their ability to make even the most clear-cut issues as muddy as New Orleans in a hurricane. Most of all, I love the rude, snarly, difficult ones.

The fantastic thing about teenagers is that, as a general rule, they haven't yet learned the adult skill of how to say 'fuck you' in a thousand different subtle ways; they just come right out and say it, which saves time and all the guessing games.

The other upside of working with teenagers is that I get to swear a lot myself, which is much more fun for me. I like swearing, always have, and now I get to do it professionally. Even the toughest, most determinably resistant kid can be won over with a stream of well-honed fuck-this and fuck-thats. I would be ill-suited to the corporate world, where they do their fuck-yous in a much slipperier manner. Me, I like my fuck-yous the old-fashioned way: out in the open for everyone to see.

It is perhaps this great enjoyment of snarly, rude, objectionable kids that has led me to become somewhat of a specialist. I have spent many years now working with kids at the far end of the scale. This has been, by and large, a strange kind of joy. You will meet some of those kids and their families in the pages that follow, but you will also meet some very normal kids as well: everything from teenage armed robbers to highly-strung high-achievers. We'll talk about lazy kids, angry kids, rude kids, scary kids, sad kids, and just plain bad kids. They're all here.

Dealing with teenagers is all about applying a few basic principles. They have youth and energy on their side. We have age and experience on ours. In this book I'm going to give you all the bits and bobs I've distilled from years of working with kids like this one.

Most of all I'm going to show you that the game is far simpler than most of us have been led to believe, in these modern child-centred, self-esteem-obsessed times.

Be warned, though: this is *not* a book about how to be a perfect parent, because perfect parents are a pain in the arse. Perfect parents are annoying and make the rest of us feel bad. Perfect parents are like those kids you went to school with who always had a clean desk, clear skin, and won all the prizes. They may excel, but no one really wants to hang out with them.

Perfect parents are also absolute liars (as there is no such thing as a perfect parent), and their kids tend to grow up to be serial killers, bureaucrats, or sometimes both.

So this, most definitely, is a book about how to be a 'good enough' parent, because good enough really is good enough. Any better than that and you start getting irritating.

Speaking of irritating, let's dwell on reality television shows for a brief moment. In recent years these shows have blossomed like pustulant sores on a plague victim. Don't blame the networks, though — they only make that stuff because we watch it. Reality television is a self-inflicted wound. The reason I bring this up is to highlight the issue of strategy. If you want to be the last one standing and win the million dollars, then you have to have a strategy.

Outwit, outplay, outlast.

What you'll see in the pages that follow is that you can do all three. The prize in this case isn't money, it's your sanity.

To emerge from the grand adventure of raising kids with your sanity intact is a worthy goal. The nice thing is that, by and large, this is a fairly achievable goal. The other nice thing is that you'll also probably enjoy your family more if you're not nuts.

So, before your teenagers drive you crazy, and even if they've already started peeling your fingers from the cliff-edge of sanity . . . read on.

note

The details of the individuals and families I talk about in this book have been changed so that they are not identifiable. Not even the great Sherlock Holmes himself would be able to trace these stories back to their source.

That said, Danger Mouse probably could find the real families, but then he's just a cartoon character so no one's going to take anything he says very seriously. My advice would be that if Danger Mouse shows up at your house and starts asking personal questions, you should probably just slip him some rat poison.

No one ever went to jail for killing a cartoon character.

introduction

bank robbers and fish

The teenage years are the developmental equivalent of a bank robbery. For some, childhood leaves slowly and politely, with gentle demands neatly written on folded pieces of paper passed over the counter with very little fuss. For others, it's as if someone drives a truck through the wall, then rips out all the fluffy childhood stuff, leaving only smoking rubble and insurance claims.

Sometimes it's all very professional, because everyone understands that the other side is only doing their job. Parents must parent and teens must rebel, just like bank robbers must rob and cops must catch them. There is no resentment in such an understanding, no hard feelings or grudges. Other times, it's all gunfire, sirens and cordoned-off roads. In these situations it's clear that no prisoners will be taken, no quarter will be given. All you can do is keep your head down and pray you get out alive.

This book is about how to get out alive.

Having said that, this was a much harder book to write than *Before Your Kids Drive You Crazy, Read This!* Primarily, this was because parents of little kids all tend to have the same core concerns: they want Johnny to eat his greens, poo in the toilet, generally do as he's told, and go to sleep at a reasonable time. So long as we can tick those boxes, most parents of younger children are justifiably happy.

With teenagers, it's more difficult because the issues parents face are *incredibly* diverse.

I started trying to write this book by making up my own list of issues based on all the families I've seen. It was a long list. I decided maybe it would be simpler if I asked parents directly, so

I put a page up on my website asking people to email me with suggestions for topics they'd like to see covered in the book.

I got a lot of emails. It quickly became apparent there were a *lot* of people really struggling to understand what was going on with their children.

It was also apparent there were a *huge* range of issues parents were dealing with; everything from your garden-variety rude 13-year-old boys, to pregnant 15-year-olds with drug and alcohol problems, to 14-year-olds who seem to have made it their mission in life to piss off every single person on the planet. After a while the list was ridiculously long. There was no way I could cover all of these scenarios without making the book longer than Tolkien's, something I didn't want to do, despite the fact that *Lord of the Bling* would make a catchy title. The issues were piling up faster than I could write the words, entirely due to the fact that teenagers have an innate ability to confront their parents with utterly unique problems and situations.

Don't blame them, it's their job.

I was a little confused why — having spent years working with kids with all kinds of problems — it was suddenly so hard to find a way to write about it. I knew what I wanted to say, but for some reason I couldn't get my head around how to do that in a way that would be truly helpful.

So I went back to the drawing-board, or in my case the drawing notepad, because, after all, thinking takes time.

I drew a series of amusing doodles.

I had a coffee.

I watched some television, had another coffee, and doodled a bit more.

I checked my emails.

I went on YouTube and watched every Eddie Izzard, Billy Connolly, and Flight of the Conchords video I could find. They were very funny, but not much help.

I thought briefly about mowing the lawn, but decided against it, checked my emails again, and had some more coffee.

And I pondered; most of all, I pondered.

The problem was, I finally decided, that I was trying to give hungry people a fish instead of teaching them how to fish for themselves. Even if I stayed up all night and wrote all day, there would never be enough time to fix all the individual problems people were having with their variously shaped and individually wrapped teenage children.

Every situation is completely new. No one has ever parented your kids, and, even though you have parented your children, you haven't ever faced the particular issues that today will bring. You don't need to know what to do about things that have already happened; you need to know what to do with the completely unpredictable thing that's going to happen *next*.

Which is why this book is not a fish, because a fish is a one-time-only deal. A fish, both literally and figuratively, has a limited shelf-life. Once you've made fish pie, you're out of options. The next time you're hungry, the cupboard will be depressingly bare. I knew I needed to write something that would help parents when they came up against things that neither of us had even dreamed of yet.

That was when I decided I wouldn't give people a fish; instead, I'd tell them all I'd learned about catching all kinds of fish in all kinds of conditions.

After this *kerplunk* — or more accurately *kersplash* — realization, I thought some more about what it was that *I* do when I'm working with a family. After all, it wasn't as if there's some big fat psychology textbook of answers on my bookshelf about what to do in each and every situation. I didn't have the luxury of ducking out of the room to look up what to do with 16-year-old boys who want to drop out of school to become professional musicians despite the fact they can't actually play the guitar, and who, rather than practising guitar, which might seem the best way to begin a guitar-playing career, spend all their time smoking cannabis and playing video games.

I couldn't thumb through an index to find out what to do with

14-year-old girls who've decided the best way to achieve personal freedom is to become pregnant to a complete stranger — whom they try to find by creeping out their window at 2am and roaming the city streets — because if they have a baby they'll get their own life and then the adults will *have* to leave them alone. I kid you not, I've met more girls than you'd care to imagine who had that exact plan.

Every single time I sit down with a new family, I'm faced with something utterly and completely unique. There are patterns to be sure, but within those patterns there are 1.98 gazillion individual variations.

There is no big fat book for any of us.

Instead, what I do is try to understand what is going on using some tried and trusted bombproof frameworks I keep inside my head (they need to be bombproof to withstand the sustained assault of teenage irrationality), and then apply a few basic principles to come up with a practical, simple plan.

If that doesn't work, I repeat the process and come up with a new plan.

No matter what I come across, no matter how complex it first appears, no matter how hopeless the situation seems, that is what I do: bombproof frameworks, some basic principles, and simple plans.

So it seemed to me that the best thing I could do was to give you all that stuff so you could do it for yourself. Perhaps not surprisingly, then, this book is broken up into five parts:

I Bombproof Frameworks
The nuts and bolts of the things you need to understand to make sense of teenagers' behaviour and what lies beneath the weird stuff they do.

II Basic Principles
The 10 basic principles that underpin the successful navigation of the teenage years.

III Simple Plans

A very simple three-step process to figure out what to do the next time you have no idea what to do.

IV Putting It All Together

Real-life examples of how families have used the strategies and principles that I will talk about to get things under control.

V The End Times

With the plague, and the vampires, and the angry confrontation. More of this later.

It has been my experience that when it comes to teenagers, problems don't come neatly separated off. They are messy. One thing spills over onto another. If parents come in saying the problem is drugs, inevitably you find there are a whole bunch of things going on, which you'll see for yourself in the penultimate section of this book: Putting It All Together. It's never just drugs, or sex, or school all by themselves; instead, it's a big tangled mess of all kinds of things.

Which is why this book is about what to *do* when you don't know what to do. There are no paint-by-numbers solutions for any of us, but if I was to sit down with your family today I'd use these same frameworks, principles and simple plans to work out how I could help you. It doesn't matter whether the problem is that your son is smoking drugs, stealing cars, or both; or that your daughter is rude, pregnant, or both — the strategies we're going to talk about will provide you with ways to understand what is going on for them, and what you can do to help.

Most of all, this book is about what to *do*.

part I

bombproof frameworks

All good generals know that if you're going to win on the battlefield you need to occupy the commanding heights. You need to be able to see what's going on to make the best decisions.

The process of parenting teenagers is much the same. You need to be able to see the big picture even when you're taking fire. *Especially* when you're taking fire.

On the battlefield of parenting, the commanding heights aren't so much about *altitude* as they are about *attitude*.

In my experience, the attitude with which parents approach the task is everything, so in this section I'm going to give you the essential information you will need to develop bombproof frameworks to understand what is happening to your kids, and why they do the things they do.

Once you understand what moves them and why, you might find it all making a little more sense. Or, more accurately, you'll understand why sometimes not much that they do makes sense, and why that's OK.

Essentially, teenagers are not right in the head. That might sound cruel, but that's only because the truth sometimes hurts. They might look vaguely like normal people, but that doesn't mean they are.

Far from it.

If you understand the weird stuff going on in both their bodies and their brain, it's going to make the journey much easier.

1

the first framework

lessons from an amputation

A few years ago I returned home from walking the dog to find that my younger son, still a toddler at the time, was in two parts. There was the larger part, which looked surprisingly relaxed, and the other smaller part, which consisted of the tip of his left ring finger, which lay in a small blood-stained paper towel. He'd cunningly put his fingers in the hinge side of the door just as my older son had closed it. Simple physics had taken care of the rest.

The dog was happy, because he immediately set about clearing up the rather large pool of blood on the floor. My mother-in-law, who is in all other respects a wonderful person but sadly the worst person to have around if someone cuts themselves, was lying on the couch looking green. My wife was holding our little guy, his hand swaddled in blood-stained bandages, and his brother hovered about looking mortified. Blessed with an over-abundance of conscience, he was worried he'd killed his little brother. My father-in-law, having recently retired from a long career in anaesthetics, had things well in hand, so to speak. The bright side of all this for him was that he'd get to catch up with some of his mates down at the hospital, so it wasn't all bad.

After briefly stopping to reassure everyone who needed it — and to drag the dog outside, who by now was red-jowled and well happy — I scooped and ran, decamping the house and heading straight for the hospital. On arrival we were ushered through to a small, white room where knowledgeable people took off the bandages and examined the stump.

'It looks pretty clean,' said the paediatrician. 'I'm sure we can reattach this.'

Great. Then she turned to me. 'Can I see the rest of the finger?'

I frowned. 'The rest of it?'

'Yes, the little piece that was cut off.'

Bugger.

'I uhhh . . . I threw it in the bin,' I said, suddenly realizing that the Father of the Year Award was at that moment slipping rapidly from my grasp.

She looked at me as if I was a fool, which I suppose was fair enough. 'Can you get it?' she finally asked.

I said I could and took off.

I drove like a maniac, figuring I'd explain it to the cops if I got stopped and they'd give me a police escort. I didn't get stopped, but I made few friends on that drive.

The situation at home was less clear than I'd thought. It turned out that our bin was suddenly full of any number of small objects that all looked like the tip of a little boy's finger. I narrowed it down to the two wee bits I thought were the most likely suspects and took off again.

As I repeated my desperate drive to the hospital, I realized this was the first time we'd ever been out with our son and left part of him at home.

I screeched up to the door and sprinted down the corridor like an extra in *ER*. Breathless, I passed the two bits to the nurse. She said one bit was finger and the other was probably orange. I briefly wondered about having the piece of orange reattached, but decided this would be impractical for a number of reasons.

So it was that a half hour later we were walking down the corridor with our poor wee man as he was wheeled off to be stitched back together. We were stressed, upset and worried for our poor little bloke's finger. Partial amputation seemed about the worst thing in the world right then.

At that moment, a woman came around the other end of the corridor pushing a wheelchair. Sitting in the wheelchair was a girl who looked about 11 or 12, wrapped in a blanket with a pink teddybear. She was pale, very thin, and had no hair. Attached to the wheelchair was a chemo bag which dripped clear fluid into a tube which snaked down under the blanket. The mother was chatting to her daughter as they came down the corridor, and even though it was light-hearted stuff I could hear the abject terror beneath it.

As she passed us, she looked at our little man with his bloody bandaged stump and smiled sympathetically, as parents do, but her eyes looked hollow.

Then they were past us and gone.

I do not know what happened to that little girl. I do not know how that story ended.

What I do know is that as soon as they passed us, my wife and I looked at each other: *Harden the fuck up and stop whining* was what we said to each other in that glance. Right at that moment, the partial amputation of his sweet little finger seemed about the least worst thing in the world. At that moment, we truly felt like the luckiest parents in the world.

At that moment, we were.

Problems are *not* relative. Some problems are *way* bigger than other problems. Watching your child die of starvation in a refugee camp in Darfur is, in my humble opinion, quite a bit worse than having a daughter who gets pregnant at 14. Sitting in the paediatric oncology ward waiting to see the leukaemia specialist is a million billion times worse that sitting outside Youth Court waiting for your son's lawyer.

Problems are *not* relative, not even a little bit. Once we forget that, we're on the slippery slope to self-pity, and once you get bogged down in that particular quagmire it's much harder to get going again. I'll take a lawyer's waiting room over an oncologist's waiting room any day.

I'm not saying there aren't times when you're perfectly justified in feeling utter despair, or paralysing fear — it's my belief that both these things are an unavoidable part of the package — but I *am* saying that where there's life, there's hope. As long as everyone's still breathing, you've got options.

Keep it in perspective is all I'm saying, because it could always be worse . . . instead of this book you could be reading one on childhood leukaemia. Someone, somewhere, *is*.

That might not be a nice thought — it's actually pretty jarring — but it's true nonetheless. So the first framework, and perhaps the most important one, is this simple equation:

Breathing = Options

2

the second framework

the weirdness of puberty

Becoming a teenager is both miraculous and incredibly weird. It's like they just get through childhood, having mastered toilet training, walking and learning to read, when suddenly and for no apparent reason their body explodes. They've at last made their peace with the fact that the opposite gender sucks, then they wake up one morning to suddenly realize the opposite sex has all manner of hidden, mysterious attractions. Then they can't stop dreaming about those hidden attractions.

What's more, in a strange and ironic twist of biology, their body picks just this moment — when they desperately want to make an impression on the opposite sex — to completely lose its mind. Suddenly their private places act as if they want to list on the stock exchange, and, just when they start to *really* care about how their face looks to other people, it bursts into a cesspit of oily spots. If you're a boy, your voice turns into a bad trumpet; if you're a girl, you become gangly and awkward and consumed with how your body looks because you know that boys (and other girls) are also consumed with how your body looks.

At the very point in your life when you become concerned with attracting the opposite sex, you inexplicably turn into an oddly shaped, pimply, neurotic freak of nature. It's as if your body has been waiting all these years for a signal to go completely mental.

This is confusing if you're a teenager, but also for parents whose beloved little cherubs suddenly become bristly, bulgy and globally bent-out-of-shape. It isn't just their bodies that change though; sometimes it seems as if everything has gone — reason, good humour, words, the whole works. Sometimes the shift seems almost spiritual, when an angelic daughter is mysteriously replaced with a demonic she-bitch.

How could such a thing happen?

We tend to think of the teenage years as a single event, but the reality is quite different. We become adults through the convergence of two separate processes: the first is puberty, or the physical maturation of the body; and the second is adolescence, or the behavioural maturation of the person. These two processes are distinct yet connected, and their timing and relationship has a significant impact on the adult trying to get out.

The biological clock

We all know a bunch of things happen in puberty, but have you ever stopped to wonder how your body knows *when* to unleash all this stuff? How do our bodies know it's business time?

Well, not surprisingly, scientists — ever a hardworking and curious lot — have done more than just wonder, they've spent a considerable time studying teenagers, castrating hamsters, and messing with sheep to try to find out.

We used to sum up puberty as 'hormones'. There was a kind of simplistic view that somewhere inside them a big bucket of hormones got dumped into their blood stream, they went completely mental for a while, then eventually things settled down.

Well, it turns out that it's a little more complicated. We all have a developmental alarm clock set off when the right combination of growth, available energy stored in our bodies, and time all collide. Once the biological alarm clock has gone off, structures deep in the brain release a special type of hormone which in turn triggers the release of sexual hormones. These lead to physical maturation of the sexual organs and remodelling of particular circuits in the brain.

This all leads to what scientists somewhat awkwardly describe as 'the development of sexual salience of sensory stimuli' and 'the expression of copulatory behaviours in certain social contexts'.

You *what?*

More simply put, it's the combination of hormone release from brain structures and then from the sex organs themselves, which leads to a rampant interest in, and desire for, rumpy pumpy.

Where once there were simply Barbie dolls and Lego towers, there is suddenly make-up and making out. The childhood posters of cars and cartoon characters are replaced with sometimes alarming posters of half-dressed pop stars of questionable morals.

The alarm is going off earlier and earlier

It seems there is a considerable degree of truth to the oft-stated view that children are growing up faster. Most of us think about puberty as something that kicks in neatly on a child's 13th birthday. Not anymore.

In the 19th century, the average age girls began menstruation was 17 years, but by 1960 that had fallen to 12–13 years. Whilst the age of menstruation has remained stable since 1960, the onset of puberty *per se* has continued to drop. The figures vary, but studies from different parts of the world have shown that about 15% of girls begin showing signs of physical development at eight years, with some as young as seven years. Boys are a couple of years behind. The average age of onset of puberty for girls is now age 10 years, and 11.5 years for boys.

There are a number of possible reasons for this decrease, which scientists are currently debating. At the moment the dominant theory is that changes in diet, and more specifically increases in childhood obesity, may be responsible. Pesticides have also been suggested as a possible cause, as have a number of psychological theories. Whatever the reason turns out to be, and it will probably be hideously complicated and involve multiple factors, all we need to know is that there is an increasing gap between the onset of physical maturation and psychological maturation.

Too much, too soon

All of this has great significance for teenagers. Some of them are starting to develop signs of sexual maturity when they are still children. This brings with it all kinds of issues. The painful self-consciousness over a developing body is beginning earlier and earlier, and with that the possibility of problems with other less developed peers.

We've also seen a concomitant rise in the rates of eating disorders and depression in children. The Children's National Medical Centre in Washington DC is treating children as young as six. Now, whilst America leads the pack in eating disorders, clinics all over the Western world have seen a steady decrease in the age of onset of these life-threatening conditions. At younger and younger ages, our children, and particularly our girls, are being pushed and pulled headlong out the door of childhood before they're ready.

So if earlier onset of puberty is doing the pushing, who's doing the pulling? Consider these consumables for pre-teen girls:

✧ After public outcry, a large British chain of department stores removed a pole-dancing kit from the toys and games section of its website. The kit exhorted the user to 'unleash the sex kitten within'.

✧ Abercrombie & Fitch came under fire for marketing thongs for pre-teen girls with the phrase *eye candy* stitched onto the front.

✧ You can buy padded bras for nine-year-olds.

✧ Or how about a T-shirt for your six-year-old that says *So many boys, so little time*?

Add to that the sexualized portrayals of children in all corners of the media, coupled with an increasing tendency for parents to lose confidence in their own judgement, and it's easy to see how things can rapidly get out of hand.

What can be done about all this? Well, the simplest thing you can do is make a stand as a parent about what you will and won't tolerate. Make sure you know what magazines your pre-teen girls are reading, and what they're watching on television. Similarly the best way to stop your pre-teen/teen girls from wearing underwear that says *eye candy* is not to buy it: if you don't want them looking like skanks, don't buy skanky clothes.

This doesn't mean they have to dress like the Amish (unless of course they are Amish, when it's pretty much compulsory), but if you have to pay for the clothes then you have a say in the clothes. There is a world of difference between trendy and skanky, and you can control which side of that line your daughter dresses on. The only reason companies make this stuff is because parents buy it.

So don't.

Sex

Such a little word, such a big issue.

It would probably be the singular issue parents struggle with the most. Like it or not, one way or another you're going to have to deal with it. The whole point of puberty is about making babies — it ain't just for show. The very idea that our children are capable of making babies is enough to make your heart skip a beat, but the cold, hard truth is that they are, and they do just that at increasingly younger ages. Go to any maternity ward in the developed world and you'll find mums who might be as young as 12 years old.

Babies are having babies. The question is: how do you stop *your* babies from making babies?

Some people opt for the approach of simply ignoring the problem and hoping it somehow sorts itself out. Not a good strategy. You need to ask yourself who you want educating your daughter about sex. You or her dropkick 17-year-old boyfriend? Do *you* want to educate your son about sexual relationships or leave that up to his mates?

To help you a little with that decision, these are some of the things many teens actually believe about sex:

- ☆ Oral sex isn't really sex.

- ☆ It's OK to give a 'friend' oral sex.

- ☆ I won't get pregnant, because I always tell him to pull it out before he 'does it'.

- ☆ I don't need to worry about diseases, because he said he hasn't done it with anyone else.

- ☆ She said I didn't have to wear a condom, because she doesn't sleep around.

- ☆ Only gays get HIV.

- ☆ All my mates say they're having sex, so I'm the only one who isn't.

- ☆ It's just sex, what's the big deal?

- ☆ He said if I loved him I'd do it.

- ☆ If she does get pregnant, at least all the adults would have to leave us alone.

If that isn't enough to scare the crap out of you, then you weren't really paying attention. If you have teenagers, you'd better make damn sure they get the right information from you, because the quality of instruction they'll get from their friends begins with 'c' and ends with 'rap'.

Talking about sex with your kids

Some people worry that talking to teens about sex and contraception will make it more likely they'll try it. Actually the opposite is true, because research consistently shows that teens who talk about sex with their parents are more likely to postpone having sex, and more likely to use birth control when they do.

It's also important for fathers to understand that they need to be involved in discussions about sex with their teenage daughters. This is not simply 'women's stuff' to be delegated to mothers. Your daughter needs to know what you think, and she needs to hear from you that she is special and should be treated with respect. She's unlikely to get that message from her boyfriend. It's also interesting to note that research shows that girls who have a closer, more emotionally supportive relationship with their fathers tend to postpone the decision to have sex.

Like most difficult subjects, the best way to talk about it is just by talking about it. There is no magic formula, so don't sweat it too much. To help you a little, I've included a few of the standard tips below:

 ☆ If you don't know how to start the conversation, you can always use television as a way in. There's enough sex on television to start a million conversations.

 ☆ If you're embarrassed, use humour as a warm-up. Use words like shagging, doing the horizontal mambo, burping the worm in the molehole, four-legged frolic, rumpy pumpy, or playing the game of twenty toes . . . Anyway, you get the idea.

 ☆ Once you're past the initial giggling and discomfort, it's important you give them accurate information to help them make good decisions. Euphemisms are an OK warm-up, but park them at the door.

 ☆ Be direct. A colleague who delivered Sex Ed classes as

part of a programme for teenage boys used to get the boys to rub the inside of their cheeks to demonstrate what the vagina feels like when it is lubricated. It was a strange thing to watch a room full of teenage boys feeling up their own cheeks, but it was a good demonstration of the point.

☆ Ask them what they would like to know about sex; and if you don't know the answer, find out. This is one time when you shouldn't try to bluff your way through the conversation.

☆ Don't freak out if they do ask lots of questions — it doesn't mean they're actually going to go out and do all this stuff. They just want to know about it.

☆ Ask them about how they would deal with someone pressuring them for sex. Make sure they have strategies they can use. You'll also want to include a good discussion about how alcohol and drugs make them more vulnerable.

☆ Ask them what they would do if they saw someone being pressured for sex at a party, or someone trying to take advantage of girls who are too drunk to know what's happening. They need to know it's not only OK to step in and stop something bad from happening, but they are just as much to blame if they see something bad happening and don't try to stop it.

☆ Tell them about your values when it comes to sex. It will help them to know where you stand on issues like sex before marriage and contraception.

☆ The other thing you can do is make sure they have access to books, pamphlets, or appropriate websites if they want to find out some things for themselves.

The other important point is to make sure the conversation doesn't stop there. This is not something you can tick off your list and move on from. Don't get all intrusive about it, but let them know its OK to come and talk to you about it at any time. The more you talk with your kids about this stuff, the safer and healthier they will be.

Sexuality

Just as an increasing interest in sex is part of puberty, hand in hand with that — so to speak — is the process of working out things like sexual orientation. It's quite normal for teenagers to have a mixture of feelings about sexuality and sexual orientation. Most boys become, at least publicly, intensely homophobic. They act as if 'gayness' is something you can pick up from a dirty toilet seat. That said, many young men have a mixture of feelings about both girls and boys.

Obviously, it's not a great idea to rock up to your kids and say something like: 'So, have you figured out which team you're gonna play for?'

Instead, you should look for ways to raise the issue indirectly, and again television is great for this. All you have to do is wait for it to come on the television and then you have an inroad to the discussion. You can ask your teen what he or she thinks about people who are gay or lesbian. What do their friends think? Do they think it's a good thing? A bad thing? Irrelevant?

I know this is a tricky one for some people. Some parents have strong views about it all. Fair enough. Just make sure that you make it OK for your kids to be who they are. If your son or daughter is struggling with issues around their sexuality it can be extremely difficult for them, and they will need your support.

If you have issues about this stuff, then figure out how to deal with it. If you're stuck, then find someone to talk to who can help you. Your kids need to know that, whichever team they decide to bat for, you will always be on theirs.

So what does it all mean?

Basically, puberty is a time of enormous physical, psychological and emotional changes. It's not surprising that teenagers feel a little out of sorts. They're having to adjust to all these changes, pay attention at school, do their homework, and deal with first relationships, first kisses, and about a billion other things.

With all that in mind, just try and be a little patient.

Low-down on puberty

★ Puberty is a time of significant physical change, as well as significant emotional and psychological change.

★ It can be just as confusing for them as it is for you.

★ The age of onset of puberty is decreasing, so kids have to deal with this stuff at younger and younger ages.

★ If you don't want them to wear skanky clothes, don't buy them.

★ Talk to your kids about sex and sexuality.

★ The more you talk about sex with them, the better prepared they will be to make good choices.

3

the third framework

mad uncle jack

It's been said that all roads lead to Rome, but I'm not sure that's true. I remember once in 8BC (eight years Before Children), my wife and I were driving through Italy, trying to find Rome. You wouldn't think it would be that hard, because Rome is a pretty big place. Strangely, we discovered that no roads led to Rome, not a single one. We came within spitting distance of Rome at one point, then the road inexplicably veered off towards Germany. It was a stressful and difficult drive that tested our relationship.

'Why don't you just stop and ask someone?' she suggested.

'That's a waste of time,' I replied, somewhat curtly.

'Don't be such a male,' she said.

I rolled my eyes in the way long-suffering husbands do: 'They all speak *Italian*. What would be the bloody point?'

'The point,' she said, with the patience of a long-suffering wife, 'is that they can *point*.'

I thought for a moment. She was right, of course — pointing was a distinct possibility. But pride was in control at this juncture, so I drove on for another half hour or so before finally agreeing to ask someone to point us in the direction of Rome. Frustratingly, a man who spoke very good English not only pointed us in the right direction, but drew a map and explained it to us as well.

'See?' my wife helpfully added as we drove into Rome a mere 40 minutes later. 'I told you.'

I saw nothing, and even if I did I would never have admitted she was right.

Now, whilst on the basis of my personal experience I'm prepared to debate the fact that all roads lead to Rome, I know unequivocally that all difficult teenagers lead to Mad Uncle Jack.

Let me, by way of explanation, introduce you to the Boop family and their darling daughter, Betty.

Mr and Mrs Boop had once been nice people. Not anymore. They'd left niceness behind a hundred years ago when their daughter turned 13. Once upon a time she'd been a princess, and she still was, in a way . . . a princess of darkness. We'll cover the reasons why more in the next chapter, but for now let's just say things were less than rosy in the Boop house.

Mrs Boop started crying before I'd even finished my amusing little introductory spiel. Mr Boop looked similarly distraught, but more resigned. When I asked them to tell me about Betty, it was as if I'd just applied the business end of a scalpel to the business end of a boil. Stuff just poured out.

'She used to be so lovely,' Mrs Boop said, and I could hear the pain in her voice as if it were a wound. She *was* wounded. She had been cut truly, madly, deeply. 'I don't know what happened. She's just so . . . so *horrible* now, so *vicious*.'

Mr Boop nodded sadly, looking stunned, angry and heartbroken, all in the same moment. He was hopelessly out of his depth, pummelled by a daughter who was doing everything except vomiting green bile and spinning her head 360° whilst speaking Aramaic, and trying to help a wife whose heart was broken into a thousand tiny, bitter pieces.

They told me about all the usual hoopla, all the usual hurtful, nasty, spiteful things adolescent girls can produce with frightening ease. Betty had become a horror, and they couldn't understand it. I let them talk for a bit to bleed off some of the pressure.

Finally, when the moment seemed right, I broke in. 'Has she ever called you a bitch?' I asked Mrs Boop.

She nodded sadly.

'A fucking bitch?'

Another sad nod.

'A fucking evil bitch?'

She looked slightly hopeful. 'No,' she said, her voice mirroring the slightly hopeful look.

I waved my hand dismissively: 'Don't worry, that one will turn up soon.'

The little bubble of hope burst, a quiet, barely audible *pop*.

'I think I need to tell you about Mad Uncle Jack,' I said.

They both looked worried I might be about to tell them about a crazed relative of my own. I wasn't.

'Imagine for a moment,' I said, 'that the rest of the family have got together and decided that Mad Uncle Jack should come live with you. Nobody else wants him, because he's mad and he smells of pee. So, they give him to you to look after.'

I looked, they were still with me. 'Then imagine you're sitting watching telly one night. The ads come on and you lean over and ask Mad Uncle Jack if he'd like a cup of tea. He looks at you for a minute, then leaps to his feet: *"Fuck ya,"* rants Mad Uncle Jack. *"Fuck ya, you're a bitch, a fucking bitch . . ."* and then storms off to his room in the basement, cursing and swearing. Now, would you let that ruin your evening or would you just think: *Ah well, it's just Uncle Jack being mad again, no surprises there.*'

Mrs Boop shrugged. 'I guess I'd just think he was mad and I wouldn't worry about it.'

I nodded sagely (not an easy thing to do): 'Would you take it personally?'

'No.'

'Would you wonder if mad old pee-smelling Uncle Jack had a point? Would you start to question your inner bitch-ness?'

'No.'

'So why,' I said, 'would you get upset when Betty does the same thing?'

She shrugged. 'When you put it like that, I don't know.'

'People say that adolescence is a developmental stage,' I

continued, 'but that's a myth. It's actually more like a mental illness.'

And for the first time, Mother Boop laughed.

'When I was a teenager,' I said, drawing on my own history of adolescent craziness by way of example, 'my brother and I would have huge fights over who should put the dish rack away. We would literally fight for 30 to 40 minutes most nights over who should dry it and put it away. There was complicated case law involved, which made the disputes long, involved, technical, and occasionally violent. One of us would wash the dishes, and the other would dry; but for some reason the putting away of the dish rack was the sticking point.

'We were like North and South Korea lined up at the Border, neither one willing to blink. On the occasions we did come to blows, I was prepared to die for the principle that my brother should put the dish rack away because he was still holding the pot lid when I had just put the last spoon in the drawer. I was quite literally willing to lay down my life for the point rather than concede.

'The weird thing is,' I continued, 'we still have that same dish rack at home, and a few years ago I was home for a visit and doing the dishes when I remembered those fights. I timed how long it took me to dry the dish rack and put it away. Three seconds. That's what it took, three seconds, yet it never once occurred to me that the smart thing to do was let the other guy think he'd won, put it away, and just get on with my life. Not once did that ever occur to me. What I did think, without any hesitation, was that if I had to die for something, I would do it for this. I would make my stand over the dish rack, and if I died doing that then at least I could say I was a man of principle.'

The Boops, who now looked a little better, smiled, perhaps remembering their own teenage follies.

'Nutcase,' I said. 'That's what I was, a fucking nutcase. I asked my mum a couple of years ago what she thought as we waged these long battles, and you know what she said?'

They shook their heads.

'She said she thought we were mad. She's a sensible woman, my mum. The single biggest mistake I see parents make is that they take the nasty stuff seriously. If you wouldn't listen to Mad Uncle Jack, why would you listen to Crazy Betty?'

'So we should just not worry about the things she says?' asked Mr Boop.

'Nope.'

'Is there any cure?' asked Mrs Boop, who looked lighter by the moment as she grasped what I was saying.

'Yes,' I said, nodding definitely: 'Definitely.'

'What is it? Medication?'

I shook my head. 'There's only one cure for crazy 13-year-old girls, but the good news is that it works every time, and it's completely organic.'

'What is it?' they both asked together.

'Fourteen. Which we can fix with 15, and follow that with 16.'

They laughed again, which was an altogether better thing than crying.

Now, I don't want to trivialize in any way the tragedy of families coping with teenagers with diagnosable mental illnesses like schizophrenia, depression, eating disorders and the like, far from it, but I am *absolutely* trying to trivialize the nonsense which comes from many kids' mouths as they're trying to find their own way in the world.

You cannot take that stuff seriously, because if you do it will break your heart. No one is going to let Mad Uncle Jack break their heart — maybe a few plates, but not their heart. What we know is that Mad Uncle Jack isn't really seeing the world as it is; he's seeing it through a broken lens, so he gets things a bit mixed up. He might call you names because he thinks you're involved in some plot with the aliens to repopulate the earth with bloodsucking spiders from Mars, but you'd probably not be too offended by that. He might think you're in league with Martian arachnids, but you know you're not, so you don't get all wound up about it.

It's the same thing with teenagers.

What you have to tell yourself is that this is just a passing affliction, a state of confusion that will fade with time. One day, the clouds will part and the sweet kid will be back again, just bigger. Until that time, all you can do is plod along in the rain and don't take it too personally.

This doesn't mean you should accept the shitty behaviour, because you shouldn't — and we'll talk more later about how to respond to the rudeness — but it *does* mean you don't let it hurt your feelings.

The other thing is that, whilst all roads might lead to Mad Uncle Jack, they don't stop there. These same roads lead off into the distance as far as the eye can see, so all you have to do is keep going, and one day you'll find you've left old Jack far behind and your son or daughter is back again. Just keep walking and don't pay him too much heed. Instead, let it flow off your back as if you're the proverbial duck. It worked for the Boops.

Of course, that alone wasn't enough to get them through, there were a few more things that had to be done, but that was what they needed to let their poor, wounded hearts begin to heal.

What we need to do now is take a look inside the head of your average teenager to explain the Mad Uncle Jack metaphor.

Passing madness

★ The most important thing to understand about your teenager is that they're not right in the head.

★ Just as you wouldn't take Mad Uncle Jack's ramblings to heart, you shouldn't take theirs.

★ Don't tolerate rudeness, and don't let it hurt your feelings.

★ It's just a stage — it will pass.

4

the fourth framework

the teenage brain . . . not the whole walnut

There is something a little spooky about walnuts, something a little too deliberate. They look way too much like tiny brains encased in little wooden skulls. Some might say that this is evidence of a divine plan. Others might say that it's simply Nature's grand design repeating; form repeating form.

But my question is this: who's the echo, the walnut or us?

Philosophy aside, the humble walnut is a pretty amazing little beast. Not only are they rich in antioxidants and plant-based omega-3 fatty acids, but researchers have shown that if you eat walnuts after a fatty meal you can reduce the damaging effects of cholesterol on blood vessels. Maybe one day we'll see the McWalnut burger?

Amazingly, despite its spooky resemblance to the walnut, and its incredible complexity, there are no known health benefits from eating a teenager's brain. I'm not aware of any reputable health professional who would recommend a daily helping of teenage brain as a beneficial dietary supplement.

It's also perhaps no great surprise that many parents of teenagers are of the opinion that, aside from any nutritional benefits, the average teenage brain has the functional ability of a walnut. This is, of course, not true. A walnut devotes its whole self to being a fully functioning walnut. Teenagers on the other hand do not possess a fully functioning brain.

Many is the time I've sat with a young person and been reminded that they're not the whole walnut. One young man I talked to some years ago had decided he could outwit the police dog tracking him after he'd committed a burglary by running in circles. His rationale was that this evasive manoeuvre would confuse the dog, who would then become dispirited and give up the chase. Needless to say, this particular young man was limping and heavily bandaged the first time I saw him.

If you need any further proof of the fact that teenagers are operating on less than the full walnut, I suggest you go to YouTube and search under the term 'crazy skateboard stunt', where you will see endless examples which nicely illustrate my point.

Why do so many teenagers do so many patently stupid and frequently life-threatening things? Why do they look at a cliff and see an opportunity to make a great video, while we look at the same cliff and feel a little queasy?

But it isn't just that though, is it? They're also frequently moody, demanding and completely unreasonable. They can take umbrage at the slightest perceived offence, and then use that umbrage to generate emotional outbursts of sufficient intensity to register on the Richter scale. They're more likely to be using alcohol and drugs, and they're more violent than grown-ups. On top of all that, they often make bizarre fashion choices and listen to music that that can variously shock, confuse and appal their parents.

Resisting social pressures is also a lot more difficult for your average teen. In one particularly telling experiment, teenagers and adults were given a simulated driving test where they had the opportunity of being rewarded if they ran a yellow light and still managed to stop before they hit a wall. The teenagers were far more likely than the adults to take increased risks if their friends were watching.

The really interesting thing is that it isn't as if they don't have the baseline ability to make good decisions — they do. In theory, teenagers can make quite good decisions. When asked questions about theoretical situations, teenagers are able to make sensible choices, but in the real world they're nowhere near as sensible. They might be able to say they wouldn't get into a car with a friend who's drunk, but in real life they find it much harder to walk the talk.

So what's going on?

It would perhaps be fair to say that the scene in Quentin Tarantino's *Pulp Fiction* when John Travolta's character, Vincent Vaga, unintentionally shoots his criminal associate, Marvin, in the head as the unfortunate young man sits in the backseat of their car was one of the funniest and most disturbing scenes from the film.

'Oh man,' Vincent says, as he wipes blood and brain tissue from his eyes. 'I shot Marvin in the face.'

'Why'da fuck you do that for?' Samuel L. Jackson's character, Jules, yells at him, understandably annoyed.

'I didn't mean to do that,' says Vincent, more concerned about the mess than poor Marvin. 'It was an accident.'

Profoundly disturbing, but bloody funny. We laughed, but knew that somehow we shouldn't. It was also, funnily enough, very bloody.

Now, whilst this was a great scene, it also highlights an important point: generally, movies are not much help when it comes to understanding brain function. Whilst Hollywood does a great job illustrating how brains look as they explode out the back of someone's skull, it's done a very poor job at explaining much beyond that.

It could be argued that the single biggest step forward in understanding our brains, apart from the guy who first decided just to yank one out and have a look at it, was the development of the MRI or Magnetic Resonance Imaging device. It was originally called the NMRI, where the 'N' stood for nuclear. Understandably, there was a concern that patients might freak out at spending an hour in a small tunnel inside a giant noisy whirling machine whose name began with nuclear, so for marketing reasons they dropped the n-word.

It used to be that we thought the first three years were the point at which there was the most significant brain development, and — don't get me wrong — some amazing stuff happens during that crucial early period, but increasingly we're seeing evidence that the teenage brain undergoes startling changes as well. To understand those, however, we need to understand a little about how brains are put together.

Some people spend their whole lives studying the anatomy and physiology of the brain. Smart people in white coats have spent decades mapping out all the various bumps and wiblets. I'm going to spend a little less time than that. A page or so should be fine.

This is the Big Kahuna of frameworks, the el Grande, the great white shark of frameworks. This stuff is to understanding teenagers what Al Gore is to understanding climate change. You really, really, *really* need to understand the brain stuff if you're going to get through parenting a teenager. OK, that might be overstating it a bit, given that all of our parents got through it without understanding the brain stuff, but it will make the whole thing a lot easier.

Most people tend to think of the brain as a single organ, but that's not very accurate. The brain is more like the European Union than it is England. Rather than a single, seamless entity, it's a connected group of separate systems joined as much by geography as function. Because they're all in the same place, they have complex links, but they all have their own separate thing going on. Nerve impulses travel around from state to state without the need for a passport, but they have vastly different effects depending on where they are.

The very walnut-like outer layer is called the *cortex*, and that's where a lot of the really complicated work goes on. Not only is that where the actual thinking gets done, but it's also where we make sense of what we see, hear, smell and feel.

Underneath that are layers which deal with the more basic stuff — hunger, thirst, sex and emotions. It's down here in the basement of the brain that much of the work of creating problems in your home is done. One of the culprits is a thing called the *corpus callosum*. This large, rather nondescript strand of fibres is the information superhighway that connects the left and right sides of the brain planet. If you have teenage girls, this strand of fibres will be making your life difficult at times, but more of that later.

Another part of the brain that will periodically have a big presence in your home is the *amygdala*. This is the seat of our gut instinct and emotions. It isn't so much that emotions are generated by the amygdala, so much as this is where a lot of the processing of emotional experiences goes on. Rest assured that if there's been some kind of explosive outburst from your teen, then the amygdala will be in there up to its knees.

Now that we've had a very brief poke around the brain, the big question is this: how does a teenage one compare to the fully ripened adult version?

As I said before, we used to think that the first three years of life were the most significant in terms of brain development, and that by age 10 it was all pretty much a done deal. In fact, the truth is that — despite outward appearances which often suggest there's very little going on in the average teenager's brain — there's actually a whole lot of stuff buzzing away.

A newborn baby has lost about 100 billion brain cells by the time they emerge into the world wrinkled, helpless and covered in goo. This might seem like a tough break, but take comfort from the fact that they still have 100 billion left, which for most of us will be ample to get through.

The really big deal, though, are the connections between brain cells, because connections are everything. Whilst it might well be useful to have a cousin who works on *The Oprah Winfrey Show* or an uncle who works in the tax department, there's probably a lot more to be said for having connections in your brain, and not just one or two, but lots.

How much is lots you ask?

Last count, 1,000 trillion.

It should come as no great surprise that this is the number of connections your average three-year-old has in their brain, which is about three times the amount you and I have. This might seem like a lot of connections for a toddler, but that's only because it really *is* a lot. If you were to write it in numerical form it would look like this: 1,000,000,000,000,000,000,000, which almost makes you dizzy.

Still, having said that, right now the computer whiz kids are looking at using individual atoms to store information in electronic devices. When they figure out how to do that — which they will, of course, because we're far better at working out stuff like iPods than solving the problem of world peace or global poverty — this means you could get 1,000 trillion pieces of information on your iPod.

Isn't that great?

Who needs world peace when we can carry around unimaginably vast amounts of crap in our pockets? Brilliant. In this modern, amazing world of ours, even iPods are catching up on brains. Having said that, I'll bet it'll be a long time before you can teach an iPod to walk, and it will certainly never grow up and want to borrow your car. Still, you can't store MP3s in your kid's head either, so I guess it's all swings and roundabouts.

So what happens to this iPod-of-the-future-load of connections in the toddler's brain?

Pruning.

The more the little person does something, the stronger those connections become, and the more of the other connections are lost. Essentially, what we don't use, we lose. In this way our everyday experiences literally carve the connections in our brains into a useable state. Simple really.

Where all this becomes even more interesting is when we start looking at how teenagers' brains are different to the mature adult brain. It turns out there is a burst of activity in the teenage brain which is quite specific.

Don't worry too much about keeping it all in your head as you go, because at the end of this chapter I'm going to give you a handy little summary. By the same token, don't skip to the end, because you'll miss out on a lot of really cool stuff . . . swimming with sharks and amorous vampires to name but two.

Recall that the cortex — the outermost, wrinkly, walnut-like layer — is where a lot of the real thinking goes on. In fact, you're using yours as you read this. If there was a brain equivalent of Google Earth and we were to zoom in on the brain (say from 15,000 feet to less than a foot), we'd be able to see a rather nondescript area called the *pre-frontal cortex*. Scientists are more descriptive than imaginative, and so it should come as no great surprise that the pre-frontal cortex is the bit just in behind the frontal cortex, which, equally unsurprisingly, is the bit at the front (about where your forehead is). So the pre-frontal cortex is the bit just behind the bit at the front. Clearly you wouldn't want to operate on someone's brain with this level of detail, but you get the general idea.

At face value the pre-frontal cortex isn't much to write home about, just a bump amongst a bunch of other bumps, but it turns out that this particular bump is really quite important. Simply speaking, if we had a little voice in our head that was the one whose job it was to say 'Umm, now let's just stop and think for a minute before we jump off that . . .', it would come from a little mouth in the pre-frontal cortex. Indeed, this area has been described as the *seat of reason*. We think that this is the part of the brain involved with things such as learning rules, understanding consequences, working memory, and how we make sense of emotions.

Wow, I hear you say, that sounds like a pretty darned important wee bump, and you'd be right.

And here's where it gets really, *really* interesting, because at the beginning of adolescence there is a virtual explosion of new connections between the brain cells of the cortex. It's a little like the way gardens go boom in spring. All of a sudden there's new growth sprouting everywhere. What's also happening though is that, just as in any garden, there's also a lot of pruning going on. Remember that in young children the connections and pathways in the brain that are used are reinforced, and the connections which aren't are binned. This is also very much the case with teenagers, because the connections which are used are strengthened, and the ones that aren't are 'pruned'.

With all this growing and trimming going on, there are going to be some big implications for how teenagers go about their business.

Now, having said all that, would it come as any great surprise to you that the pre-frontal cortex, the veritable 'seat of reason', is one of the last areas of the brain to come fully online, that in fact there's actually a *decline* in the relative size of this area in the teenage brain?

Did you fall off your seat in amazement when you read that? Probably not.

The important thing here is not the lack of surprise, but rather the fact there is something very real underlying teenagers' problems in making decisions, sticking to rules, and thinking through the consequences of their actions.

In fact, the pre-frontal cortex — the seat of reason — isn't fully operational and fully connected to its neighbours, until we're in our early twenties.

Bugger, you say, and you'd be right. The big message here for parents is that we can't expect our teens to make reasonable decisions all the time because they simply don't have the right equipment. There's a huge range of variation amongst teenagers to be sure, but we always need to keep in the back of our minds that they don't have as much in the *front* of their minds as we do. That all important pre-frontal cortex is still being built.

But it doesn't just stop there. Teenagers have stuff going on all over the place.

There are really only two things almonds have in common with the amygdala: the first is that they both start with 'A', and the second is that they have roughly the same shape. That's pretty much it, though. Almonds can be found in trees, and amygdalas are found in the deeper, more primitive, layers of the brain. To find an amygdala, you would have to cut open a person's skull, slice off the top, walnut-like layer of their brain, and grab a handful of the gloopy stuff right in the middle.

Don't do that, though; not only is it very messy, but you'll also get in all kinds of trouble with the police. Far easier just to google it if you're really interested in seeing what one looks like.

Why these little almond-shaped devils are important to you is more a consequence of how important they are to your teenager. For one thing, the amygdala plays a crucial role in the recognition of emotions in others, essentially enabling us to decode the facial expressions of other people, so we can figure out if they're feeling happy, sad, angry or afraid. If you're in a room and you see an unfamiliar face, or someone who looks afraid, or even someone who's staring at you, your amygdala clicks into gear and starts trying to figure out what's going on. What's more, the amygdala also plays a key role in emotional reactivity and in how we respond to stressful situations.

When you stop and think about it, this seems like a pretty important skill to master if you're going to be in the vicinity of other human beings. We need to know how other people are feeling to adjust our own behaviour and to make sense of what's happening in the world around us.

What is particularly interesting is that it seems it's the partnership between the amygdala and the pre-frontal cortex that's most important in correctly identifying emotions in others. When teenagers and adults were shown pictures of people with a fearful expression on their face, teenagers showed far more activity in their amygdala and far less activity in their pre-frontal cortex than adults did. What's more, teenagers are far more likely to make a mistake in deciding what the emotion is they're looking at, with kids under 14 more likely to say the face is showing sadness, anger or confusion than correctly identifying fear.

Again, if you stop and think about what this means, it helps to make some sense of how teenagers sometimes behave. Their basic ability to correctly figure out what other people are feeling is still developing, and they're prone to make assumptions that are incorrect. They also tend to react from these emotional centres rather than bump the decision upstairs to the smart people in the pre-frontal cortex.

From such little mistakes, cataclysmic arguments are born.

You've probably heard people use the term 'the old grey matter' when referring to the brain, usually as they're tapping their head and winking. What they're referring to are the actual brain cells, or neurons, which look grey on MRI scans. But there's another matter that matters just as much, which we don't hear so much about: white matter. It should come as no surprise that white matter is called 'white matter' because it looks white on MRI scans. Not very stunning, I know, but there you go. What is quite a bit more interesting is the role white matter plays — or more correctly doesn't play — in the developing teenage brain.

White matter is *myelin* (like violin but with a *my*), the fatty substance that in-sheathes the nerve cells. Myelin performs much the same function as the plastic insulation around electrical cables which helps to transmit the current by preventing it from leaking out of the wire. Nerve impulses travel down the nerve cell in much the same way as the current in an electrical cable. The presence of myelin greatly increases the efficiency of the transmission of nerve impulses around our brain. When you're a teenager, you're still forming this white matter, and the process isn't fully completed until well into your twenties.

Remember the corpus callosum, the large bundle of fibres that connects the left and right sides of the brain? Well, it turns out that the corpus callosum is composed almost entirely of white matter. So the added burden teenagers face is that, whilst adults have the equivalent of high-speed connections between the left and right sides of their brains, teenagers are still working on the uninsulated dial-up version. Whilst we can point and click at mental web pages which load pretty much instantly, teenagers have to spend a bit longer waiting for the site to load before they can make a decision.

Ever thought of swimming with sharks? I bet most of you would have instantly thought 'well that doesn't sound like a good idea'. In many ways it probably seems like a no-brainer. For your average teenager, though, the answer isn't quite so obvious, and getting to it isn't quite so simple.

We all know teenagers sometimes make poor choices when it comes to assessing risk, and we've already talked about how the pre-frontal cortex plays a role in that, but there seems to be another even more interesting layer of hootengafluf involved. In a fascinating experiment, teenagers and adults were shown simple phrases such as 'swimming with sharks' and asked to push a button to say whether they thought this was a good idea or a bad idea. On the good idea scenarios, the teenagers and the adults reacted with about the same speed. On the bad idea scenarios, the teenagers were markedly slower. They still said that 'swimming with sharks' was a bad idea (which is reassuring), but it took them longer to get there.

What was really fascinating, though, was that when they looked at the MRI scans of the adults and the adolescents they found there were two quite distinct processes going on. The adults used the parts of their brain that were more involved with generating mental images of possible outcomes, whereas the teenagers used the parts of their brain that were more involved with reasoning capacities.

So it seems that adults were more able to instantly 'see' that swimming with sharks was a bad idea, whereas teenagers had to break it all down into steps and work it through, which took them longer. The grown-ups' heads instantly filled with pictures of bloodstained frothy water (and probably the theme from *Jaws*) whereas the teenagers went: 'Hmmm, swimming with sharks? Let me think about that for a minute . . .'

Whilst the adults' heads filled with scary pictures, the teenagers had to take the long way round. Clearly this suggests that even in an abstract laboratory situation teenagers need more time to think through whether or not a suggestion is a good idea or not. When you push out from the lab into the real world, then you can start to see how teenagers sometimes make stupid choices. When you're standing on the edge of the great white shark tank with your mates, the music's playing, the girls and/or the boys are watching, and everyone else is jumping in, then you don't really have time to sit and figure it all out.

You just go with the flow and figure the rest out later.

Even teenage rats live life on the wild side. Studies have shown that teen rats are more likely to seek out novel stimuli and explore unknown areas than they are at younger ages or as grown-up rats. Even rats, it would appear, like to get a little crazy during adolescence. There is some consolation in knowing it isn't just human teenagers who do crazy things. No doubt somewhere in Africa right now there is probably a bunch of teenage zebras throwing rocks at lions.

'Come on, Larry,' one will taunt another. 'What are ya? A zebra or a *gazelle?*'

And despite the fact that Larry's mum and dad have told him a thousand times to stay away from the lions, he'll probably throw the rock anyway.

So why would this be? Why does Larry kick the rock? Why would teenage animals of all kinds engage in risky behaviour? Surely they can't all be doing it just to stress out their parents?

Some scientists have argued that there might be a number of evolutionary rewards for teenage risk-taking. For example, it might help species to disperse and thus decrease the risk of inbreeding if teenagers feel a need to roam just as they are becoming sexually mature. It's also possible that if teens have an inbuilt drive to try out new behaviours, this will force them to leave the proverbial nest of childhood (or the literal nest in the case of teenage birds) and get on with their own life.

It's actually completely normal for teenagers to engage in risk-taking behaviours. You put a teenage zebra, a lion and a rock on the same savannah, and chances are it will end in tears. Understandably, this statement always causes more alarm than it soothes. What it does confirm, though, is that there's a good reason for putting in place firm boundaries, and we'll talk more about how to do that later on.

In a nutshell (and any kind of nutshell will do here—even a pistachio would be fine), alcohol, drugs and teenage brains do not go well together. In fact, the more we learn about various combinations of teenagers, alcohol and drugs, the worse things look. The evidence seems pretty clear that teenage brains are affected differently by alcohol and drugs than are adult brains. One example is that teenagers are more susceptible to alcohol-related impairment of memory and learning. When you think about the fact that most teenagers are involved in some kind of education, memory and learning are two things you wouldn't want to be messing with.

What's more, the way that teenagers physically respond to drugs is different as well. The pathways that connect the pre-frontal cortex to the more primitive reward centres of the brain are still under construction, and there is evidence that this makes teenagers hypersensitive to the 'kick' of novel experiences. By way of example, teenagers (both rats and humans) are more likely to become addicted to nicotine and also at far lower doses.

This said, one wonders, given the generally gutter-based lifestyle rats lead, if rat mums and dads are concerned that their little teen ratlings are smoking? Not that one wishes to stereotype, but one would think that rat mums and dads probably aren't the most supportive parents. If you let your kids roam the sewers, you can't be too surprised if they pick up some bad habits.

In any case, it makes sense that teenagers get addicted more quickly than adults given that teenage brains are undergoing extensive remodelling and renovations, much of which is conducted according to the principle of 'use or lose it'. Can you imagine the havoc alcohol and drugs wreak in that kind of environment? It would be like getting the kitchen done, only each day before he starts the builder gets off his face on high-grade hashish and cheap wine.

I'd bet there'd be a fair chance that not all the cupboards would close properly. In fact, it's likely some of the cupboard doors would be completely missing. If the builder is stoned and drunk, then the kitchen is unlikely to end up in *Better Homes and Gardens*.

It always amazes me that parents of teenagers complain so much about the fact that their kids sleep all day. Clearly they've forgotten the joys of preschoolers who rise at 6.00am, ready to go. Teenagers, on the other hand, are quite the opposite. They tend to stay up late and sleep all day. Getting teenagers out of bed for school in the morning is a trial for many parents.

So why is this? Are teenagers inherently lazy or is there something else going on?

In the previous chapter we talked about how puberty is a time of hormones, lots of hormones. The average teenager's bloodstream is coursing with sex hormones, growth hormones and stress hormones. We've talked about how all this affects their bodies — but what about their brains? Well, it turns out that the sex hormones in particular (testosterone and oestrogen) act in the part of the brain which controls the production of a particular substance called serotonin.

Serotonin plays a pivotal role in mood and affects our hormonally regulated body clock. The teenager's constant state of hormonal overdrive knocks their body clock on its head, which is why teenagers tend to be awake all night and then want to sleep all day. They're not so much lazy, as they are suffering from a hormonal hangover. Fortunately, though, just like all hangovers, with a bit of a nap, a milkshake and a few years this too will pass.

It would be easy at this point, having just read all that, to start thinking that teenagers were all hopelessly messed up in the head. Whilst that's understandable, it's also far from the truth.

In reality, all of these changes to the way teenagers experience the world are neither good nor bad, they're simply part of the ride. You went through all this stuff, just as I did. Indeed for most of us, when we reflect back on our teenage years, there are many things we did that now seem breathtakingly reckless. The nice thing about understanding all this brain stuff is that it might even make some of your own teenage behaviour a little more understandable.

I myself recall late one evening when I was a student, about 19, being goaded into walking over a pipe suspended 20 feet above a stony river-bed whilst I was so drunk I didn't so much walk along the pipe as stagger over it. I still see that pipe from time to time as I'm driving around, and when I look at it now I can't believe I could ever have been that stupid. Still, it got me some points with my mates and became one of those stories you tell when you get old and boring. Having said that, I could have fallen off and died, or been paralysed, or brain-damaged, or drowned, or any one of a number of catastrophes.

What's my point?

We all do stupid things when we're young: that's part of the joy of being young. If we're lucky we aren't seriously hurt or killed, and we live to tell the tale. All of the things I've talked about in this chapter are signs that your teenager is moving from childhood to adulthood. You don't need to worry about trying to fix this stuff *per se* because it fixes itself. Connections are formed, pre-frontal cortices ripen, amygdalas settle down into their rightful place, and myelin neatly wraps the whole thing up.

What we do need to be able to do is to understand what drives teenagers to think and act the way they do. Sometimes they'll be doing things deliberately, to be sure, as do we all; but sometimes when they shrug and say 'I dunno' when you ask them what they were thinking after they've just done something breathtakingly stupid, they just might be telling the truth.

The teenage brain

* The teenage years are a time of significant changes in the developing brain.

* There is an explosion of growth in connections in some areas, and at the same time a large amount of 'pruning' of redundant connections.

* The pre-frontal cortex is the 'seat of reason', the bit that helps us to make wise choices. This is the *last* part of the brain to develop fully.

* Teenagers are more prone than adults to misjudge emotions in others.

* The wiring in the brain isn't fully insulated by the myelin sheath until in the early twenties. This decreases the speed and efficiency of thinking.

* Teenagers can make good decisions in theory (such as not to swim with sharks), but it takes them longer than adults to reach those decisions and they use different parts of their brain to do it.

* It's natural for teenagers to seek out and engage in risky behaviours.

* Teenagers' brains are affected differently by alcohol and drugs than adult brains. They are more vulnerable to the effects of using alcohol and drugs, and — because their brains are still not fully wired together — are more likely to become addicted.

* The reason teenagers stay up so late at night and want to sleep all day is that their hormones knock their internal body-clock off-balance.

★ In general, teenagers find it harder to think before acting, to stop themselves once they've started down a course of action, and to choose between safe and risky options.

★ Teenagers are also more likely to be influenced by the presence of their friends to engage in risky behaviours.

★ Teenagers are biologically programmed to be emotionally reactive and to get wound up over things that might seem relatively minor.

★ All this is quite normal and will, for most of us, pass with time.

5

the fifth framework

weapons of mass disruption

I would love to have been in the Oval Office the day they finally had to admit to themselves that Saddam wasn't hiding anything in Iraq. No Saran gas, no anthrax, no nuclear weapons. Not even any nookular weapons. Nothing.

What a day that would have been . . .

'And you really didn't find *anything*?'

'No, Mr President.'

'And you looked everywhere?'

'Yes, Mr President.'

'Did you look in his bed? People hide stuff in their beds — did you look in his bed?'

An uncomfortable shuffling of feet. 'Ah . . . yes, Mr President.'

'Right down the bottom of his bed, where the sheets tuck in — did you look there?'

'Yes, sir.'

'Under his bed? Did you look *under* his bed?'

'Yes, Mr President.'

'Right back in the corner under his bed? Did you look there? Cause if I was gonna hide some kind of super-weapon that's where I'd put it, right back in the corner.'

'We checked all the corners, sir.'

'Closet?'

'Yes, sir, we checked there, too.'

'So basically you checked out his whole room and there wasn't *anything?*'

'That's correct, Mr President.'

A pause.

'Did you check outside his room? Maybe he left some in his desk at work?'

A second pause, more awkward than the first.

'We pretty much checked out the entire country, sir. There was nothing there.'

'Darn it.'

'So . . . what do we tell the people, Mr President?'

Anxious fidgeting. 'Well, Karl, you're my most trusted tell-yer-what-to-say guy — what do I tell 'em?'

'Tell the people that this was a great victory for freedom, and democracy, and that we have brought a new era of peace to the people of Iraq.'

'Iraq?'

'That's where Saddam lives, Mr President.'

'Where is that? Somewhere near Idaho?'

'No, sir, it's in the Middle East.'

'Oh. Near Boston, then?'

'Kind of.'

'And they'll buy all that democracy stuff?'

'Absolutely, sir. This is America, they always buy it.'

'What do you think, Donald? You're the Secretary of Defence: is it bad we didn't find those super-weapons?'

'No, sir.'

'Why is that?'

'Because we found freedom, sir, lots of freedom . . . and some oil.'

'Good job, boys.'

'Thank you, Mr President.'

Contrary to popular belief, the Bush Administration wasn't the first to invent weapons of mass destruction. Way back in 429BC the Spartans — who were later to star in a fantastic movie called *300* — used chemical warfare when fighting the Peloponnesian war. They piled sulphur against the walls of a besieged castle and burned it, releasing clouds of toxic sulphur dioxide.

In the second century BC, the great Roman General Hannibal pioneered biological warfare, and utter bastardry, when he found himself outnumbered in a naval battle. The quick-thinking Hannibal sent his troops ashore to gather venomous snakes, which he then put in earthen pots and fired at the enemy ships to great effect. Over the course of human history we've fired scorpions and dismembered plague victims at each other as well.

It's only in the past 50 years that the delivery of these agents has become a little more sophisticated and a lot cleaner. Now we don't cut the heads off dead plague victims and biff them with a catapult; instead, we grow nasty things in laboratories and drop them from planes.

Alongside this historical development of weapons of mass destruction, teenagers have been perfecting their own arsenal of WMDs, except their intended outcome is more about *disruption* than destruction.

Teenagers don't so much want to hurt people as disrupt the command and control centres. Teenagers want to take down the government by stealth, subterfuge, confusion and sometimes flat-out assault.

What follows are the major WMDs employed by teenagers to undermine, overwhelm, and overthrow governments. These are lifted straight from an intercepted copy of the *Teenagers Revolutionary Training Manual* so you can see exactly how they intend these tactics should be used. It's important to familiarize yourself with the more common WMDs because then you'll be less likely to be thrown off-balance, and therefore will be more likely to make better decisions.

1 Confusion

This is one of the oldest tricks in the book. Basically, you simply continue to argue with your parents as long as you can whilst changing the subject at every opportunity you get. In this way the argument may start off being about why you're late home, but it can end up half an hour later with your mother having to justify why the government has done so little to help the starving in Africa and why she thinks your being late is more significant than some poor little baby in Africa starving to death.

2 Deflection

Related to CONFUSION, DEFLECTION is a fantastic tool. The trick is to keep the argument going, but to quickly deflect the questions back to your parents. In this way, rather than you having to explain your behaviour, they will have to explain theirs. You always answer a question about your behaviour with a question about their behaviour. Simply keep batting the ball back without actually answering the question. An example would be as follows:

Parent: Why were you late home last night?

Teenager: Why are you always going on about why I'm late?

Parent: Because I worry about you.

Teenager: Why are you always so worried about me?

Parent: Because I love you.

Teenager: If you love me, why don't you trust me?

Parent: I do trust you.

Teenager: So why do you always want to know where I am?

Parent: I don't, I just . . .

Teenager: How can you say you love me when you don't trust me?

Parent: I don't . . . I mean . . . I do . . . trust you, that is, but . . . ummm . . .

As you can see in this exchange, you have successfully shifted the focus from your behaviour to your parent's behaviour. As long as they keep answering your questions, then you have nothing to worry about.

3 Distraction

One of the most powerful principles that you can exploit is simple DISTRACTION. If your parent is distracted by something, then they will not be able to pay their full attention to the request you are making or the confession you have just made. The key here is to pick a time when they are busy with something (the more important or overwhelming the better) and then make your play. The distracting situation could be anything from a phone call, a favourite television programme, spending time with their own friends, an argument with one of your siblings, the death of a beloved pet or grandparent, housework, or even the lucky appearance of a door-to-door salesperson. As soon as they are distracted, get in quick, speak quietly, use as few words as possible, and use every skill you have to convey the appearance that the issue you are raising is inconsequential.

4 Fear

One of the most effective tools that you have is your parents' FEAR. Essentially, they are afraid of so many things it's hard for them to keep count. They're afraid of you getting hurt, abducted by serial killers, hooked on drugs, pregnant, pregnant and hooked on drugs, failing in school, not getting a good job, being unhappy, having a crap boyfriend/girlfriend and/or both at the same time, and just about everything else you can think of. Because of this, all you have to do is threaten any of these things and they will become almost paralysed with FEAR. For example, you can threaten to walk out of the house at 2.00am, you can threaten to run off with your loser girlfriend, drop out of school, or just about any stupid thing you can think of. All you need is for them to buckle in the face of one of your threats and then you've got them just where you want them.

5 Guilt

This is closely related to FEAR, but there are some subtle differences. As well as being naturally fearful, your parents will also feel guilty about everything. Anything good you do they will credit to you, anything bad you do they will blame on themselves. Because adults make poor decisions when they are burdened with GUILT, you will need to become skilled at creating it so you can then exploit the vulnerability which results. All you need to do is find a weak spot and play to that. This is much easier if your parents have separated, because you can then blame the one who is present for their relationship ending. This nicely leads back into FEAR, because you can then threaten to go live with your other parent if you don't get your way. Another option for exploiting guilt is to nag, whine, and generally harangue your parent until they crack and yell at you and say something harsh, then immediately exploit the massive amount of GUILT they will instantly feel.

6 Splitting

Don't worry if your mum and dad are still together, because the good news is there's still a way you can exploit this situation. SPLITTING is the art of pitting your parents against each other. This can be done either directly or indirectly. In the indirect approach, you simply ask both parents for what you want and then choose the answer you like best. In the direct approach, you invite each parent to side with you in an argument. Statistically, regardless of whether you're a boy or a girl, the odds favour trying to co-opt your father. Father's are generally well-meaning, but sometimes don't think through the long-term consequences of siding with you. Also, because mothers tend to go on a bit about most things, this will naturally incline the father who has not thought through the issues adequately to side with you. Obviously if your parents are separated then the options for further splitting are only as limited as your imagination. However, do not confuse SPLITTING with spitting, which is an entirely different thing.

7 Exhaustion

Here we borrow a leaf from the SAS handbook, where soldiers are given an experience of being 'broken' in a training exercise when they are made to stand for hours in what is called the 'stress position'. This is an incredibly uncomfortable position which, after several hours of pain and discomfort, breaks the will of the soldier and they give up all their information to the enemy. You are able to do the same thing with your parents to get what you want.

Essentially, all you have to do is just go on, and

on, and on, and on, and on, and on, and on, and on, and on, and
on, and on, and on, and on, and on, and on, and on, and on, and
on, and on, and on, and on, and on, and on, and on, and on, and
on, and on, and on, and on, until they finally give in and let you do
what you want.

8 Collective bargaining

Parents want to be seen as being fair, and to a certain extent as
being 'cool'. They want to be liked. Obviously there is tremendous
variation in this need to be seen as fair and cool, but there will
always be some element of these needs at work when your parents
are making decisions. So much of their self-esteem is wrapped
up in being a 'good parent' that they can sometimes be forced
into making errors of judgement. For this reason we suggest
that if you want to ask if you can do something that you know
will be marginal, then always have at least one or more friends
present when you ask. The presence of friends will introduce an
extra element of distraction for your parents (see WMD3) and will
make it more likely they will not focus on the important issues.
They might be more inclined to seem reasonable in front of your
friends, and also will want to avoid having an argument in front of
other people. There is the added advantage that if your parent is
wavering you can tell them that your friend's parents have already
said that she/he can go, thus taking advantage of the fact that if
one adult thinks something is OK everyone else will follow along.

9 The pseudo broken heart

Parents hate to see their children suffering. In fact this is one of
the most distressing things a parent can experience, and as such
it is a fantastic weakness that you can exploit with great effect.
This strategy should be used if you have been told you can't do
something, or if you have just received a substantial punishment.
In such a situation, you must immediately conjure up a display of

such emotional pain that they will have no choice but to give in for fear that you may suffer some long-term emotional trauma if they do not. You must cry as if you have just lost all that is precious to you in the world. You must convey such utter and complete heartbreak, such total despair, such grieving as the world has never seen. It must be so convincing that it will cause them to buckle and let you have your way. A word of caution, though: use sparingly because this strategy can backfire if overused.

10 False hope

This is a stunningly effective strategy, but sadly — unless your parents are extraordinarily gullible and/or stupid — it can only be used a maximum of two to three times in your career. Essentially, this works best for those of you who have reached the exalted level of Grand Master Snot. Shortly before an event that you will need your parents' permission for, or conversely immediately after having done something seriously bad, you display an apparent change in attitude and profess a heartfelt desire to be 'good' if they will only give you one more chance. It has to be convincing, but if you are focused and stay on message, then chances are you'll get your way. Your parents desperately want to believe that you have seen the light, and this weakness can play into your hands nicely. Remember, though, you will only get to use this WMD two to three times max, so think carefully before deploying it.

11 Start high

This is a simple bargaining technique that is useful in a range of different scenarios. The rule is to start with an initial demand that you know is so patently unreasonable that your parents will never agree to it, argue for that position ferociously until they are exhausted, then offer to settle for something only moderately unreasonable. If you time it right, they will leap at the compromise. For example, you might begin by asking if you can go away with your boyfriend for the weekend to a tattoo convention. They will say no. Argue that for as long as it takes to wear them down, then at the 11th moment appear to give up and ask them in a frustrated tone if you can 'at least' stay at your friend Mary's house (Mary being the friend you know they think is a bad influence and who they would never normally let you stay with). If you've timed it right, they will collapse in an exhausted heap and say yes, feeling relieved that they've kept you from a tattoo convention you never wanted to go to anyway.

12 Tactical hatred

Recall that parents like to be liked, and in particular they most like to be liked by you. As you know, they would willingly die for you — which is only right given that you never asked to be born anyway — and this deep love for you leaves them vulnerable to attack. A well-timed 'I hate you' can have the same effect on your parents as a pipe bomb. If you say it at just the right time with just the right tone, they will be so hurt they will stop thinking. This is the moment when you want to sweep in with your demands. If you can subtly convey the impression that you will like them if they let you have your way, this will help greatly. Get them while they're weak and you stand a far better chance of success.

13 Violence

In some cases you may have to resort to actual violence. You have a number of options available to you: verbal, emotional and, last but not least, physical. We've already described some of the ways you can verbally manipulate and cajole your parents, but in some instances you may need to resort to actual physical violence. You may have to break and smash things. You may have to hit people. Once you have been violent for a while, you will be able to relax a little and simply use the threat of violence. Fortunately for you, in recent years politicians and lawmakers have given you more and more rights so that it is harder and harder for parents to deal with your violent behaviour. For example, if you verbally abuse your mother and your father gives you a shove in response, then you can threaten to call the police and have him charged with assault. Just a word of warning: you should be very careful about actually carrying through the threat of calling the police, because many of them are parents as well and will often see through your protests of victimization. Lawyers are a different story, though. Luckily for you, there are now a number of community agencies where you can go and get lawyers to fight for you. Isn't that just peachy?

As you can see, there are many options open to the average teenager. It is important as a parent to familiarize yourself with the various WMDs teenagers can deploy so that you will be able to respond appropriately when you encounter them. You may not encounter all of these, but you will encounter at least some. If you're familiar with the common WMDs, you won't be surprised, distracted, or hurt when they are used against you, and because of that you'll probably make much better decisions.

Weapons of mass disruption

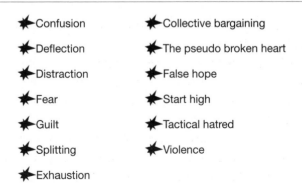

- Confusion
- Deflection
- Distraction
- Fear
- Guilt
- Splitting
- Exhaustion
- Collective bargaining
- The pseudo broken heart
- False hope
- Start high
- Tactical hatred
- Violence

6

the sixth framework

a tank will always be a tank

My view has always been that kids are like vehicles, they are what they are. You can paint them, change the seat covers, even get expensive alloy wheels, but you can't change the basic nature of the vehicle itself. A tank will always be a tank, and if you try and pretend it's a Ferrari Testarossa then you're going to come unstuck. The opposite is true as well, because Ferraris are completely useless in the rough.

We now know quite a bit about personalities, what they are, and how much they change over the course of our lives. Whilst it's true that we mellow with age, we also remain remarkably stable over the course of our lives. Who we are at 3 years of age is who we are at 26, and odds on at 56 and 86 as well. The best evidence would seem to suggest that we come out with our personalities having been pretty much cemented in place from the get-go. Over the course of our lives we learn some things that might change our views and challenge our values, and we also learn how to take off our rough edges and moderate the less palatable aspects of ourselves, but the underlying person doesn't change all that much.

We mature, but we don't really metamorphose, if you see what I mean.

If you think about your own life, you'll probably find yourself agreeing with me. Are you really all that different to who you were as a kid? Or as a teenager? The external appearance may have changed a little, you may have learned a few more subtle skills for getting what you want, and maybe picked up some more manners along the way, but who you fundamentally *are* remains relatively stable.

If you began life as a stubborn little soul, you probably still are. If you were shy as a kid, you probably still are now. You will undoubtedly have learned some strategies to cope with your shyness, but it will always be there. Sadly, if you were a boring pain in the arse as a little person, you will undoubtedly retain some vestiges of this as an adult. On the upside, if you are a miserable, sour bastard, research suggests you will die earlier, which is good news for the rest of us.

The trick for us as parents is to understand that, just as this is true for ourselves, it is also true for our kids. We might think we can change them, but really we can't. It's important to understand this, because if you don't then you'll waste a great deal of time and energy trying to make your son or daughter into something they're not. You will also suffer great hurt, and cause great hurt along the way. You can lecture, threaten, cajole, and tutor a tank in the ways of a Ferrari as much as you like. You can even paint the tank red, but a tank will always be a tank. To expect anything else is mad.

The first crucial step is to understand what kind of car (or armoured vehicle) your kid is, and then accept it. Once you've done this you will be much happier, as will they.

The next step is to help them to learn how to drive whatever they happen to be. If your precious one began life as a tank, this is not a bad thing at all because tanks can accomplish great deeds. You know when a tank has arrived because they don't wait for someone to open the door and invite them in, they simply drive through the front wall. Tanks are good. The downside of being a tank is that they have a tendency to squash their own guys if they aren't very careful. Tanks need to learn to stop and look around before they go crashing in through someone's front wall.

One of our most important jobs as parents — in my humble

opinion anyway — is to teach our kids how to be who they are, to accept both their strengths and their weaknesses, and to make the most of the cards they've been dealt. We have to remember, too, that we shouldn't rush to judge what is a strength and what is a weakness, because usually it'll be both. Stubbornness can be a great gift. It can help you persevere when other weaker souls would give in. It can also create all kinds of problems for you.

Being popular and good at sports is a wonderful thing, but by the same token you are less likely to be a billionaire, as they tend to be neither of those things. Not fitting in at school and not liking sports can make life hard initially, but then these are the personality types more common to people who really do become billionaires.

Our approach as parents needs to change depending on what kind of vehicle you're dealing with. Some need a more hands-on approach, and some need a hands-in-pockets approach. There is no one-size-fits-all method that works best with all cars. You need to figure out what kind of car your kid is driving, then teach them all you can about how to drive as best they can.

The 'how' of how you do that we'll cover in the sections on Principles and Simple Plans, but just for now keep these questions in your mind: What kind of car is my kid driving, and what are they going to need to know to make the best use of what they've got?

Tank or Ferrari Testarossa, it's all grist for the mill.

Personality

★ Our personalities are basically there from the get-go.

★ The person we are at 3 years of age is essentially who we'll be at 30 years of age, just with more manners and bowel control.

★ Part of our job as parents is to try to understand what kind of vehicle our kids are, and then help them to learn to drive it as best they can.

7

the seventh framework

*teenage boys and the rise
of the neanderthal*

The Neanderthals weren't here for long. They first appeared in Europe about 200,000 years ago, and the very last group lived in a place called Gorham's Cave in Gibraltar about 24,000–28,000 years ago. So far as we know, they left no forwarding address.

Now I know that 170,000-odd years might seem like quite a long time, but when you think about the fact that dinosaurs managed 250 million years, it really isn't that great an effort.

So what happened to the poor old Neanderthals, I hear you ask? Well, it turns out that a pushy group of hominids called *Homo sapiens* blundered down into Europe about 50,000 years ago and gently elbowed the Neanderthals off the edge. Typical, isn't it? Once the humans show up someone always ends up crying, or becoming extinct in this case.

We don't know an awful lot about the Neanderthals. They seemed to be a fairly simple group who used basic tools, hunted, procreated (although obviously not so well), and generally lived a simple life. Their needs and wants were somewhat crude, as were their abilities. We weren't even sure they spoke a language until someone in France found a Neanderthal hyoid bone (the small bone in the throat to which the tongue attaches) and we knew that they at least had the basic ability to produce speech. In any case, it's likely their conversations were pretty basic.

It makes you wonder what would happen if we found Neander-thals living in a forest somewhere today, doesn't it? Would we put them in a zoo?

In many ways the experience of teenage boys is one of evolutionary digression. For a brief few years they slide sideways and backwards, mimicking our extinct Neanderthal cousins. Not only do they get hairier, but they also become obsessed with their more primal urges, they often lose the gift of speech, resorting to rudimentary grunts, and return to their caves.

It would be a big mistake, though, to take from this that boys are simple creatures — far from it. Boys are just as complex as girls, they just don't make such a big song and dance about it. The reason these modern adolescent Neanderthals grunt and retreat to caves is not because they're not as smart as the humans, because they are — as were the original Neanderthals: it's just that they can't stand all the yabbering.

Indeed, my theory is that the prehistoric Neanderthals didn't die out because they were killed off by the humans, it was simply that they couldn't stand the idea of putting up with all the inane yabbering any longer.

There is no question that boys and girls are very different. They think differently, act differently, communicate differently, and take very different paths on the journey to adulthood. The purpose of this chapter on boys, and the following one on girls, is to highlight some of these differences and give you some direction about how to approach them. If you know how your kids experience the world, then you'll be far better equipped to get through the teenage years with both your, and their, sanity intact.

'He'll be OK'

In 2005, Celia Lashlie published a remarkable book called *He'll Be OK: Growing gorgeous boys into good men*. The book was the public end-product of an equally remarkable piece of research called the Good Man Project. Over the course of 18 months, she interviewed boys at a total of 25 high schools about what constitutes a 'good man'. The book is articulate, compelling, and presents a unique inside view of the world of teenage boys. The fact that it's written by a woman is, in my opinion, its great strength, because in many ways it reads like a travel guide for tourists in a strange land. If you have boys and you want to learn some more about their world, then I would strongly recommend the book.

It's also, as luck would have it, bloody funny.

Ages and stages

When I was a psychology student doing a developmental psychology paper, I remember there were three 'adult students' in my class who had children. They pointed out at several stages that the textbook versions of ages and stages didn't match up with their kids at all. I've always remembered that and applied a little caution as to how exact a science developmental psychology really is.

In that spirit I offer you a rough guide to teenage boy ages and stages. This is a rough guide only, but I've tried to capture the major themes of boys as they travel down the road. Some start early, some start late, but they all make the journey using roughly the same roads.

As you read this, keep in mind the things we've talked about in the previous chapter about brain development as well, because when you put the two chapters together you'll see that many of the things teenage boys do which don't make a lot of sense when you first encounter them make a lot more sense when you've got some useful frameworks to understand what's behind them.

Early Neanderthal (11ish–13ish)

The early teenage boy is a coltish beast. They are gawky and awkward and gallop about quite a bit. When not galloping, they tend to lie about looking bored. They alternate between childishness and a self-conscious attempt at manliness. At this stage they're more like boys playing dress-up than men. Girls are an object of fascination and growing obsession. The problem is they don't know what to do with one when they get one. Fortunately for them (or unfortunately if you're a parent), young women of today are far more forthright in letting boys know.

This is when the gently simmering pragmatism that is the background rhythm of all boys' lives begins to make itself truly heard. Their early attempts at surliness are also very rudimentary. This is the point where they first become aware that there's a cave they can go hide out in, but they still have to keep popping out all the time to make sure you're still there. They're reassured by the fact that you are, but they tend to express this with much rolling of the eyes and sighing, as if to say *What are you still doing here?*

The early Neanderthal's whole focus is on having fun.

At this point there can be a tendency for mothers to start to worry because their previously affectionate little boy starts to pull away from her. He suddenly doesn't seem to want to be cuddled, or to give cuddles. Mothers invariably begin to worry that he will turn into an angry young man, that he will do drugs, rob banks, and begin relationships with strange young women who dress in black and have multiple piercings. Mothers fret at this point because they don't understand why he is suddenly withdrawing from them. Paradoxically, even though all the early Neanderthal wants is to be left alone in his cave, his behaviour often provokes a rash of motherly over-involvement, which in turn can provoke a series of bitter arguments if left to get too out of hand.

Fathers tend not to worry. Fathers understand that caves are simply what boys do. Fathers understand that there isn't anything sinister going on; this is just how it's done. Fathers know that teenage boys don't want or need mothers fussing about. Fathers can't say this, however, because this will get them in all kinds of trouble. Instead, they try and gently hint at it, and begin the long process of running interference between teenage boys and their mothers.

Strangely, fathers hope that sometime in the next few years their boys will briefly hook up with strange young women who dress in black and have multiple piercings. Fathers don't want their sons to necessarily marry these girls, but they do want their boys to live a little.

It's a guy thing.

Middle Neanderthal (14ish–16ish)

This is when teenage boys do the Neanderthal thing hard-core. Their concerns are solely in the here and now, and communication with parents is seen as something usually best avoided. They work on a timetable where the only minute that ever matters is the last minute, because that's when everything gets done. At this age, their mothers' tendency to sweat the small stuff drives them crazy. They don't understand what the big deal is about the bathmat being left on the floor. This seems like a ridiculous thing to get so wound up about. They love their mothers, but they tell themselves that when they eventually get together with some chick for the long term there's no way they are going to let her tell them what to do with the bathmat. They love their dads, but they wonder why he doesn't just tell his chick to back off and leave the damn bathmat on the floor. They are invariably a little disappointed that their fathers don't stand up to their mothers about the bathmat, and they tell themselves they'll *never* be like that. When they eventually settle down, they'll leave the damn bathmat any damn place they want.

Yeah, right.

Middle Neanderthals sleep a lot, look at porn on the internet, and eat as if their stomach was a door to another dimension. Adults look at a loaf of bread and see a week; the middle Neanderthal looks at the same loaf and sees a single sitting. The education stakes are getting higher and the middle Neanderthal is starting to feel the pressure of that. It will alarm his parents that he doesn't seem to have much of a plan, but he knows that no one his age has much of a plan. He might know what he wants to do, but he's loathe to talk about it because he doesn't want to look stupid if he doesn't manage to do it. Fear of failure drives boys' dreams underground. They still have them, but they keep them close.

The middle Neanderthal is an arch pragmatist, and this will stay with him for his entire life, although as he ages it will be blunted somewhat and refined. The middle Neanderthal evaluates everything from the same stance: What's in it for me? He needs to see the immediate relevance to himself. If there is none, then he loses interest almost instantly. If he thinks there's no point, he turns away without a second glance.

Girls are important to the middle Neanderthal, but not as important as his friends. Loyalty is the undercurrent of his social life. This will often be expressed as piss-taking, punching, and shoving, but it is loyalty through and through. The modern Neanderthal might scoff at all the naïve young men who joined up to go fight in the various wars and say that he'd never do that, but even the modern Neanderthal wouldn't leave his mates to face the enemy alone. He understands that a man stands, and falls, with his mates.

The middle Neanderthal has his own philosophy. It may not actually make a lot of sense, but it will be deeply held and fiercely defended. The middle Neanderthal is never wrong, just misunderstood. He feels 50 feet tall and bulletproof. He will never surrender his beliefs, but instead is more likely to storm off and slam his door. He will then sulk to the tune of something that you hate played at very loud volumes.

He will be drawn to risk at this point, as if it were some deep itch that needs to be scratched. He will seek out things to try and rinse the boredom from his life. He will hate boredom, and for a while will seem to find it everywhere. In his search for novel and thrilling experiences, he will likely do things that are unwise and downright dangerous. His parents usually won't know the half of it. This is how it has been with Neanderthals since time began.

Mothers of middle Neanderthals often find themselves fighting against a wall of stony indifference. They remember bedtime stories and flowers left on their pillow only a few short years ago, and wonder who this tall, hairy, sullen stranger is. They struggle to understand where their little boy went. All they want to do is hug this solid young man and tell him that they love him, but often he will not let them near.

Sometimes he might, though, just for a moment. He might suddenly lay his head on her shoulder, or give her a hug for no reason. This fills mothers with misplaced hope. They think that their little boy is back again and that all will be as it was. They are invariably hurt when the next moment he pulls away and rolls his eyes when they go to hug him again.

Mothers of middle Neanderthals often make the mistake of trying to talk their way out of all the worry. They will drill and press. They will probe for information. This will achieve little except making the middle Neanderthal angry. He will then likely lash out and say something rude, which will provoke further conflict. Mothers on their own will find this a hard time, and it will test them greatly.

Fathers will now be quite experienced at running interference between mothers and their sons. If they're good at it, they will likely put out many fires before too much damage has been done. If they're not very good at it, they will usually make things far worse. Fathers who are not very good at running interference always take the wrong side and tend to react to situations rather than provide leadership.

The middle Neanderthal is where we see the first real signs of the man to come. His focus will still be on having fun and, even though it might appear that he is only ever living in the now, he will have the growing awareness that his actions define who he is and what kind of man he will be. Every day he will be making choices. It may not be obvious, often not even to him, but it is true nonetheless.

Late Neanderthal (17ish–19ish)

There is often a striking difference between the late Neanderthal and the earlier stages. Principally, this is seen as a gradually increasing calmness, a sense of self, and purpose. This is not to say that the late Neanderthal has got it all worked out, because he likely will not have, but there is an increasing sense that he at least knows what kind of questions he wants to be asking. It isn't so much about having the answers as it is about knowing in which direction to look. His horizon will still be close, but it will at least be further than the end of his toes.

For the late Neanderthal there is an increasing sense that soon he will be standing on his own feet, and living the life of his own choosing. This will bring a certain seriousness of purpose which, although it may not always be carried through into actual sustained effort, will provide some measure of reassurance to his parents.

He will slowly be rediscovering language again, and beginning to string whole sentences together. He may not be pouring out his heart to you (that's what his girlfriends and girl friends are for), but he may well be starting to converse more freely.

Mothers at this point may let themselves start to believe that he really will be alright. They will still worry, but they will at last begin to have the first fledgling sense that maybe he really will be OK. For the second time, mothers face the crushing realization that their sons will be leaving the nest again, just as they did when their sons first went to school. Except this time it won't just be from 9.00am until 3.00pm; this time it will likely be for good. Mothers also know that boys follow girls, so it is likely that they'll fall in love with some girl from another country and go with her since girls tend to stay closer to their families.

At this point, mothers start to think that even a strange young woman who dresses in black with multiple piercings wouldn't be so bad if she lived in the same town.

Fathers experience a shift in their relationship with their sons at this point as well. There is a sense of pride that their boy is now truly becoming a man, and a sense of sadness that he will be leaving the pack to establish his own territory. It is necessary, but a little sad.

A little while after this, both mothers and fathers sometimes realize that their children appear to have no immediate plans to leave home. Oddly, the empty nest can suddenly start to feel a little full. They realize that children really are leaving home later and later, and it dawns on them that the actual problem may be getting their kids to leave. This confuses them, but, given that they have now had many years' experience feeling confused, it doesn't necessarily bother them.

Early *Homo sapiens* (first year away from home)

It is worth noting that when boys do leave home they will often become complete idiots. This first year away from home is often marked by constant partying and other wastrel-related activities. This seems to have become a modern-day rite of passage in a world where male rites of passage have become largely obsolete. This time is spent in the mindless pursuit of inebriation and girls.

This is not necessarily a bad thing. It's not a great thing, but it's not necessarily a bad thing.

I myself spent my first year away from home at university getting drunk on Friday, Saturday and Sunday. We also had a Monday-afternoon-getting-drunk club and, for a short time, a Wednesday-afternoon-getting-drunk club as well. After a whole term of this, we gave up the Wednesday session because we simply weren't getting anything done. A little while later, we also cut back the Monday-afternoon-getting-drunk club to a bi-weekly event. I hate to think how clever I might have been if I hadn't consumed so much alcohol during that year (and to a lesser extent the four years following it). I'm pretty sure I would have discovered several really important things.

Most early *Homo sapiens* will survive this and eventually settle down and sort themselves out. In Celia Lashlie's book *He'll Be OK*, there is a wonderful quote from a boy who, when asked whether or not he'd ever have a plan to figure out what to do with his life, replied: 'No.' When she asked this boy how he would then sort his life out, he replied: 'Oh that's easy. I'll be about 25 and some gorgeous-looking chick will walk past. She'll have a great plan and I'll just hook onto her.'

When I read that I laughed, and shook my head at the crazy

things kids say. Then, when I stopped and actually thought about it, I realized that he'd just described pretty much what I did. I was a little younger than 25 when my gorgeous-looking chick walked past, but I'd hooked onto her just the same.

In my view, this highlights the profound wisdom of male pragmatism. Why bother going to all the trouble of working out a plan when women spend so much time thinking about it?

Just find a good one and use hers.

The sisterhood myth

We can't talk about raising boys without a little diversion into Genderpoliticsville. This will probably get me killed, but it needs to be said nonetheless. You see, the theory is that women are the kinder, gentler, wiser sex, and that if us men just stopped oppressing them and got the hell out of the way then the sisterhood would fix all the world's problems. Women are painted as wise, intuitive, and generally right about everything, whilst men are seen as fairly simple creatures, emotionally repressed, and generally wrong about just about everything.

I'm far from convinced about any of that. Women, the gentler sex? I think not. Pray that if you are ever hijacked the terrorists are male, because if male hijackers decide that their demands aren't being met they'll just blow you up, nice and clean. If the hijackers are women, then they'll drag out their box of evil shit and get to work. Female terrorists are ruthless.

Or what about political leaders? Margaret Thatcher was slumping in the polls, so she went to war with Argentina over the inconsequential Falkland Islands, which were notable primarily for their natural reserves of sheep and windswept bugger-all. Clearly Maggie wasn't willing to give up either of those things.

I work in the stiflingly politically correct world of shrinks, social workers, and 'helping professionals'. At times the rampant sensitivity to the otherly gendered/cultured/physically-abled is stretched so tight it can pick up the vibrations of a mouse fart a mile away. Seriously, you have no idea the nonsense I've heard over the years. Certainly one of the holiest of holies is the unquestioned ideology of innate female nurturing/wisdom and male hopelessness.

It's this tendency to see women as good/wise/intuitive and men as bad/incapable/negligent which has resulted in the current view that mothers are the true experts in raising children, whilst fathers are seen more as the backup team who hold the fort when the mother is busy with other things. To be sure, women still occupy the primary spot when it comes to the actual provision of childcare because they do more of it than men. In that context, it's inevitable and not at all unreasonable that mothers are seen as knowing more about raising kids than fathers who are often away much of the day.

Mother knows best.

Well, sometimes she does, but not all the time.

Now, I'm not wanting to get all whiney and go on about us 'poor men', because we've done OK out of patriarchy to be sure, but I think it's time we *all* grew up and moved on. Not just the gentlemen, but the ladies as well.

Why?

Because where all this history and politics can really come unstuck is when mums and dads are raising teenage boys. If mums think they know best about the needs of teenage boys, and if dads simply give way without having their say, then everyone is being set up for a big collision. Mums are wonderful in all kinds of ways, don't get me wrong, but they are starting from the back of the field when it comes to understanding teenage boys. The trick if you're a mum, in my humble opinion, is to first acknowledge the fact that you're playing a game where the rules are very different to everything that has gone before, to resist the urge to try to change your teenage son into what you think he should be, and to simply trust the process.

What the hell does that mean, I hear you ask?

Let me explain.

Growing teenage boys

The following are my 2¢ worth of tips for growing teenage boys. Below I've given some general guidelines for raising teenage boys, then some that are more specifically aimed at mums, and then some more specifically aimed at dads. In the next Parts ('Basic Principles' and 'Simple Plans') I'm going to talk more about the practicalities of how to get through the day-to-day issues of raising teenagers, but the following tips are aimed predominantly at giving you ways to build your relationships with your boys, or at the very least to minimize the damage.

General guidelines

Just be there.   The Neanderthal doesn't need to be having great deep and meaningful conversations all the time to know you're there. If you are there, he'll simply know it. All you have to do is be there if he needs you. Just be there.

Simple. A word to the wise, though: he will also know if you aren't there.

Work his pragmatic streak.   He's going to do things only if he can see that there's something in it for him. If you want him to do something, then make sure there really *is* something in it for him (even if that is understanding that doing whatever you've asked him to do will avoid some heinous punishment), and then make sure he understands that. He needs to see a very direct connection between your expectation and the benefit to himself. Make it as clear as you can and you increase the likelihood of a good outcome.

Structure.   Neanderthals like structure. They need boundaries. They like to know what's what and what you expect. They don't have to agree, or to even like it; but even when they don't like it, they still need it.

Understand Neanderthal time management.   It would be nice to think that one day your Neanderthal will understand it's better to get things done well ahead of time, but he probably won't. For the vast majority of boys, it always gets done *just* before the deadline. This is a consequence of their innate pragmatism — after all, what's the point doing your assignment a week early when Earth could be destroyed by a meteor before the assignment is due?

Plans take time.   Don't worry about the fact that he may not seem to have much sense of direction. That will come in time. It may already be here even, it's just that he may not be talking about it much. The best way to help him get there is give him time to think. If you have a grumpy Neanderthal, don't seek the conversation out; but if he brings it to you, then ask good questions and listen to what he has to say.

They feel all, but usually only show anger.   Don't make the mistake of thinking that just because he grunts and looks angry that this is all that's going on. Boys are every bit as sensitive as girls. They feel all the hurt, the upset, the fear, the insecurities, all that stuff. Girls might show more of a range of feelings, but they don't have the market cornered on the number or volume of feelings by any stretch of the imagination. Boys just don't make such a big deal about it, even when it is a big deal. Your job is to see past the angry displays to what might lie beneath.

Trust yourself.   You've spent a long time getting him to this point and you've taught him a lot of things along the way. All the values and morals you've taught him will be in there, and they will become more evident at the other end. It might look like he's rejected everything you've ever taught him, but that's just part of the journey. He's got to act as if he's rejected everything first so he can pick up the bits he wants for himself. Men choose their own road, but they end up with a surprising amount of their mother's stuff mixed in.

Tips for mothers

Don't mollycoddle him.   Mollycoddling is a great word, but a lousy strategy. Boys don't want it, or need it. In fact, in my opinion mollycoddling is very bad for boys because it means they're not practising self-responsibility. You will get no thanks for mollycoddling him either; instead, you'll probably get inordinate amounts of rudeness. It will annoy him and will be the source of constant conflict between you.

Don't make his lunch for school.   I'm with Celia Lashlie on this one. It's such good advice that I just couldn't leave it out of my book. This is one simple thing you can do to encourage him to stand on his own feet. If he goes to high school, he should be making his own lunch. You will worry that he won't make it right, or enough, or put the right things in, but the beauty of making mistakes like that is that you get hungry, and the hunger aids in the learning process.

Don't sweat the small stuff, or for that matter most of the middle-sized stuff either.   A large part of the reason that adolescence is so challenging for many mums is that up until that point their boys have been — generally speaking — happy to do things mum's way. Once they become a Neanderthal, however, they begin to question everything. They want to do things their own way, and, because the compass which marks their way is arch pragmatism, they will likely take a somewhat different approach to you.

They may not, for instance, see the point of making their bed each morning. This will likely seem completely pointless to them. They will retain this view until they marry and realize the error of their ways. Boys will not change their view about making beds for mothers, only for wives. You can fight that one if you really want to, but my advice would be there's going to enough going on to worry about, so don't get hung up on unmade beds.

Don't sweat the small stuff; leave that for his wife to sort out.

Keep the fussing to a minimum.   There is a world of difference between taking an interest in his wellbeing and fussing. It is completely understandable, and reasonable, that you would want to tell him to drive carefully, to be responsible, to call you when he gets there, to take a coat, to make sure his lunch is in his bag, to remember to say thank-you and all the other things good mums tell their children to do. Just keep it to an absolute minimum. You telling him to do it is no guarantee that he actually will do it. In fact, he's more likely to leave his coat at home even though he knows it's cold just to prove a point. Boys hate fussing, they just hate it. They really, really do.

Not so much with the talk, talk, talk.   There's nothing that can't be said with fewer words. Nothing. Indeed word count is one of the more obvious differences between men and women. If you have a Neanderthal, then endless talking won't work. Neanderthals are creatures of few words, if any. They prefer their communication as direct and pragmatic as possible. The more you talk, the more you increase the chances of eye rolling, lip curling, and general rudeness. For the Neanderthal, talk isn't cheap — it's downright painful. You might think that talking is the best way to maintain your relationship with him, but you'd be wrong. Sometimes the best way to communicate is with respectful silence. Sometimes you can say more simply by shutting up. Oddly, he's also more likely to hear the silence than all the words.

Do tell him you love him.   He'll moan, and sigh, and roll his eyes, but tell him anyway. Don't tell him all the time, though: pick your moments. You're his mum, so you get to say stuff like that.

Talk when the going is good.   Bearing in mind all the stuff I've said above, when he does come to you for a conversation, debate, or whatever, then seize the moment.

If you're separated, remember that the man might be your ex, but he's still your son's current and only dad. Many mums struggle with the issue of separated dads. You may not like your ex very much, and there may be very good reasons for that, but he's the only dad your son has got. If his father expresses an interest in being involved in his son's life, then you should encourage the contact as much as you can. I know that can sometimes be very hard, but try your best is all I'm saying.

Tips for fathers

Step up. The most important thing you can do for your son is step up and be involved. Don't leave it all to his mum. Mums have a tendency to take over because dads have a tendency to stand around looking a bit lost (even when they're not) in the hope that she'll just step in and take over. This isn't her work, it's yours.

Don't undermine his mother. Even though you might disagree with his mother from time to time, you must never undermine her with your son. The last thing you want to do is set up a de facto Boys Club where women members aren't allowed. He must see you and his mother as a team. How you treat his mother is his first view of adult relationships; far better to show him best practice than teach him bad habits. If you and his mum are separated, it's even more important to work as a team.

Don't give way all the time. We all give way to our partners some of the time, but we should never do it all of the time. You've probably given way over things like whether or not the toilet seat should be up or down, how the towels are folded, and getting the slightly smaller television than the one you wanted, but you shouldn't give way all the time on the parenting stuff. By definition, you will know more about teenage boys than his mother will, so you need to trust your instincts and make your voice heard.

Accept him for who he is. We all have ideas of how we would like our sons to be. That's nice. These ideas notwithstanding, our sons need to know that we accept who they really are, that we're not wishing they were someone else. Your son might have no interest in sports, he might love poetry more than kickboxing, he might dress funny, listen to weird music, have strange friends, he could even be gay. Whatever the case — gay, straight, sports or music — he needs to know that you accept who he is. You're his dad, and your acceptance of him is of huge importance. He probably won't say it, but he desperately wants you to be proud of him.

Give him your time.   It's a cliché I know, but it's no less true for that. You don't have to give him much, sometimes even five or ten minutes a day will do, but you have to give him some. Just remember that one day when you're old, retired, and lonely, he's going to have to make a decision about either visiting you or doing his own thing. Give him reasons to come back and visit you when you're old long before you get there.

Tips for living with Neanderthals

* Teenage boys tend to withdraw from their parents and become more Neanderthal-like.

* They lose the gift of speech, become arch pragmatists, and constantly lose stuff.

* If they had a T-shirt, it would read: *and I should care because?*

* Teenagers are just as complex emotionally as girls, they just don't make such a big fuss about it.

* The way through it is to understand how they function and adjust your responses accordingly.

8

the eighth framework

the bitchy physics of the girl-niverse

Physicists can't explain what's at the bottom of a Black Hole. They have some ideas, some theories, but no one really knows. For those of you unfamiliar with Black Holes, they're essentially what's left after a star — like our sun, for instance — collapses in on itself in a fit of cosmic exhaustion. The result is a kind of celestial 'hole' with a gravitational attraction so strong it pulls in everything, even light, hence the black part of the Black Hole. These things are so massive that nothing escapes them, not light, not time, not anything. The scientists know there's something down there at the very bottom of the Black Hole eating everything up, they just can't explain exactly what it is. They have some ideas, some theories, but no one really knows for sure.

Black Holes and the bitchy physics of the Girl-niverse: two of life's great mysteries.

For a while this bothered me intensely — not so much the Black Hole stuff, more that I didn't understand the bitchy physics of the Girl-niverse — because I thought I really *should* understand it, given what I do for a living. After a few years, however, I realized that no one understands them, indeed not even teenage girls really understand teenage girls, and after that I felt much better.

We can make a whole lot of predictions about boys, but girls are far more of a mystery. We know, for example, that for teenage boys with behavioural problems staying in school is a protective factor, meaning they're less likely to get in trouble if they're in school. Not so for girls. It doesn't seem to make much difference whether they're in school or out of school; if they want trouble, they find it. If they can't find it, they have a million different ways to conjure it up from the ether.

As another example, we also know that the little boys who are the most violent in preschool are likely to be the big boys who fill the jails as adults. Not so for girls. You might be a fairy princess in preschool, and a demonic she-bitch at 13. Conversely, you could be a horror in preschool and Hanna Montana later on. In fact, there are many things where straight lines can be drawn for boys that cannot be drawn for girls. Boys, we can predict. Girls, we shrug our shoulders and frown.

Certainly in my experience working with many families, I have seen time and time again the striking differences between teenage boys and teenage girls. If a boy goes off the rails, he generally drinks alcohol, takes some drugs, gets into some petty crime and hits a few people. When girls go off the rails, they have a capacity to create degrees of chaos that are hard to believe. When girls go off the rails, the earth shifts on its axis.

So why is it so much more complicated with girls?

Girls' brains and boys' brains

Can the answer be found in their brains?

Right now, there are some very clever people locked away in lead-lined rooms with expensive machines doing their best to see if there are any differences between male and female brains, but to date they haven't found much.

We do know that, on average, the male brain is larger than the female brain. This usually makes blokes sit up and look rather pleased with themselves. Unfortunately, when you compare brain size to body weight, the differences disappear. Even if it were true that there was a relative difference in brain size, this wouldn't necessarily mean anything anyway.

After Einstein's death, they pulled out his brain to see if there were any extra bits which could explain his super-duper cleverness. Sadly, it was a bit of a disappointment and looked very much like the brain of a plumber — it was nothing special to look at by any stretch of the imagination. If you're curious, just search 'Einstein's brain' on any picture search engine and you'll see what I mean.

So are there any real differences between girls' brains and boys' brains that might explain all this?

You can certainly read any number of pop-psychology books which make all kinds of outrageous claims, but so far the best picture seems to be that there are some small average differences in brain structures with lots of overlap between boys and girls. In short, the answer is pretty much a great big fat 'not really'. While some researchers have found some minor differences, they are nothing to write home about.

So at this point the best we can do is shrug our shoulders slightly, ponder on the mystery of the human condition, and just get on with the business of parenting.

Ages and stages

The standard warning applies here about ages and stages, just as it did in the previous chapter when we talked about boys. Development is a pretty imprecise affair given that we all travel at our own pace. Most of us get there in the end, but we don't always do it at the same speed, or even sometimes in the same order. Also, given what I've just said about how hard it is to predict what girls will do, you'd be a mug to treat any information about developmental pathways as gospel. Having said that, there are some broad patterns about what you can expect.

Early Girl-niverse (10ish–13ish)

The early teenage girl is a gangly, self-conscious thing. She will be going through the changes of puberty and both looking and feeling very different to how she felt when she was on the other side of it all. Things are happening, and the things that happen to her are far more obvious than they are with boys. With all the pressures that young women feel about how they look, she will be feeling anxious about everything to do with herself. She will likely be constantly measuring, comparing, and weighing herself.

At this age, she will flip-flop between wanting to be a little girl and wanting to be Catwoman. She will not really understand what being free means, and the glimpses she has of it will likely cause her more stress, but she will want it just the same. She will want to be independent, and yet will need the constant reassurance that she can depend on you.

Her place in the social pecking order will be tremendously important to her. That place will be determined largely by surface details: how attractive she is, the clothes she wears, and most of all by how socially accepted she is.

In the Girl-niverse, social status is more important than oxygen.

Unfortunately, it is also in the nature of girls to be completely bitchy. There are probably nicer ways to say that, but bitchy probably captures it best. Unlike boys — who value loyalty to friends over just about all other things (including sometimes common sense and their physical safety) — the Girl-niverse is a tangled web of shifting loyalties and allegiances. The depths of Girl-niverse nastiness are bottomless and beyond the comprehension of most of us. What's more, the communication age means girls can mount orchestrated campaigns, which include text-bullying, using websites like *bebo* and *myspace*, and any other way they can imagine to pick on their target. Girls hunt in packs and, when they decide to target another member of the Girl-niverse, they can be ruthless.

The ever-changing shape of teenage girls' social structures is dizzying for most adults, and completely mystifying for almost all fathers. Don't try and understand it would be my advice, because as soon as you think you've worked out who's in and who's out, it will change again. The same girl who was your daughter's best friend yesterday will be the one who wounds her deeply today. The day after that, they'll both be lined up against a third girl you've never even heard of before.

In the Girl-niverse, friendships are intense, sometimes melo-dramatic, and often over-the-top.

There will also be another change occurring at this time which will scare the living crap out of fathers. Their daughter's developing sense of sexuality will mean she suddenly becomes aware of the sexual economy, the subtle trade and counter-trade which underlies male and female relationships. Skirts will get shorter, bellies will be exposed, make-up will stop being a toy and will assume the importance of a strategic asset, and all manner of things may be pierced. She will become increasingly aware of the fact that, just as teenage boys can use physical means to get attention (noise and bravado), girls can achieve far more with the gentle bat of a single eyelash. Knowledge is power, and the sense of power some girls get from this recently acquired knowledge can turn fathers (and mothers) prematurely grey.

With this increasing maturity, both physically and emotionally, the generally smoother roads of childhood begin to give way to far rockier ground. In fact, it has been my experience that 13 is the new 14. It used to be that if parents came to see me with a previously lovely pre-teen who has gone completely off the rails, the child would always be 14. With the lowering age of puberty/adolescence, it is now increasingly common for parents to arrive with 13-year-olds.

Middle Girl-niverse (14ish–16-ish)

These are interesting years. As she gets older she is beginning to venture further and further out into the world, and further and further away from your supervision. This is the point where negotiations over independence begin in earnest. As a result, the emotional landscape of the home is going to change, sometimes drastically. Conflict moves in and wants its own room.

She will be trying out various external incarnations of herself to see who and what she is, although this will be heavily influenced by her peer group. In many ways her appearance and behaviour will be a reflection of them. She will spend huge amounts of time texting, and immersed in social-networking internet sites such as *bebo* and *myspace*.

Her developing sense of sexuality will also be expressing itself in her behaviour and thoughts. This said, she will largely find boys her own age rather silly and immature; largely because at that age they are.

Despite how sweet she may appear, she can be emotionally ruthless at this point. Sadly, mothers often bear the brunt of this. The reason for this is that daughters have to separate themselves from their mothers to establish their own identity in the world. It's also about now that many dads become paralysed with a mixture of fear and profound confusion. The intensity and unpredictability of the middle Girl-niverse years can pull the ground out from under most dads' feet. Mums are usually much better at dealing with this stuff initially, because they understand more about where it comes from. The difficulty is that, because mums are often the primary target of all the vitriol, they can become ground down to the point where they give up in exhaustion.

What is nice about girls at this stage, and indeed girls in general, is that they are much more open about their hopes and dreams. If she has them, then often she'll be talking about them. This is tremendously reassuring when it happens. At this age she will inevitably be thinking more about her future. She may not necessarily give evidence this in her behaviour, but she will be feeling the world pressing closer all the time.

She will be having conversations with her friends about things that would likely cause her father to drop stone-dead to the floor.

Just as with boys, her view of the world at this time will be self-centred and focused on what's in it for her. This can be very frustrating and/or worrying for parents if they make the mistake of thinking this is a permanent feature rather than a passing cloud.

Late Girl-niverse (17ish–19ish)

By now, she will not only be looking like a grown-up, but encouragingly she'll be sounding more and more like a grown-up as well. This is the point where parents start to think they just might get out alive. Reasonableness will be creeping in. Her brain will increasingly be able to grapple with more complex tasks, such as perspective-taking and logical thinking. She will tend to have a greater appreciation for the rights of others, which will flow through into increased consideration of how others feel.

She will be more settled in herself, who she is, and what she believes in. This will bring with it new challenges as she contemplates her journey out into the world. It will be a pleasant surprise for her parents at this stage that she may show more interest in sitting down and actually talking with them about what she wants and where she is going.

If the middle years have been difficult, parents may wonder at this stage if their daughter has been replaced with a being from another dimension. The flighty, fiery, irrational conflict of previous years is increasingly replaced with reason and a grounded common sense that is both welcomed and mysterious. There will likely still be times when how she acts seems in conflict with the views she espouses, but in general there is a sense that things are settling.

Most of all she is finally beginning to understand that she is not the centre of the Girl-niverse, but instead that the Girl-niverse is actually part of the Universe.

Growing teenage girls

The trick with teenage girls is knowing that there is no trick. There is no single thing that you can do. The way you get through is simply one step at a time, one foot after the other.

General guidelines
Just be there.   Just as with boys, girls need to know that you will be there, that you are on their side. The changes they go through during these years are dramatic, and so they need to know that you will always be in their corner. Even when they say mean things to you, they still want to know you will be there.

Provide a refuge. The Girl-niverse is a dizzyingly fast place where the rules change as fast as the allegiances change. She will need somewhere away from all of that where she can relax and be herself, even though she may not be sure what that means.

Make it OK for her to talk to you about bullying, and be prepared to help her in whatever way you can if it happens. The bitchiness of the Girl-niverse can at times be merciless. If your daughter is on the receiving end, be prepared to step in and help her. Contact the school if need be, get her mobile service provider to block the numbers of girls texting her, and also be aware of what is happening online. Talk to her about her feelings and reassure her that the nastiness says everything about the perpetrators and nothing about her.

Be the rock. We'll talk about this more in the next section on 'Basic Principles', but it needs to be said here nonetheless. In the Girl-niverse, storms blow up suddenly and with little warning. When that happens, you must be the rock, not the rolling seas. You must be the calm, solid, immovable object upon which the waves break.

Provide structure. All kids need structure, and one of our most important jobs as parents is to provide that structure. Some girls will push against this structure with a level of energy you might have expected more from a Sumo wrestler than a 13-year-old, but you must hold the line.

Don't judge a book by its cover. She might be looking more and more like an adult, but that doesn't mean that she is. Remember that she won't have the true capacity of an adult until she is in her early twenties. At 16 she might sound convincing, just make sure you don't let yourself be fully convinced.

Be the reality check. Many teenage girls are obsessed with their physical appearance. We all know that this is driven by external forces far bigger and more pervasive than you can ever control, but you can still be a reality check for her. It is important that you help her understand how the images of women in the media are tightly controlled and highly photo-shopped. You need to be giving her messages about how she is OK, regardless of the external appearance stuff. When her friends turn on her, she needs to know her family will always be there for her.

Tips for mothers

Remember Mad Aunt Jane. Sadly, mothers are often the targets of the majority of teenage hostility, and this is especially true for girls. This is largely as a consequence of the fact that mothers and daughters, as a general rule, tend to have emotionally closer relationships than fathers and daughters do. This becomes a problem when she enters her teenage years and has to try and carve out her own identity, to work out who she is and what she stands for. Sometimes, but not all the time, that can involve making a conscious effort to reject all of her parents' values and beliefs. In these situations it's mum who gets the most heat, because mum is the one she needs to break away from to figure out who she is. In amidst all that nastiness, you must always remember Mad Aunt Jane. Her rantings are simply the product of a very curable mental illness. Time will fix it.

Be a model. Obviously, I'm not talking about the Kate Moss kind of model; in fact, quite the opposite. She needs you to be a role model when it comes to your own body image. From the very early days, she will be looking at how you look at yourself. It is important that you model to her healthy attitudes towards food and body image. If you are always complaining about looking 'fat' or, worse still, about *her* looking 'fat', then you are starting down a dangerous road. She needs to see that you are comfortable with who you are and how you look.

Girl talk.   This is a complete mystery to me, because I'm a bloke. I don't know what happens in 'girl talk', but I do know that whenever mums and daughters do it, it's a very good thing. If your daughter wants to engage in girl talk, by all means indulge her as much as you can. You will anyway — but it needs to be said just the same. You may need to use every ounce of your mother's intuition to know just when she is edging closer to you for a few moments' respite from the world. She will still need you: it just might get hard to tell when she is signalling you to come in from the cold.

Tips for fathers

Don't be scared.   Teenage daughters can be a little scary, but it's important you don't lose your nerve. They can be as unpredictable as an old hand-grenade, and this can make some dads pull back for fear of saying 'the wrong thing'. Forget that. You will invariably say the wrong thing, but there's nothing wrong with that. The only wrong thing you can really do is to say nothing for fear of getting it wrong.

Don't try to be a girl.   Obviously, if you have the urge to cross-dress that's a whole other book; instead, what I'm talking about here is that you shouldn't try to follow her rules as a way to build a relationship with her. It's important that you learn as much as she is prepared to show you about her world, but that doesn't mean you have to give up your bloke-hood citizenship. She only has one dad, and she needs you to be a dad.

Don't give way all the time.   Just as with boys, it's important that you don't give way all the time when it comes to parenting girls. You might not understand the bitchy physics of the Girl-niverse, but you will still have a perspective that can be useful. Don't roll over and give up — this isn't fair to her mum, because she then has to sort all the problems out by herself. Get active and get in there.

Be a model.   Your daughter will look to you as her first experience of how men treat women in relationships. You need to model the kinds of behaviours you would like to see her partner display.

Give her your time.   Girls need their dads, teenage girls especially so. There's a whole bunch of 'women's stuff' she'll do with her mum, but there's still a huge amount that she will need you for as well. She needs to know that you will always be on her side, no matter what trials life will bring. The easiest way to show her you're on her side is to be by her side as often as you can.

Tips for living alongside the Girl-niverse

- No one really understands teenage girls — not even teenage girls.

- Teenage girls tend to become a tad emotional and reactive at the slightest provocation.

- The Girl-niverse is all about social standing; its all about being popular.

- It can also be a vicious, bitchy world where your friends turn on you one day, then love you the next.

- The way through is to understand what moves her and her world, and be the stable anchor. She needs you to be involved in her life.

- Home needs to be the place where she can gain some perspective.

9

the ninth framework

systems thinking —

wheels within wheels within wheels

We are surrounded by systems of every kind, from the infinitesimally small subatomic world to the infinitesimally huge Universe
itself. Everything is connected. You, as a for instance, are composed
of elements that were formed during the birth of stars and which
have bumped around the Universe for hundreds of billions of years
before finally ending up inside you. Your own body is a very large
system composed of many smaller systems. What you do to one
part has impacts on the rest, just as what one person does has
impacts on many others.

If, for instance, I was to tap you on the shoulder right now, that
would probably scare the shit out of you, possibly literally. Your
brain would dump adrenaline into your bloodstream, your blood
pressure would climb, your heart rate would spike, and you might
well jump.

'What in God's name do you think you're playing at?' you might
bellow at me.

I would simply laugh, thinking I'd just played a very jolly
prank.

In that moment you and I would be a system, each of us
affecting the other: You feeling pissed off, and me cackling away
at my good-natured tomfoolery.

You might then become so enraged at my apparent disregard

for your distress that you pull a gun and shoot me dead. Fair enough, who could blame you? The gunshots would, of course, alert your neighbours (part of your social system), who would in turn call the police (part of the legal system). You would be arrested and put on trial for murder, which would in turn be covered in the papers under the banner 'Joke leads to brutal execution', which would in turn affect all the people reading the paper, who were themselves considering playing pranks. The world would become a more serious place.

You'd get off the charge, of course — that goes without saying — but your relationship would end because of all the stress, and your children would hate you. Eventually, destitute and alone, you would creep up behind an armed police officer and tap him on the shoulder as you suddenly start laughing insanely. The police officer would shoot you, and the whole tragic cycle would begin again.

We are all connected, and the things that we do influence everything around us in more ways than we can possibly imagine. All of which makes a great deal of sense. We all know this, yet for some reason we all tend to completely ignore this fact when we are in families.

Whenever I talk to parents who have come to see me, they usually talk in very linear terms about the problem.

'What is the problem?' I ask.
'Jimmy is argumentative and rude,' they say.
'And why is that?' I ask
'Because he's bad,' they say.

This is linear thinking, it's like a straight line with an arrow that points straight at Jimmy. It goes only one way, and it doesn't include any other information. The problem is Jimmy's behaviour, and it starts and stops with him and him alone.

Systems thinking is a little different. Systems thinking is about taking a step back from things and looking at how different parts are all connected:

'What's the problem?' I ask.

'Jimmy is argumentative and rude,' they say.

'And why is that?' I ask

'Because we get frustrated and argue with him rather then enforce clear boundaries. This in turn means he escalates his behaviour and starts yelling at us. We then feel attacked and yell back. He feels attacked and yells back. This continues until we all become hoarse and are no longer able to yell.'

Now, it's important to understand that systems thinking is *not* about making excuses for bad behaviour. Instead, it is about trying to understand how everyone's behaviour impacts on everyone else. If Jimmy gets angry and tells you to fuck off, then that is his fault, not yours. By the same token, you might reflect on the fact that this only happens when you start yelling. Having reached this conclusion, you might then try harder not to yell at him, which would decrease the number of times you get told to fuck off.

There is no excuse for rudeness or bad behaviour, because those behaviours are a clear and conscious choice. Having said that, the smart thing for parents to do is to try and create an environment where your teenagers are more likely to make good choices.

Systems thinking is about not simply blaming conflict on the other person. It takes two to tango, and two to tussle as well, which is far too many ts for one sentence; but that notwithstanding, it still needs to be said. Systems thinking is about stepping back and taking a long, hard look at how we all contribute to the problem.

The one question I always ask that parents often have the most trouble answering — but which is actually the most important question of all — is this: *What do you do that makes it worse?*

Unless you are blessed with inexhaustible patience, and wisdom beyond the grasp of us mere mortals, you *will* do things that make it worse. Usually the more conflict there has been, the harder it is for parents to admit that they might be doing something that contributes to the problem. This is understandable, because conflict tends to polarize us. We retreat to our bunkers, dig in, and blame the other side.

In my own life as a parent, this is the question I most often ask myself, not always in the heat of the moment, but certainly afterwards. I have learned more from answering that question than any other.

Systems thinking

★ All life exists within systems.

★ Family life is a system just like any other.

★ How we behave affects the way everyone around us behaves.

★ If you can work out what you do that makes things worse, then you will be a whole lot closer to making things better.

10

the tenth framework

bombproof frameworks
— the edited highlights

The teenage years are, in many ways, a little like the US-led invasion of Iraq. It generally starts out OK, but quickly becomes a lot more complicated, is filled with profoundly stressful moments, and suddenly where once it was so simple there doesn't seem to be any way out. The cheering crowds give way to insurgency and roadside bombs, and you're spending all your time behind sandbags taking fire.

Now, whilst teenagers aren't quite as complex as Middle Eastern politics, they come pretty close. All this makes you feel sorry for people in the Middle East raising teenagers, because they've probably got more complexity going on in their lives than anyone could begin to imagine.

In this first section we've covered off what I think are the most important frameworks you need to understand if you're parenting teenagers. If you're like me, though, your memory is just good enough to know that there was a bunch of stuff in there that seemed really important to know, but you just can't quite remember what it was. Or if you do, it's gone by the next day.

To help make all the information more manageable, I've summarized all the major points from this first section so that you have a quick refresher course available if you suddenly find yourself under fire and need to remind yourself about the important stuff.

1　There are two different but related processes at work here: puberty (physical development) and adolescence (behavioural development). By the end of it, with any luck, the two will come together so they look and act like a big person.

2　The age of the onset of puberty has been getting steadily younger. In girls, on average it now begins somewhere around 10 years of age. In boys, it starts at about 11 or 12 years.

3　There are lots of theories about why that might be, but all we need to know is that it's happening much younger than it did for us.

4　With the decreasing age of the onset of puberty, the gap between the physical maturation and psychological maturation is becoming bigger and bigger. Marketing companies already understand this, which is why you can now get padded bras for nine-year-olds.

5　Along with all the physical changes in their bodies, there are some huge changes going on in their brains as well. The teenage years are an incredibly significant period when the brain undergoes a number of important changes.

6　The end result of the brain remodelling itself is that teenagers have a reduced capacity to make good decisions about risk. It takes them longer to decide if something is a good idea, and they're more likely to be influenced by their friends to do dangerous things.

7　Teenagers also have a reduced capacity to process emotional responses, despite the fact that they rely more heavily on these emotional responses.

8　It is also completely natural for teenagers to want to sleep all day, because their body clock gets knocked off its legs by all the hormones coursing through their veins.

9 The best way to understand teenagers is to use the Mad Uncle Jack analogy. You wouldn't be hurt by anything he said, so don't be hurt by anything they say.

10 Boys are best understood as completely pragmatic souls who work on a 'what's in it for me?' economy. They will tend to do everything at the last minute, because there is no point doing it before then. They have a loathing for excessive talking, and respond best to clear and firm boundaries. They may appear to be mindless, wordless Neanderthals, but there is still a lot going on. They just don't make such a big song and dance about it.

11 Boys need you to be strong, and to be there when they need you.

12 Girls are complex and almost impossible to understand. For girls, social standing tends to be the defining feature of their sense of self-worth. They will be heavily influenced by their friends as a general rule, although with age will come an increasingly strong move towards choosing friends who share the same values and beliefs that they do.

13 Girls need your patience, and your understanding. They need a stable centre to whirl about, so that when they need to find the ground again they always have a way back down.

14 Remember to think about your family as a system, that it isn't always as simple as saying it is one person's fault. We all affect each other, and we need to constantly reflect on this when we're trying to sort out a problem.

15 Last of all remember this simple equation:

Breathing = Hope

Basic frameworks

★ Breathing = Hope

★ The weirdness of puberty

★ Remember Mad Uncle Jack

★ Not the whole walnut

★ Weapons of mass disruption

★ A tank will always be a tank

★ The rise of the Neanderthal

★ The bitchy physics of the Girl-niverse

★ Systems thinking

part 2

basic
principles

After many years working with teenagers and families with all kinds of problems, I have become convinced that there is no paint-by-numbers solution. This isn't like baking a cake, where if you follow the recipe and put in just the right amount of flour, butter, milk, and sugar you'll get a good result. There is no recipe.

With little kids it's much easier, because you can follow a recipe and get them to sleep, eat their vegetables, and poo in the right place. With teenagers it is a whole different ballgame. The relationships are more complex, and the power balance is very different as well.

Often it will feel as if you're driving through fog at high speed, fighting for control of the wheel. In such moments you need a compass, you need to know which direction to turn. It has been my experience that the way forward with teenagers is to follow a few simple principles and trust that you will find your way through.

In this section I will give you the 10 basic principles I believe provide the best chance of making it through. These are not mine, I did not invent them. These were simply the lessons I have learned along the way from watching what works — and what doesn't.

You will need these.

Seriously.

11

So why all the hoo-hah about principles?

The reason for all the hoo-hah is that basic principles are the things you fall back on in both the good times and the bad. You use basic principles to back out of your drive, and also when the fogs comes down so thick you can't see the end of the bonnet, when the only option you have is to put the proverbial pedal to the inevitable metal.

Good times, bad times, sad times, and out of time — in all these scenarios you're going to need a compass.

Let me clarify by way of example.

The boy who wanted to kill his mother

The warnings about Patrick started long before I saw him.

'He'll kill his mother,' I was told by one of his foster parents. 'One of these days, he'll kill her.'

Crikey, I remember thinking.

'Oh yes,' they said. 'He's so angry. You mark my words, if something isn't done he'll kill her. Whatever you do, don't get them in the same room together, because he's so angry he'd probably attack her there and then.'

Statements like that are always a little worrying when you're the guy who has to do the mysterious 'something' that will stop this from happening.

Patrick was 16 and a ricochet. He'd come back around a second time. Six years before, when he was just 10, I'd been asked to assess him. At that time he'd been an angry little boy. He was in foster care in a residential facility. They were having all kinds of problems and wanted a bit of guidance. He was typical of boys who grow up in foster care: angry, quiet, not wanting to talk about anything much at all. His mum, for her part, was a nice woman. She'd been battered and bruised by life and was simply doing her best. She'd had a dropkick of a husband who'd done a fine job of messing up the kids and then taking off, leaving her to deal with the aftermath.

Dropkick dad had hit her, hit the kids, and done almost every other nasty thing he could think of. At 10, Patrick had been a fairly messed-up wee man. Even back then, his behaviours were setting off all kinds of alarm bells with his caregivers. I'd done the usual blah blah and written up my report saying all the usual things. One thing I had said quite clearly was that I thought there should have been some focused family therapy with the clear aim of getting Patrick back into his mother's care.

Maybe those things would have helped, maybe they wouldn't have. It was all academic anyway, because for a range of complicated reasons none of that stuff happened.

Now, six years further down the road, people were saying he wasn't just angry, he was dangerous. There had been some violence directed at mum, and a mountain of threats. It seemed there were good reasons for the concern, not the least of which were Patrick's own statements. They hadn't seen each other for six months, because the last time they'd seen each other Patrick had lost his rag and smashed a window.

'So what do you want?' I'd asked him. It sounds like a simple enough question, but you'd be surprised how often no one actually asks kids in care what *they* want. We do a lot of telling with kids like Patrick, but not a lot of asking.

'I wanna kill her.'

He didn't even stop to think about it.

'What do you mean?' I asked.

He looked at me like I was stupid. 'I mean, I want to kill her.'

'I see,' although in truth I didn't see much of anything, but it bought me some time. 'And why is that?'

'Cause it's all her fault.'

'What is?'

He looked at me again and his eyes went dark, 'It's her fault that my life is so fucked-up.'

'It's your mum's fault?'

Again with the dark, brooding, James Dean stare. 'Yeah.'

'And how do you work *that* out?'

'If she hadn't left me in that place for all those years, none of this would have happened.'

'You really believe that?'

'Yeah.'

'OK, then.'

We sat there in silence for a little while.

'There's just one thing . . .' I said.

'What?'

'She's coming along today. She wants to talk with you about all this.'

He looked at me, and he suddenly didn't seem so much angry as scared. 'Really?'

I nodded. 'Yup.'

'I'll kill her,' he said, although it didn't sound quite so convincing now.

I smiled at him: 'Did you bring something to do it with, or would you like to borrow something?' In my view it's always good to show kids you're not scared, even if you are. Especially if you are.

'Are you taking the piss?' he asked.

I shrugged, 'I wouldn't say I'm taking it, more like borrowing.'

'I really will kill her,' he said, starting to find his feet again.

'You keep saying that. Why is that? You think I'm hard of hearing or something?'

He gave me the broody teenage glare thing.

'I came close to gunning down two old ladies on a plane once,' I said. My cardinal rule in working with angry teenagers is that you first need to get their attention. I figured this would do it.

A single eyebrow squeezed out from beneath the glare, it made a half-hearted attempt at raising itself until the layers of cynicism coating Patrick's forehead defeated it.

'It's true,' I said. 'I was on a plane and they were behind me. They talked for an hour and a quarter about the weather in some stupid little town.' I shook my head. 'I swear to God that it was so painfully boring that I honestly thought it was either me or them. If I didn't kill them, they'd kill me with the complete and utter boredom.'

'So why didn't you kill them?' he asked.

I shrugged. 'I had the window and a big fat man had the aisle. I couldn't get out.'

For just a second he cracked a smile, then realized what he'd just done and glued his glare back together again.

'I know what you're doing,' he said.

'Discriminating against fat people and stupid old ladies?'

'Trying to make me think you're a good guy so I won't kill my mum.'

I shook my head. 'Nope.'

'What then?' he snared.

'Who do you think you are in my little story?' I asked.

'I'm you.'

'Nope.'

'Who am I then?'

'You're the fat guy's seat.'

He frowned. 'What?'

'You're the fat guy's seat.'

'What do you mean?'

I smiled, 'You're thinking way too small for the big, fat arse the world's dumped on you.'

He sat there for a minute, just looking at me. When he spoke, his words were measured and tightly buttoned: 'If that bitch walks into the room, I'm going to fucking kill her.'

Just at that moment there was a knock at the door, very quiet; it opened, and who should walk in but the aforementioned 'bitch'.

This was not how the plan was supposed to go. She should have been sitting out the front waiting for me to come get her if the moment seemed right. I'd been very clear about that. She'd nodded and said she understood.

I looked over at Patrick.

His eyes had turned black.

I opened my mouth to say something suitably calming, something to establish a little John-and-Yoko vibe. If I'd had a guitar I would have started humming 'Give Peace a Chance'.

Too late for that, though — Patrick was on his feet, fists clenched.

Shit, I thought profoundly, *buggery shit bollocks* . . .

So what would you do next?

Now, imagine for a moment that you were me. What would you do next? What would you say? This is not a book about how to run a family therapy session, but that doesn't mean that you aren't a family therapist. Every time you sit down to dinner with your kids, you're doing family therapy, you're building stuff. The only difference is that you're not paying some stranger to sit in the room while you're doing it. If you live in a family, then — like it or not — you're a family therapist. We'll talk more of this a little later on in Part III, but just for now understand that, whether you're a shrink or a parent, the principles apply the same.

In this case, the stakes are a little high right now because Patrick is saying he's going to kill his mum, and mum has a long and complicated history she's just dragged through the door completely unexpectedly. You had a nice plan in place to avoid precisely this moment, but the best laid plans of mice and shrinks frequently end up in tatters on the floor.

Whatever you do, you have about a second and a half to think about it. To complicate things, you don't know exactly how anyone is going to react.

Recall from the previous section that teenagers are more impulsive, more violent than older people, and tend to make decisions based more on emotions than on any sensible processing of those emotions. Get this one wrong and there could quite literally be blood on the floor.

If you're thinking to yourself that you wouldn't know what to do next, then you're experiencing what happens when you don't have some basic principles to guide your decisions. We become paralysed when we are filled with doubt, and doubt goes with the territory with teenagers.

In the next chapter, I'm going to give you 10 basic principles. As you're reading them, think about how they might apply to you and yours, and then I'll show you how I used these principles to fill in the gap that came straight after the *buggery shit bollocks* moment.

12

basic principles

I need to make it clear at the outset that I didn't invent this stuff, I didn't dream these principles up one day sitting under a tree somewhere. All I did was pay attention to what families were telling me over the years. I believe these principles are *of* the world in much the same way as gravity is *of* the world. They're simply part of the way things are. We could get into a whole lot of complex hoopla about why these principles exist, but we don't need to, because it doesn't really matter.

You won't be able to stay true to these principles all the time, no one can, so don't feel bad about that. Just try to stay as close to them as you can. These are the rules by which the game is played: if you know them, then you're going to be a step ahead of the pack.

1 Success = $R^3 - F$

Without doubt the three most important things in raising teenagers are these: relationship, relationship, relationship. This is the stuff that binds us together, and the stuff that sets the underlying tone of our lives. Without it, everything starts to fall apart pretty quickly.

Relationship is the glue which fixes the emotional wear and tear of life.

To a large extent, you reap what you sow in this department. Your child has been keeping their own scorecard along the way, and the teenage years are when they tend to add it up, and allocate the prizes. If you haven't put much work in through their childhood, then you are going to have problems. You can't buy their good behaviour in their teenage years with money or mobile phones, and you can't demand respect when you've done bugger-all to earn it.

Well, you can, but it's unlikely to get you anywhere except deeper in the shit.

All discipline systems are built on a solid bedrock of relationship. Without it you have no leverage. There has to be some underlying connection before you can start issuing directions.

If you're the kind of parent who achieved discipline through fear when your children were little, then, if you aren't already in trouble, you probably will be soon. Fear only works until they get bigger than you. Once they stop being afraid, you're royally screwed. Don't blame them, though: if you govern by fear, then eventually you will be called to account for that, and rightly so.

This has always been the fate of dictators.

Relationship is important because they will desperately need a parent to help them get through these years. They need some-one they can depend on, someone they know will always be on their side, come good or bad. Having said this, they don't need a simpering patsy who will believe everything they say and fight all their battles for them. Instead, they need someone who under-stands that sometimes the best way to protect someone you care about is to let them bloody their knees a little. They need to know that you will always love them, but you will also hold them accountable for their behaviour.

What they do *not* need is for you to be their friend. This is a bad thing and almost always ends in tears. The world is full of potential friends, but your children have only one mother and one father. If you fall out with a friend, you can always make new ones, but you can't make a new dad or a new mum. You just get one of each. You cannot be a friend *and* a parent. Parents do things that friends either could not, or would not, do. Parents make the hard decisions, and parents say no.

You are their parent, *not* their friend.

This does not mean that you can't spend time with them, talk with them, or goof around, because you absolutely should do all of those things. Have fun with them wherever you can, just don't give up being a parent to be their friend.

If for no other reason, you shouldn't because it's embarrassing to watch. Parents trying to be their children's friends are like the uncool kids desperately trying to impress the cool kids. It'll never happen, and they'll just be mean to you. At least if you're a parent, you get to growl at them from time to time.

Sam's parents were having big problems with him disrespecting them at home. At 13, he was rude and frequently verbally abusive. His parents were both busy professional types who had spent long hours at work for most of his life. He had every toy you could imagine, his own credit card, and lots of freedom. They let him do pretty much whatever he wanted whenever he wanted in the hope this would buy some goodwill. Instead, he just got angrier and ruder. Mum was frequently at school trying to sort out various discipline problems.

Dad kept calling him 'mate' when they spoke, when it was clear they were anything but mates.

After talking, we decided they should cut up his credit card, put some rules in place, and punish the rudeness. His dad was no longer allowed to call him 'mate', but he could call him 'Sam' or 'son'. Mum agreed not to fight all Sam's battles at school, and let him deal with the fallout from his behaviour. Dad was also set the task of trying to clock up at least 10 minutes a day with Sam. Watching television together didn't count. They also planned a family holiday together to a mutually agreed destination. Amazingly, as the plans were enacted, the relationships improved, as did the behaviour, despite the fact that Sam had less money and less freedom than he had had before.

2 Remember Mad Uncle Jack

By far the most common error that parents of teenagers make is that they think they are dealing with a normal person. You aren't. Just because they look like a normal person doesn't mean that they are normal. In the previous section, we spent quite a bit of time looking inside the teenage brain. I hope this has helped to give you a new appreciation for the enormous amount of growing (and shrinking) that goes on during these important years. If you understand this, then you will be more able to put their behaviour in its proper context.

At all times you must remember that you are dealing with Mad Uncle Jack. They are not normal people relative to adults. How they think and behave is quite normal for people of their age, but it isn't the same — at least in theory — as how we think and behave. They may be looking more and more like adults, but they still don't function like adults. Over time, as brain development continues, they will become more and more able to think like an adult, but for most of them the process will not be complete until their early twenties.

Once again let me say very clearly that I am in no way wanting to trivialize the distress and heartbreak suffered by families with sons or daughters who have mental illnesses such as schizophrenia or depression. I have seen many families affected by mental illness and I know the burdens that places upon them all.

What I *am* saying, however, is that we should not take to heart many of the hurtful and nasty things teenagers say and do. This doesn't mean you tolerate rudeness or disrespect, but it *does* mean that just because they say they hate you doesn't necessarily mean that it is so. We'll talk more about how to deal with the rudeness later on, but just for now all you need remember is that what they say, think, and feel aren't always the same thing.

In over 17 years of working with teenagers I have never met one who hated his or her parents. Not one. I've met a great many who said they did as a way to get a response, and a great many who were actually deeply hurt rather than hateful, but I have never met one who genuinely hated his/her parents.

Your teenage son asks you if he can go to his friend's place for the weekend. You know that the last time he went there his friend's parents let them roam the streets till 3.00am. You say no. He goes off his block and, amongst other things, screams at you that you are 'a total fucking control freak' and that he hates you because you 'always act like a fucking controlling bitch/bastard'.

At this point do you:

a) wonder if you really are a total fucking control freak?
b) cry?
c) beg his forgiveness?
d) all of the above?
e) tell him that his behaviour is unacceptable and punish him?

3 Don't be a Big Jessie

There will be plenty of times when you feel like being a Big Jessie: just don't. For those of you unfamiliar with the phrase, a 'Big Jessie' is a Scottish term referring to someone who is a 'Big Girl's Blouse' (see the disorder I have invented on page 146) or a bit of a softy. If you make the mistake of being a Big Jessie with your kids, it will end badly. Big Jessies are too soft or too scared to lay down the law and enforce it, and so they let their kids basically decide how things will be.

The Big Jessie does not exhibit any kind of leadership, and instead makes rather hollow-sounding statements about how disappointed they are with their children. Alternatively, they say nothing at all for fear of upsetting their teenage children. The Big Jessie thinks it is easier to simply stay out of the way than to jump in with both boots on, because if they stay out of the way at least there will not be any conflict.

A leader understands that sometimes you need to show you have metal, and sometimes you need to show you have teeth. Conflict and arguments are never fun, but they are a necessary part of life when you are dealing with people who have a tendency towards being unreasonable, demanding, and reckless. Sometimes letting them know you have teeth is how you show them that you love them.

If you're a Big Jessie, then you will let your fear and anxiety shut you down. You will abdicate from the throne, and the peasants will revolt. Just when they need clear and consistent leadership, you will desert them. Don't.

This is an example of how Big Jessies behave.

'Simon, is that you?'

'Jesus, Dad, what do you want?'

'It's 2.30am, you were supposed to be home at midnight.'

'So?'

'So why are you late?'

'I'm home now — do you have to go on about it?'

'I thought we'd talked about this.'

'Fucking hell, Dad. Shit happens. It's not my fault.'

'Don't talk to me like that.'

'Well if you didn't fucking go on about it, I wouldn't have
    to. Fuck it, I'm going to bed.'

'No, you aren't. You're going to tell me where you were.'

'Fuck off, I'm going to bed.'

'Simon, come here, please.'

The sound of a bedroom door slamming.

'Simon?'

No response.

'Simon?'

Somewhere down the hall, a stereo is turned on.

Here is what a leader would do.

'Simon, is that you?'

'Jesus, Dad, what do you want?'

'It's 2.30am, you were supposed to be home at midnight.'

'So?'

'So why are you late?'

'I'm home now — do you have to go on about it?'

'No, we don't. You're grounded next weekend.'

'What? That's not fair—'

'I'm not discussing it now, we can talk about it tomorrow.
    Go to bed.'

'But—'

'You can either go to bed now or I can make it two
    weekends.'

'But—'

'Last chance.'

Mumbling, stomping, sound of a door closing.

4 Not too loose, not too tight

There are many things that underpants and parents have in common, but the key similarity is the necessity for a structure that is not too loose, and not too tight. When I was a penniless student I had a range of underpants, from my lucky red ones which I always wore to exams, to the stock-standard, middle-echelon underpants, and at the lower end of the market I had my last-resort underpants. The last-resort underpants were the ones I was forced to wear when I hadn't done the laundry for a few days.

The reason they were my last-resort underpants is that the elastic was almost completely gone. They were as loose as underpants can get whilst still retaining an underpants-like shape. Primarily, how I experienced this looseness was that my last-resort underpants would always fall down under my jeans. This left me with the uncomfortable feeling that my arse was hanging out when actually it was still safely covered by my jeans. Psychologically, though, I walked around feeling like my arse was exposed to the world.

Vulnerable, that's how I felt, vulnerable.

I don't think I need to explain in any kind of detail the dangers and discomforts of underpants that are too tight. I think we can all appreciate those particular horrors.

The teenage years are a time when young people have to begin to find their own way in the world. As a result, the rules and boundaries are going to need to be negotiated, and continually adjusted as your teen matures. The secret with rules is that they need to be not too loose, but not too tight. Teenagers need enough room to make decisions and take responsibility for themselves, but not so much room that they end up doing stupid stuff. If you are too tight with your rules, then you're setting both you and them up for some big conflict. They have to rebel, it's their job, and they need room to do that safely. On the other hand if you're too loose, chances are they will crash.

We're going to talk more about how to do all this, because there are some things to think about when setting family rules, but just for now keep hold of the basic principle that — just like underpants — the rules need to be not too loose, and not too tight.

Wendy brought in her daughter, Kate, who was 13 and a major handful. When I asked Wendy about the rules at home, it took her 10 minutes to explain them all. Kate had a specified time to be out the door for school each morning, a specified time to be home, a process for asking if friends could come over, and another process for asking if she could go out somewhere. If she did go out somewhere, there were rules covering every aspect of that — right down to what she was allowed to wear. As Wendy explained all this, Kate rolled her eyes continuously. Wendy, Kate and I renegotiated that all down to three: be respectful, let people know where you are and who you're with, and be home at the agreed time. Fewer rules, fewer fights.

Graeme brought in his son, John, because he'd got into trouble at school. He'd been smoking, fighting, disrespecting the teachers, stealing and damaging property. My clinical diagnosis of Johnny is that he was a snot.

When I asked Graeme what the rules were at home, he just looked at me blankly. 'Rules?' he said. 'What do you mean?'

Enough said.

5 Find points of contact

Communication is your greatest tool, but there's more to it than simply sitting in a room and talking at them. Real communication involves contact with the other side, because it's only through contact that we achieve anything. This doesn't mean you need to always have deep and meaningful conversations with your teenager, because for many of you those moments will be few and far between. Instead, what you're aiming for are the little moments of connection, the times when something important happens. That might happen with a joke, a hug, a simple exchange of smiles, or even a moment of silence that could so easily have been ruined with words.

Points of contact are those magical moments when you are both there with each other, and the world is somewhere off in the periphery. It might be hard to define exactly what has just happened, but you still know something has.

The more conflict you have with your teenager, the more important it becomes to find these moments. Think of them as the moments when the storms of adolescence clear slightly and you catch a brief glimpse of each other. It might be fleeting, but that is when you need to let them know that despite all the wind and the rain you are still there.

I cannot tell you what points of contact look like, because they are different every time, but I can tell you this: if you look for them, you'll find them. It's as simple, and as spooky, and as serious as that. You cannot orchestrate these things. This is not a technique or a trick. This is simply about paying attention to what is happening, and marking the moment when it does.

All you need to do is notice.

Here are some examples of points of contact that parents created themselves where there was a long history of ill-feeling and conflict.

Giving him a ride to school and listening to his music without complaining.

Plaiting teenage daughter's hair as she watched telly.

Sitting on the back-door step. Not talking. Just sitting.

Parent saying sorry for something that happened.

Parent saying they were not sorry for something that
happened.

A look.

A well-placed nod.

Eating fish and chips together.

A carefully aimed hug.

Sitting with him outside Youth Court.

Standing in the rain, watching her play netball.

Passing a spanner.

Buying girly shoes.

A conversation.

6 Punctuation is everything

The effective use of punctuation underlies all good parenting. In fact, I would go so far as to say that there are some types of punctuation which have no place at all in parent-teenager communication.

Perhaps the worst offender is the humble comma. This simple punctuation device is responsible for more conflict between parents and their teenage children than any other. Whilst it might seem extreme, my advice would be to declare your home a comma-free zone. The comma will only bring trouble, and if you are wise you will have none of it. The rule of thumb is that anything which comes after the comma is nagging. Anything after a comma is simply going on about things.

The full-stop, on the other hand, is your friend. The full-stop can prevent many arguments. It can be used liberally with little fear.

Question marks are a little like salt, in that a little salt is usually helpful, whereas a lot of salt ruins just about any meal. Salt and question marks should both be used in moderation.

In general, you will want to deploy a full-stop as soon as you can. If you have a choice between a comma and a full-stop, always go for the latter.

Mothers tend to have far more difficulty with this basic concept of teenage punctuation, although they will usually swear that they don't. Commas come so naturally to mothers that they are often unable to tell when they are using them. Mothers also take more convincing about the need to limit the use of question marks. Mothers often think the best follow-up for one question mark is another question mark.

Fathers are more full-stop oriented.

Bad punctuation

'No, you can't go to your friend's place tonight, and before you ask me why, let me tell you, because if you were to speak a little more nicely to me and your father, and show us just a modicum of common courtesy, then I might have let you go, but you're the one who decides to be rude, so you're the one who can stay home, and if you want someone to blame for that, then don't blame me, because I'm not the one who doesn't think about anyone else in this family, although you probably don't even notice the fact that I do lots of things for you that I never get any thanks for, like your washing, and cooking all the meals, and keeping this place clean, and . . .'

How to fix that

'No, you can't go to your friend's place tonight.'

7 Be the rock, not the sea

For many families, the teenage years are a bit like global warming: once everything starts to heat up, the weather just keeps getting wilder and wilder. The once-in-a-hundred-years storms seem to roll through every second day. There are floods, hurricanes and tropical downpours in temperate regions.

Through all these storms you must be the rock, not the sea. You must not let yourself be tossed around by the gales; instead, you must be the stable centre, the immovable mass upon which the seas throw themselves. This requires determination and focus, because the storms can sometimes be loud and prolonged. You must become rock-like in such moments. You must hold your ground.

The other property which is fairly fundamental to rocks is that they do not chase things. You will never see a rock in hot pursuit. A rock simply sits in its place and waits for the world to come to it. This is what you must do when your teenagers run this way and that. You must not chase them, you must simply wait.

When the winds blow, and the seas rage, be the rock and wait. The tide might retreat, but it will always come back again.

Steven and Caroline's daughter was 14 going on 24 going on 3, and would regularly spit the proverbial dummy for no apparent reason. They would get called every name under the sun and many that were way up back behind the sun as well. When they tried to tell her she had to be home at a certain time, she would scream at them until they screamed back at her, then she would allege child abuse. She would also take money from them without asking, and then expect to be transported all over the city at a whim.

In short, they were letting her walk all over them. When I asked them why this was happening, they said they were worried that if they didn't try so hard to please their daughter she would hate them and reject them. Instead, they chased her all over town trying to please her. They had become the waves, letting themselves be blown all over the place because they had nothing to hang on to.

We decided their new strategy would be to become a lot more rock-like. Instead of buying into arguments and getting into escalating screaming matches, they would simply refuse to play the game. They would ignore her, and if she escalated and/or became verbally abusive they would punish her. If she threatened to run, they would ignore her and calmly read the paper. If she did run, they would not chase her. In short, they became an immovable object in her path.

She did not hate them, nor did she reject them. She threatened to run once and was gone for about two hours. Oddly, the more rock-like they became, the more she seemed to settle.

Steven and Caroline discovered that, even though their daughter acted as if she wanted them to do whatever she told them to do, she really wanted them to be a rock: to set limits, to behave like adults, and to be there no matter what.

8 Don't make *their* problem *your* problem

Let me ask you this: if you are driving along the road and you see a police car approaching, do you automatically slow down? Most of us do. Even if you aren't speeding, you may get that little guilty feeling and take your foot off the gas in spite of the fact that you're doing nothing wrong. And why?

The reason we slow down is not because we think about car

accidents or running over pedestrians; it is because we instantly worry about getting a speeding ticket. We take our foot off the gas because it is conditioned into our brains that if the police catch us speeding, they will punish us. They will give us a speeding ticket. Speeding tickets hurt, because they cost money.

Now imagine if, whenever you were caught speeding, the police officer gave you a stern lecture about how disappointed they were in you. What might happen to the number of speeding cars then? Imagine further still that you were also given the option of telling the cop to 'fuck off' because they don't 'understand' you, and further that you were then allowed to stomp down the hall into your room and slam the door. What might happen to the average speed of cars on the road?

Let's face it, our highways and byways would be a complete death trap. This is why the police don't just give us a stern lecture about how disappointed they are and then let us stomp off to our rooms. They know we wouldn't give a monkey's arse about that, and so instead they give us speeding tickets. If we're really reckless, they take away our licence, and eventually our freedom.

They make it *our* problem.

The same principle is true of human beings, regardless of age, in that we tend to change our behaviour only when it becomes a problem for us. The big mistake that a lot of parents make is that they take their children's bad behaviour and make it their own problem. Instead of some logical consequence falling on the teenager (loss of privileges, loss of curfew time, etc), they make it their problem. They effectively say to their teenager: Your behaviour is making me feel upset, so please stop it.

Yeah, right.

Teenagers barely understand the concept that their parents have feelings, let alone have much regard for what those feelings might be.

If you want them to change their behaviour, then you must make the problem theirs, not yours. They will only show an interest in dealing with it when it bites them.

Making it your problem

Why can't you ever come home on time? I spend all night getting stressed out and not sleeping? Can't you try and be a little more considerate?

Making it their problem

If you come in later than 10.30pm, you won't be going out anywhere next weekend.

Making it your problem

Your room stinks; I can see rotting food under your bed. Why should the rest of us have to live in a house that stinks just because you're too lazy to clean up your room? Don't you care about how we feel?

Making it their problem

You have one hour to clean up your room. If you haven't done it by then, I will be coming in with a large plastic rubbish bag and throwing anything that I think looks suspect into that bag and taking it to the dump. Your time starts now.

9 Keep making decisions

No parenting book is complete without some tale of miraculous survival against the odds in the Andes, and so in that vein let me tell you the incredible tale of Joe Simpson and Simon Yates. In 1985, these two experienced mountaineers climbed to the summit of the 6344-metre Siula Grande in the Peruvian Andes. This mountain had been climbed before, but never by the route Yates and Simpson had chosen: the almost-vertical west face. The ascent went well and they made it to the top with comparatively little drama. Getting back down would prove an altogether different experience. As they were descending, Simpson slipped and broke his tibia, smashing it back up into his knee. If you were to do this while you were out grocery shopping it would be agonizing, but at that altitude, in what mountaineers call the Death Zone, any kind of injury is almost always fatal. At that altitude a rescue attempt is usually out of the question, because your fellow climbers need all their energy and willpower simply to get themselves back down alive.

Simpson and Yates had been friends and climbing partners for years, and, despite the absolute peril of their predicament, Yates was determined he would not leave his friend behind to die on the mountain. Instead, they stabilized Simpson's broken leg as best they could, and then Yates proceeded to lower his friend down the mountain to their base camp far below them at 3000 feet. They had only a limited amount of rope, and so Yates had to tie two pieces together to get enough length. The only problem was that the knot wouldn't go through the metal belay, so Simpson had to put all his weight on his one good leg whilst Yates undid the rope and retied it.

As Simpson was being lowered by his friend, he suddenly dropped over the edge of a 100-foot sheer-ice cliff. Dangling in mid-air, he could do nothing to save himself and was slowly freezing to death in the sub-zero temperatures. Yates in the meantime was slipping inch by agonizing inch down the mountain towards the ice cliff, unable to see his friend, knowing only that somewhere below him he faced the same ledge that Simpson had slid over. Yates tried desperately to hang on, and he managed to support his friend for an hour before making what one can only assume was the hardest decision of his life, and the only option available to him: he cut the rope.

Simpson fell 100 feet and hit an ice bridge over a crevasse which broke, saving his life. He came to rest on a narrow ice-shelf deep inside the crevasse. Battered and bruised, he pulled in the rope that was still attached to him and realized his friend had cut it. Simpson has always defended Yates's actions in cutting that rope, in the face of some criticism from other mountaineers.

The next morning, Yates climbed down the mountain alone. He saw the gaping black mouth of the crevasse and assumed his friend was dead. Exhausted and guilt-ridden, he returned to their base camp.

Meanwhile, deep in the crevasse Simpson was assessing his options. He was badly injured, and clinging to a narrow ice-shelf deep inside a crevasse high in the Andes. He couldn't climb up, and there was only the darkness of the void below. It is hard to imagine how a person could be any more alone. He had no idea where the bottom of the crevasse was. He didn't know if his rope was even long enough to get there, or if it did whether there would be any way out.

But what he did next was the truly incredible thing, an act of such strength of will and determination that it is barely fathomable. While most of us would probably have curled up on the ledge in defeat and slowly died of hypothermia, Simpson did not. Instead, after much soul-searching, he secured his rope to the ice, and lowered himself off into the darkness.

His rationale for doing this was that if the situation looks hopeless, then the only way you can survive is to keep making decisions. If you stop making decisions, then you are lost.

Amazingly he made it to the bottom of the crevasse, and even more amazingly there was a way out onto the slopes. Over the next three days, he descended the mountain alone and badly injured. He made it back to their base camp, delirious and on the brink of death, just as a grief-stricken Yates was preparing to leave. The story of Simpson's incredible journey down the face of Siula Grande is considered one of the most amazing feats in mountaineering history.

Simpson wrote a book about his ordeal called *Touching the Void*, which was later made into a gripping docu-drama of the same name by Film Four.

It's well worth a read, or a watch, or both.

But the moral for all of us at the end of this section on making simple plans is that sometimes all you can do is keep making decisions. If you find yourself in the middle of some great peril and allow yourself to become paralysed with indecision, if you become overwhelmed, if you give up, then you're done for.

Keep making decisions.

10 Life is suffering

Technically speaking, this is actually the first of Buddha's four noble truths. Whilst it sounds a little defeatist at first glance, it's actually a rather optimistic approach to life. You see, Buddha had the theory that the reason so many people are unhappy is that we become attached to the completely unrealistic expectation that life should somehow be easier than it is. We think it should be less stressful, and so when it is stressful we become bitter and resentful.

'It's not fair,' we say.

'No,' says Buddha, 'it isn't. Shit happens, get over it.'

Admittedly, Buddha probably wouldn't have responded quite so bluntly, but that's the gist of it.

Now, whatever your thoughts are about Buddha, he does have quite a good point, and one that is particularly relevant to raising teenagers. If you expect it to be a smooth ride, you will be sadly disappointed. If you expect to get through unscathed, again you are likely to be sadly disappointed. Disappointment isn't in itself necessarily harmful, but when that disappointment turns into anger and resentment it can be harmful. Very harmful. I have sat with many parents who have told me that they do not like their teenage children.

I nod and say that I understand.

I *do*, truly.

And then I work very hard to provide them with some frameworks and principles to give them a more helpful view of what is going on. It's fine not to like your children, most of us experience moments like this, but when these feelings go from momentary to stationary I get worried.

Life is suffering. Nothing is perfect, and parenting is one of the least perfect things of all. Most people would say that being a parent has been both the best and the worst thing they have ever done. It is.

The trick with all that stuff, if there is one, is simply to accept that the ride is long and varied. The bad and the good will be your constant companions, so don't fight it. That will just make you tired.

The 10 basic principles

1   $R^3 - F$.

2   Remember Mad Uncle Jack.

3   Don't be a big Jessie.

4   Not too loose, not too tight.

5   Find points of contact.

6   Punctuation is everything.

7   Be the rock not the sea.

8   Don't make their problem your problem.

9   Keep making decisions.

10   Life is suffering.

13

applying the principles

patrick and the hoo-hah

So recall our young friend Patrick and his death threats against his mother and her unplanned arrival in the middle of a conversation. Dust that off with a sudden rising to his feet and a clenching of fists, and you're pretty much back at the point where we left off.

So, what now?

These are the moments when you need some guiding principles to help you to figure out what to do next. Even if there was a big book of answers, you don't have the time to go out and look up what to do.

The only saving grace at this point was that I'd seen Mum before and talked about a lot of this stuff with her. We'd talked about some of the bombproof frameworks and the basic principles, so I was hoping she'd remember all that in the next few seconds.

'Hello, Mary,' I said, trying to sound calmer than I felt.

She didn't say anything, but I could see her eyes welling up with tears.

Patrick, for his part, looked absolutely furious, but at least he wasn't lunging.

'Have a seat, Mary,' I said, pointing to a chair across from Patrick. At this point we were in deep enough that there wasn't much to be lost from pushing the boat out all the way. He was a big boy and if he did lunge it was going to be quite a scene. At this point I was relying on principle 1: R^3 – F. They weren't friends, but there was a relationship there, otherwise he wouldn't have cared. Given that by now it was clear he wasn't going to attack her immediately, I wanted to give them some time to see if we couldn't shift things along.

She looked at me, back at Patrick, then sat down.

He just stood there.

'Sit down, Patrick,' I said.

In an exaggeratedly slow movement he turned to look at me. I was reassured by that, because it was a little like watching a peacock fanning his tail.

'Sit down,' I said again, affecting a don't-be-a-dick tone and using everything I'd ever learned about Jedi mind tricks from watching the *Star Wars* movies.

He sat.

Gotta love those Jedi mind tricks.

Now at this point I'm very aware of Mad Uncle Jack (principle 2: remember Mad Uncle Jack). I'm quite clear about the fact that teenagers are more impulsive, think less about consequences, tend to be more violent than they will be when they're older, and make decisions more from their emotions than their good old pre-frontal cortex.

I wouldn't say that I was sitting on the balls of my feet ready to intervene, but I sure as hell wasn't slouching.

Of all the 10 principles, the one I'm most focused on is number 5 (find points of contact). More than anything, I wanted some point of contact between them, preferably emotional rather than physical. It was clear there were big feelings going on, and those big feelings — the product of big history — were fogging up the room. They couldn't see each other for all the smoke and debris.

In moments like this, and indeed in every family session I do, I'm looking for those points of contact — the places where people come together, where the magic happens. You should, too, but we'll come back to this one.

I looked over at Mary. A single tear rolled down her cheek. It was the first time she'd seen him in six months. I could see how much she loved him, you'd had to have been blind or stupid not to see that.

Patrick didn't see it, but not because he was blind or stupid. He couldn't see it because he was 16 and his amygdala wasn't quite up to speed when it came to interpreting facial expressions.

Mary opened her mouth to speak: 'Patty—' she started.

'*Fuck up!*' he barked back at her. 'Just *fuck up!*'

At this point I jumped in with a little dose of principle number 4 (not too loose, not too tight).

'Patrick,' I said.

He looked at me.

'Here's how this goes,' I said to him, very slowly and quietly whilst Obe Wan whispered *Use the Force, Luke*, in my ear: 'You don't have to stay if you don't want to, that's your choice; but if you do stay, you aren't going to talk to your mum like that, OK?'

He just kept staring at me.

'OK?' I asked again, with just a little hint of Darth Vadar.

After the longest time, he nodded.

Mary went to speak again, but this time I cut in because I could see that whatever she was going to say was motivated by hurt and guilt and all that shitty stuff. None of it would help. Time for principle 7 (be the rock, not the sea): 'Mary?'

'What?'

'You remember last time we talked about rocks?'

She smiled a little, and closed her mouth. I watched her visibly settle herself, calming herself and slowing down. She was a remarkable woman who had suffered more than Patrick could ever imagine. Within about a half minute she was there, she was as rock-like as she could possibly be.

Patrick looked at me and frowned. 'What the fuck are you talking about, man?'

'Geology.'

'You're fucking weird,' he said.

'You're not the first to make that observation,' I said genially, safely wrapped in principle 2 (remember Mad Uncle Jack) and thus not being hurt or offended.

I turned back to his mother: 'I need to ask you a question, Mary.'

She nodded.

'And when you answer it, I need you to talk just to me. OK?'

She nodded. By telling Patrick his mother wasn't talking to him, I'd relieved him of his mandatory obligation to argue with her.

At this point I've got principle number 5 (find points of contact) banging away in my ear like a really annoying neighbour learning the jungle drums. The only thing that could cut through all Patrick's angry teenage bluster was a little contact. They needed a glimpse of each other through the clouds. He needed to see that she was still here.

'I want you to tell me again about Patrick's third birthday, about the cake.'

She looked at me for a moment, confused, then I saw the click inside her head. I knew it would be tough for her to talk about this, but as Buddha's first noble truth — and my 10th principle — point out: life is suffering.

'When he was three,' she said, 'his father was drinking and it was very bad. He was very violent, both to me and the kids. It was . . . it was a very bad time.'

As she spoke, I could hear the pain in her voice. It had clearly been a nightmare. Her husband, Patrick's father, had not wanted her to 'waste' any money on a birthday party, mostly because he was spending all their money on booze. On the day before Patrick's birthday, she went to her mother's place and baked a cake. She brought it home and hid it under a bed in their spare room, knowing that this was taking a terrible risk, but she did it just the same. Then she waited until her husband went out with his mates and brought the cake out.

'I didn't care,' she said directly to Patrick, who had listened quietly as she'd talked.

I knew she'd break the rules and talk to him directly, in fact I was counting on it.

'I knew what he'd do if he found out, but the look on your little face was worth it. I would have done anything for that.' She turned to him, tears running down her cheeks. 'I would have died for you then, and I'd die for you now.'

He sat there for a moment, still as stone, then a single, fat tear slid down his own cheek.

And that was it: principle number 5 as large as life.

Point of contact.

Ding-a-bloody-ling.

Sitting there in his chair, he looked 16 and 6. He was a little boy wearing a big-boy skin.

Mary leaned out and put a hand on his knee. It was a big call, but the right one. Then she said something sweet, and just as importantly devoid of commas (principle 6: punctuation is everything), and then he was crying for real.

I waited for a few minutes to make sure they were OK, then I stood. 'You know,' I said. 'Everyone said I shouldn't even let you guys be in the same room together, but I think they're wrong. I think there have been far too many people keeping you in separate rooms. So I'm going to get out of your way and leave you both to catch up. If you need me, I'll be outside smelling the roses.'

Then I left.

They didn't need my help any more that day. There would be more days to come where they did, but not that day. That day they were just a mum and her boy.

Basic principles.

There is no big book of answers about what to do when a mother walks in on your session just as her son is threatening to kill her. Basic principles are sometimes all you're going to have, and sometimes all you'll actually need.

part III

simple plans

The only plan worth having is a simple one. If you have to write it down, it's no good. Who remembers to bring bits of paper when the ship is going down and you're all fighting for a place in the lifeboat?

In this section, I'm going to provide you with a very simple method for making very simple plans.

This is what I do when I'm working with families, even when the problem seems hideously complex. In fact, in my experience the more complex the problem, the simpler the plan needs to be.

Once we've got the method sorted, then we're going to look at how you can use this process to tackle a range of different problems, including all the usual stuff that parents of teenagers face, and some of the not-so-usual stuff.

As I said at the beginning, the problems and issues you may face with your teen will be unique, so I'm not trying to give you a one-size-fits-all solution, but rather a flexible approach, so when you don't know what to do you can break it down into chunks, and get it sorted.

14

simple plans, elephants' graveyards, and three helpful questions

I spent the early part of my career looking for the elephants' graveyard. This seemed entirely reasonable at the time, because everyone else was looking for it as well. The elephants' graveyard is, of course, the mythical place where elephants go to die. The legend goes that if you ever find that place, you will have discovered a vast treasure-trove of ivory.

Now, obviously I'm talking about a metaphorical elephants' graveyard, not an actual one. I mean that I, and many around me, was searching for the secret place where problems go to die, where all the answers are buried. It would be silly to search for an actual elephants' graveyard for two reasons: the first is that international treaties on the trading of ivory mean it would be almost impossible to sell the stuff; and, secondly, I don't live in Africa. We don't have elephants here, and so it's highly unlikely that they'd come all this way to die.

The reason we were all searching for the place where problems go to die is that we really believed it existed. People thought there would be some magical new way of doing things that would fix all things for all people. Some still believe that. It would be nice to think it was true, but it isn't. Therapy fads come and go just as they always have, and always will.

There will never be one place where we can find all the answers, because, just like elephants, problems end in different places and in different ways.

Life got much easier for me once I gave up my search for the elephants' graveyard, because, rather than trying to fit every problem into some grand overarching theory, I could just deal with it as is, and where is. Simplicity is good, very good in fact. I'd been working with kids for many years before I discovered the value of simplicity. Before that, I'd followed along with everyone else and looked for complex answers to complex problems.

It's an easy mistake to make, because that's the way things have been going for a while now. It often seems that we've swapped trying to figure out how to fix the problem for increasingly complex ways to describe the problem. For example, kids are no longer naughty; instead, they have Oppositional Defiant Disorder (ODD) or Attention Deficit Hyperactivity Disorder (ADHD). They're no longer just a bit weird; instead, they have Autistic Spectrum Disorders (ASD). They're no longer sad; they have Reactive Attachment Disorder (RAD). I'm sure you'll agree this is an awful lot of acronyms for simple words like sad, naughty, and a little weird.

Now, I'm not saying that things like Asperger's or ADHD don't exist, because clearly there are a number of young people who present with these very real issues, but the problem — at least in my humble opinion — is that there are many kids incorrectly labelled with whatever is the current fad. Worse still, the internet has made it easy for parents to sit at home diagnosing their children after completing some half-arsed online checklist.

Not to be left behind, I've actually invented my own diagnosis: Big Girl's Blouse Disorder (BGBD). This disorder is primarily evidenced by lots of whining, bleating, and complaining about how unfair life is.

The treatment is simple: harden up.

Berkeley once said: 'First we raise the dust, and then claim we cannot see.' He's right. So after a few years trampling around raising lots of dust, I decided to stop looking for elephants' graveyards and go with something a little simpler. I decided that maybe the best thing was to accept that there was no one-size-fits-all answer; to accept that elephants and problems all end in their own way in their own place.

So I stopped chasing graveyards and instead approached each situation with an open mind. Instead of looking for the Ultimate Answer, I decided to deal with what was in front of me. As a result, I discovered three helpful questions that I now ask myself whenever I'm faced with a problem:

1   Where is it all going pear-shaped?
2   What would be better than this?
3   What needs to happen to get there?

Can't get much simpler than that really, can it? Now it might seem a little too simplistic, irritatingly so, but before you put this book down in disgust and go back to your sudoku puzzles, read on a little further. These three simple questions are just the things you need to build a simple plan. So don't sudoku off just yet; stay with me a little longer.

You just might be pleasantly surprised.

Step 1: Where is it all going pear-shaped?

I am an avid collector of good phrases, and 'pear-shaped' is one of my favourites. The phrase usually refers to a situation that has gone wrong, sometimes horribly so. The etymologists are still arguing about where the phrase comes from, but the theory I like the most is that it was a term used by RAF pilots in the late 1940s or early 1950s. Apparently it's very difficult to pull off the perfect circular aerobatic loop, and the usual result is a loop which looks 'pear-shaped'.

Etymological arguments aside, the reason I like the phrase is because it puts me in a good state of mind. Words are interesting things, and they all come with their own baggage. If I was to think to myself something like 'What is the nature of the problem?', I would become instantly bored and a little depressed. That phrase conjures up the same feelings as things like 'family mission statement' and 'achievable goals'.

Boring.

Where is it all going pear-shaped?

Nice.

The other thing I like about this phrase is that it gets me thinking about specific points. The notion that there is a point where things start going pear-shaped immediately suggests a narrowing of the search from global issues to specific ones. I am no longer thinking about broad, but instead specific. This is good, because broad is overwhelming. You think broad too much and you start to lose hope. There's nothing inherently wrong with thinking broad as a general principle, but if you're having problems with your kids you want to nail down some specifics pretty quickly.

You cannot, for example, change a youth culture which places value on drinking to excess. You can, however, do something about the fact that your teenage son came home two hours after his curfew drunker than the proverbial skunk.

The key here is to get specific and identify the points where you can have an impact. Ideally, you want to be able to answer the question in a sentence or two.

This is also where we start to pull together the bombproof frameworks from the first section, and the basic principles from the second section. There are an awful lot of pointers in there which can help you figure out what may be going on.

It could be that you have full-on puberty/adolescence issues.

It could be that there are aspects of their behaviour which could be explained by referring to all the stuff about teenage brains.

It could be that it's a boy thing, or a girl thing.

It could be they're employing a WMD.

Any of these things are possible, and it is likely it will be a combination of several factors. In the chapters that follow, I'm going to show you how you can answer the pear-shaped question using a number of examples from actual cases so you can see how it works in practice.

The key points, though, are keeping it simple, and keeping it specific.

Billy the kid, Part 1

Billy is 13 and has been brought to see me by his mother. She is having huge arguments with him about the state of his room. It's a tip, and she's brought the pictures to prove it. What happens is that she lets it go for a while until she is unable to ignore it anymore. Then the fights start. 'It's the smell,' she says, wrinkling her nose painfully. 'You couldn't believe the *stink*.'

'Do you think it stinks?' I ask Billy.

He shrugs. 'Nah, not really.'

His mother sighs.

When I ask them to describe what happens, the picture is pretty clear. Mum tries to ignore it, but eventually she can't. She then launches into Billy whose little hackles immediately rise, and then they get into an escalating cycle of yelling and unkindness. Lately it has been really bad, and just the week before, during one argument, Billy punched a hole in the wall. Hence the trip to the shrink. When asked about why he did it, Billy says: 'Because she just goes on and on and on until it feels like I'm going to explode.'

'Do you think punching holes in walls is a reasonable way to let people know you don't like something?'

He shrugs and looks down, all sullen and embarrassed. 'I s'pose not,' he mumbles.

It's always reassuring to catch these little glimpses of conscience.

So, where does it all go pear-shaped? There are two factors that make this all tip over. The first is that there is a mismatch between Mum and Billy's understanding of who the bedroom belongs to — and what the terms of that agreement are. The second is that Mum thinks the way to resolve that mismatch is to keep talking until Billy gives in, whilst Billy thinks the best way to make his mum leave him alone is to simply increase the volume.

OK, so what now?

Step 2: What would be better than this?

Where many parents get stuck when they strike problems with their kids is that they bite off far too big a chunk. If there's a problem, and it involves teenagers, then chances are it's going to be messy. It has long been my experience that if you try and figure out how to get all the way from a big stinky mess to completely spotless, it does your head in. Often the big solution seems unattainable.

The danger here is that, because people can't work out how to get all the way to the end, they get stuck. I'm a big believer in little steps, and realistic ones at that. I rarely know how to fix a problem completely, but I almost always know what would be better than the current situation.

It doesn't matter if you don't know how to fix things: all you need to know is how to make things better than they are at the moment. That can be surprisingly easy. Then, once things are better, you repeat step 1 and step 2 and see if you can make it better again.

It is this simple question — what would be better than this? — which has enabled me to make progress in cases where progress seemed all but impossible. You don't always get to the end, and you rarely end up with everything being perfect, but you do usually end up somewhere better than where you started.

Billy the kid, Part 2

'So, what would be better than this?' I asked them both.

Billy jumped right in, bless his grumpy little socks: 'For her to leave me alone.'

'Her?' I said, looking around with a puzzled expression. 'Do you have an imaginary friend, Billy? A pesky fairy, maybe?'

He frowned at me. 'Mum,' he said curtly.

I gave him my ah-ha look. 'Ah-ha,' I said. 'It's just that your tone suggested you were talking about a pest rather than talking about your mum, the only mum you'll ever have, the mum who gave you life, and wiped your bum when you were little, and took you to the doctor in the middle of the night when you were sick. And cooked more meals for you than you could count, and worked to keep you clothed, and walked you to school when you were little, and a billion other things. You can understand my confusion when you used that incredibly ungrateful tone.'

He scowled, but said nothing. Shrinks can sometimes get away with dishing out a telling-off, and I judged that Billy would concede the point. Not too loose, not too tight.

'And for you?' I asked Mum. 'What would be better than this?

She thought for a moment: 'I don't want to have to put up with the stink, and I don't want to be yelling all the time and having him yell at me.'

Smart woman.

'OK,' I said smiling, 'that seems pretty clear. If it wasn't so stinky, there was less yelling, and your mum left you alone, that would be better than what it is now, right?' I looked at Billy, expectantly. He nodded. So did his mother.

Easy. What would be better than this? Here we haven't gone for any grand plan. We're not trying to change anyone's personality, or the mailing address of any members of the family. We haven't gone for trying to make Billy into a mature, caring, thoughtful human being. Just a little less stinky and not so loud. Mum doesn't have to sink to Billy's level of hygiene, or to stop talking altogether. In fact, all that we're doing here is aiming for a little less stinky and a little less noise. I've said it before, and I'll say it again: simplicity is the key.

Step 3: What needs to happen to get there?

A few years ago we had a man deliver a load of woodchips for the garden. The idea was that I would spread the woodchips on top of the garden to stop weeds from growing. I hate gardening with a passion. I resent it to the very core of my being. I'd rather be reading a book, or watching telly, or just lying on the couch staring at the ceiling. Because of my bitter hatred for all things to do with gardens, anything that stops weeds is good with me.

'How much would you like?' the little man on the phone had asked when I was ordering it.

'Ummm, I reckon about five cubic metres should do it,' I said confidently. It didn't sound that much when I said it, really that was just five large boxes.

It was actually a very large truck that turned up, and the little man was not so little either. He was actually quite a big man, but not in a good way, more in a too-many-burgers-and-too-much-beer kind of way.

'There y'are, mate,' he said after he'd finished tipping the truckload of chips onto our drive.

I felt sick. It was an enormous pile, so big in fact that it was more like a geological feature. It looked as if you'd need oxygen bottles to get to the top. I expected to see base camps sprout on our lawn, replete with Sherpas and yaks. At night, yetis would come down from the snowy heights and carve obscenities on our fence. My sons' sons' sons would still be labouring away to get this mountain of woodchips spread on the garden. I was a little overwhelmed to say the least.

I shifted three wheelbarrow loads and it looked exactly the same. At that point I realized it was probably better to kill myself rather than spend the rest of my life shifting woodchips. I hadn't signed on for this.

Just at that moment, a friend rang up. When he heard about my pile of chips, he was more optimistic. Shortly after that he turned up with his wheelbarrow and shovels.

'Let's get cracking,' he said.

I tried to tell him there was no point trying, that we were almost certainly going to die on this mountain, but it was pointless. He'd already disappeared around the back of the house with a full wheelbarrow.

Because sitting around whining like a Big Jessie seemed less than manly in the face of all this enthusiastic action, I filled my own wheelbarrow and set about it. We'd be dead by lunchtime, of that I was sure, but at least I'd die on my feet.

Actually, we were finished by lunchtime, not dead but spread. The mountain of woodchips was safely dispersed over the garden and there was only a little sweeping left to do. My back hurt, but the job was done. I knew that if I'd been here myself I would still have been sitting around feeling sorry for myself and trying to come up with clever plans to shift it without me actually having to do any work. Instead the job was done.

I learned two very important lessons that day, which I have never forgotten: the first is that the way you move mountains is one wheelbarrow at a time, and the second is that gardening really does suck.

In that spirit, when you're trying to figure out how to resolve some issue with your kids, it's always worth remembering that you do it exactly the same way you shift woodchips: you pick a spot, load up the wheelbarrow, and get pushing. One wheelbarrow, one step, one conversation, one day at a time. That's how you get there.

The key is that once you know where you want to be, you then have to break it down into small enough chunks. I know all this is very obvious, but that doesn't mean it's not important or that it won't work. In this modern technologically-obsessed world of ours, we place a lot of value on things that look complicated and hi-tech. Watch the infomercials on television and you'll see any number of products to make you look like a supermodel with 'buns of steel' or an athlete with 'six-pack abs' all achieved in only 30 seconds a day with no exercise while you're eating cream buns and jelly doughnuts. All you need to do is call us NOW and make three EASY payments of $99.99, and we'll also give you our patented easy-slide macho-man socks which can give you sculpted toes in only 23 seconds a day. Valued at over $1.5 million today, the easy-slide macho man socks can be yours FREE.

So call toll-free now: 0800 IBELIEVEANYOLDCRAP

Call NOW!

(Please note: results shown are not typical; jelly doughnuts not included.)

Or you could just do some sit-ups at home for free.

All you have to do is break the problem down into little steps and you will get there. I've seen kids with more problems than hairs in an old man's ears, with more diagnoses than you could fit inside a monkey, and I still go back to this very simple process of breaking it down into one step at a time.

The way you fix old men's bushy ears is by plucking one waxy hair at a time.

Billy the kid, Part 3

So we'd got to the point of deciding there's a mismatch between Mum and Billy's understanding of who the bedroom belongs to, what the terms of that agreement are, and that Mum thinks the way to resolve that mismatch is to keep talking until Billy gives in. For things to be better than what they are now, Billy's room would have to stink less, there would have to be less yelling, and Billy's mum would be leaving him alone. A little less stinky, and a little less noise. And how do we get to a little less stinky and a little less noise?

Like this. The first thing is that we need to clarify who the room belongs to, then we need to review the terms of that agreement, then finally we need to specify what will happen if that agreement is broken.

'Hey, Billy,' I said. 'Who does your room belong to?'

'Me,' he said, without thinking.

'Nope.'

'Yes, it does.'

'No, it doesn't.'

'Yes, it does.'

'No, it doesn't'

'Yes, it does.'

'No, it doesn't'

He frowned. 'Does.'

'Doesn't.'

'Does.'

'Doesn't'

'Does.'

Now, whilst it's very bad form for a parent to get into these kinds of ping-pong arguments, I'm able to indulge in them once in a while, for no other reason than it's fun and helps to fill in the hour.

'It's my room,' he said.

I laughed. 'Next thing you'll be telling me those aren't your mum's underpants you're wearing.'

He laughed, blushed, and tried to look outraged all in the same breath. 'I'm not wearing my mum's underpants.'

'Did you know,' I said, 'that you can't legally own anything until you're 16?'

'Bull,' he said.

'Nope, can't own a bull either.'

'For real?' he said.

'For real.'

He stopped talking.

'So, your room actually belongs to your mum — you're just renting it. How much do you pay a week?'

He frowned. 'Nothing.'

'So you're letting him live there rent-free?' I asked Mum. She nodded. 'I am.'

'Why?'

She smiled. 'He can't afford to pay for it.'

'Is this true?' I asked him.

Billy the kid shrugged, looking confused and a little less certain of himself: 'I guess.'

'OK,' I said to Mum, 'you have two choices as I see it. The first is that you can kick him out and rent his room out to a homestay student who will keep the room spotless, or the second is that you can let him stay even though he doesn't pay rent and you renegotiate the rental agreement to something you can both live with.'

She theatrically thought for a moment, then said she'd be happy to negotiate terms.

'And *you* have two choices as well,' I said to Billy. 'You can either leave home, get a job, and rent somewhere else so you can live how you please, or . . . ' I let the sentence trail off.

'Or what?'

'Or you can accept the fact that in order to live rent-free you're going to have to make some compromises.'

He thought for a minute, clearly doing a mental budget and making a number of projections about his current earning potential. 'OK,' he finally said.

'OK what?'

'OK, I'll negotiate.'

I nodded. 'Good. Now let's negotiate.

What needs to happen to get there?

Mum and Billy need to agree to an acceptable baseline of messiness so we can arrive at a win–win outcome.

Mum needs to operate the not too loose, not too tight principle and relax a little about the room. She needs to be clear which battles are worth fighting, and what the true cost of the battle will be.

In return for the peace and quiet, Billy needs to stick to the agreed-upon level of mess. In reality he knows his mum won't kick him out, but despite this he still needs to appreciate the benefit to him of being a good tenant.

Billy needs to know what will happen if his room is at the state where it's about to breach the contract, and he needs to know what the penalty will be if he does (ie, everything on the floor goes in the rubbish), and when the penalty will be applied.

Once the lines have been drawn, we all stick to them, and we all know what will happen if we don't.

15

tools

I'm a big fan of tazers. The advertisement for one company that makes these little babies says their tazers '. . . *fire 50,000 Volts up to 15 feet, with more stopping power than a .357 Magnum'*.

Yeah, baby.

Of course, like anything that's really cool, they do cause some controversy. The anti-tazer people generally say they're prone to abuse by trigger-happy cops and that — despite the various manufacturers' claims — they can be lethal. It always amazes me that people who never have to face huge, violent, drug-crazed criminals in dark alleys at 3.00am in the morning seem to have so much expertise in this area, far more so than the hapless police officer who does have to face the aforementioned huge, violent, drug-crazed criminals.

The word 'torture' is also periodically used in connection with the police use of tazers. Well, call me Charlie Muggins, but I think if the cop is telling you to stop moving, and you look down and see that bright little red laser dot on your chest, and you still decide to keep walking, then anything after that point isn't torture, it's simply the police educating you about the consequences of your choices.

Now, obviously parents of teenagers don't have the option of using a tazer, although one can only surmise that the level of compliance with simple requests would drastically increase if such tools were available to parents.

I, myself, would always have had a tidy room as a teenager if my mother had occasionally tazered either myself or my siblings to reinforce her point.

Because we don't have the tazer option available to us, we must look a little wider.

In this chapter, I'm going to cover off some of the other tools that you have in your holster.

Information

Knowledge really is power. There's a reason that you sometimes feel like you're fumbling in the dark, which is that you probably are. The great thing about living in the information-overload age is that you don't have to go very far to find some. All you need is a little careful googling and you can find the answers to most questions.

If you can get your head around the basic frameworks from the first section of this book, then you're going to be in a good space to understand whatever they might throw at you. If you then add some knowledge in on top of that, then you're in a pretty good place.

The more you can understand about what is going on, the better equipped you will be to deal with it.

There is no reason why you can't be informed about just about anything, because most of us have access to this vast buzzing superhighway of knowledge called the internet. Just by way of example, when I googled 'methamphetamines' I got 340,000 hits, 'teen pregnancy' got me 3,330,000 hits, 'bullying' got me 7,410,000 hits, and eating disorders got me 9,430,000 hits. If you aren't sure about the facts, Google is always there to fill in the blanks.

To help you along in this regard, if you go to my website, www. goldfishwisdom.co.nz, you will find a page with links to a range of sites that deal with various teenage issues. You will also find some completely frivolous links as well, which may lift your spirits if you're feeling a little trodden down.

Networking

Some time ago, probably around 3BC, teenagers realized that networking was a powerful tool. They realized that networking enabled better plotting, and that plotting meant for better parties. Just over 2000 years after that, mobile phones and the internet were invented, and then the concept of networking took off big-time.

Now, just as they can use networking both for good and evil, so can you. There are two basic types of networking: low tech and hi tech.

The low-tech kind is where you actually talk to people. Talking is what we all used to do before email and text messaging. Some of you may even remember it. There is nothing better than actually getting to know the parents of the kids who your kids hang out with. This doesn't mean you have to go out and make a bunch of new friends and have each other over for barbeques, but knowing each other well enough to ring up to check out if what you're being told is true or not is useful.

The hi-tech kind does require a little text messaging and/or emails. In this scenario, you can use technology to spread information among parents just as it can be used to spread information amongst teens. Imagine, for instance, that your daughter tells you about a party her friends have been talking about. She assures you there will be adult supervision, and you inevitably check this out as best you can. But suppose you could then send emails or text messages out to all the parents from your child's school so they would all know about the party as well? The benefit here is that it's harder for teens to sneak off to parties when their parents already know the details. If the next weekend your son says he is going out with his friends and he hasn't told you about a big party that you've already heard about through the hi-tech grapevine, you might be able to ask him a few more informed questions.

They all do it, so why shouldn't we?

It doesn't have to be a big deal, and it can be as formal or informal as you like. All you need to do is ask other parents if they want space on the grapevine, and after that it will be largely self-perpetuating.

Is this spying?

No, of course not, Moneypenny.

Attitude

This was obviously the big thrust of Part II, because the basic principles I outlined there are all about how you put attitude into action. Parenting teenagers is *all* about attitude. If you approach the task with the right attitude, then you're 95.64% of the way there. The single biggest mistake that I see with parents who are having trouble with their teenagers is an unhelpful attitude. These are a few of the more popular flavours:

- ✩ *The whiner* constantly feels that they haven't done anything to deserve this much trouble from their kids. Maybe they have, maybe they haven't. It doesn't matter, because whining about it won't help.

- ✩ *The grudge* forgets that they're supposed to be the grown-up and holds grudges and bitter feelings which leak out all over the place.

- ✩ *The hippy* wants their kids to be free spirits and drink deeply from the vibe of the earth. Hates rules and limits. Likes freedom and individual expression of one's inner self, often to the point of tolerating all kinds of unacceptable behaviours. Then is surprised why their kids won't do anything they're asked.

- ✩ *The scaredy cat* is so frightened of the world that they stop their kids from doing anything at all. Constantly hovers around protecting everyone from any kind of discomfort or harm, then wonders why their kids hate them.

✧ *The vacant seat* simply is not there. Too busy building a career, or building model trains, or talking in chat rooms to parent their children. Isn't surprised when kids get into trouble, because doesn't actually notice.

✧ *The bottomless wallet* tries to buy good behaviour with trinkets and cash. Thinks that money and material things can overcome their fundamental absence as parents. Constantly perplexed as to why their kids have no ambition, no respect for property, and treat money like it's a spontaneously regenerating resource.

✧ *The idiot* blindly believes everything their kids tell them. Need I say more?

✧ *The cool dude* likes to be cool with the kids. Parents can't be cool, not if they're doing their job properly. To be a parent, you have to be a bit of a drag at times; in fact, quite a bit of the time. They like to hang with the kids, then are surprised when their kid gets busted for selling drugs at school.

✧ *The over-involved* is so involved in every part of their children's lives that they have no space of their own. They want to go on the PTA, the sports club board, they want to go to the music lessons and sit in offering helpful advice and encouragement, to go on the school camps, to have long, intense conversations. Then they can't understand why their adult children never come and visit them.

✧ *The deaf post* thinks they know what's best for their kids. Never listen to anything their kid tells them about what they actually want. Then swears black and blue that they *always* listen. Pushes despite all the protests, and then are surprised when they wake up to find that their kid has run away to join the circus.

It's pretty clear that all these different styles are quite different from the principles I described in Part II of this book. It's also pretty clear that most of us would stray into at least one or two of these styles from time to time. This is natural. We're only human. But if you have a consistently crap attitude, you're going to get consistently crap results. If you meet anger with anger, what do you think might happen? I know it, and you know it, but many of us forget it in the heat of the moment.

Attitude is one of the most powerful tools you have.

Negotiation

Sometimes parents worry that negotiation shows weakness. This is wrong. You can show just as much weakness by choosing not to negotiate. The trick is being clear about under which conditions you'll negotiate, and under which conditions you won't. It is not, for example, a good idea to negotiate with terrorists, and particularly with teenage terrorists. If you begin negotiations under some threat, then you're headed for trouble. Next time they want something they'll just make another bomb, or run away again, or get that tattoo, or marry their idiot boyfriend just to spite you.

Never negotiate with terrorists.

You should, on the other hand, feel obligated to negotiate with delegations who come in peace and are acting in good faith. This shows strength, and builds trust with developing nations.

Building trust is in everyone's interests.

It is also important to remember that, whether you like it or not, your kids are going to be acting with increasing autonomy from here on out. As they get older, they will venture further and further from home, and be gone for longer and longer periods. If you don't negotiate some of that, you increase the chances of them making stubborn, pig-headed mistakes just on principle. Negotiation is essential, so here are my 10 tips for how to do that:

1 Clearly signal the start of the negotiating process, even if it is right here and now.

2 Always begin by aiming for win–win (for them to be able to go to a party and for you to be reassured they will be safe and responsible).

3 Listen carefully to their request. Ask some questions to show you're listening and trying hard to make sure you understand them.

4 Establish the facts (the things which simply are), the options (possible solutions) and what you both think/feel about those options.

5 Remember, there is nothing inherently wrong with raising a bad idea, but problems inevitably arise if we are too attached to that bad idea.

6 Model good negotiation skills by focusing on the problem, *not* criticising the person.

7 If things get heated, stop the process and let everyone cool down before resuming the discussion at some mutually agreed time.

8 Be fair, and be consistent.

9 Keep the big picture in mind, don't get lost in the details.

10 Once you make a deal, stick to it.

Remember, too, from Chapters 7 and 8 where we talked about boys and girls, that most teenagers need to see the immediate relevance to themselves of whatever it is you've asked them to do. This is absolutely true for boys, but also for girls. They need to see what's in it for them first before they'll really think about a compromise.

Rules

What a lot of parents sometimes fail to understand is that if *you* don't provide the rules, *they'll* make up rules of their own. If you don't give them a curfew, they'll impose their own. Usually this self-imposed curfew will not be one you would have chosen and will likely include the phrase 'any bloody old time I bloody like' in there somewhere.

Human beings like rules because without them life takes far more effort. Oddly, despite all their protests, teenagers are also far happier with rules than without them. Without rules, you have to figure out each and every situation for yourself, which takes up a lot of time, and can be very stressful.

Setting rules tells your kids that you care about them.

These are my tips for rules:

1 Make as few as possible, 3–5 rules maximum. Any more than that and you won't be able to remember them. Also, the more you have, the more you have to police.

2 Keep them simple and fair. The more complex they are, the more they're open to interpretation. Also, if they aren't fair, then they will only make things worse.

3 Make them realistic. There is no point making rules you can't monitor or enforce.

4 Negotiate the details.

5 Revisit them periodically. There will be a lot of changes going on for your kids, so you need to make sure the rules are keeping pace with that.

Remember that the whole point of having rules is to provide a system of conduct so we can all get about the things we need to do without harming ourselves or others. The other thing is that rules aren't just about what *not* to do, they're actually supposed to be about living a particular way, about building something rather than just blocking something off. If your rules allow your kids to be kids, and you to be parents, then you will all be fine. If they don't, then you will simply be inviting a great many arguments.

Money

The nice thing about money is that you will generally have more of it than they do. Because of that, they will want your money. Except here's the thing: you don't have to give them your money. Not a cent. You can if you want, and most parents will, but you don't actually *have* to. It isn't written into the contract.

Unless they have a job, money can be a powerful incentive.

Some people are troubled by using money to obtain good behaviour. The usual objection is that this is 'bribing them'. This line of thinking holds that we shouldn't bribe our children; they should behave and do their jobs simply because they want to. In this view, bribery is seen as being a poor strategy.

I usually answer that criticism with a single question: How many of us would go to work if we stopped being paid? Maybe some, but my guess is not very many. There is nothing wrong with bribery.

My friend Eleanor was bribed to study as a teenager. Her parents said they would rather she studied than have to work at an after-school job, so they paid her an hourly rate to hit the books. It wasn't a great hourly rate because, as Eleanor herself is the first to concede, her mum was Scottish, but it did the trick nonetheless.

Bribery is just another way of saying performance-based pay.

Experience

You have much more of this than they do, so make sure you use it. This means keeping a cool head and utilizing the perspective that age sometimes brings. You will not be able to use your experience to your advantage if you let your emotions run the show. It's inevitable that there will be times when you make decisions emotionally, but these are rarely the best decisions you make, particularly if they are driven by anger, fear, or guilt. These emotions are usually behind some of our worst decisions.

So be cool of head, stand back from things, and take in the whole picture. You were young once, and if you try really hard you can probably recall a little of what it was like. You know some things about life they have yet to learn. This doesn't mean you get to lecture them, but it does mean you can exercise a little wisdom and let them learn in their own way.

The poker face

If you don't have one, get one. You're going to need it. Remember that teenagers are not very good at accurately judging emotions in others, and they're prone to be a little emotional themselves in how they react, particularly if they're talking about something they feel upset about. They will sometimes be looking for any excuse to pop their little cork, so try hard not to give them one. If you want them to talk to you about the big stuff, then you have to be able to at least maintain the façade of not freaking out.

If you want your daughter to come and talk to you about the fact that she's thinking about 'going all the way', then you have to be able to listen to what she says without screaming, fainting, or wailing.

You *must* have a poker face.

You can be doing back flips, you can swear and shout and curse as much as you like, just so long as it all stays *inside* your head.

These are my tips for generating a poker face in a time of crisis:

1 Shut up. Just shut up. Whatever you do, just shut the hell up.

2 Don't move. Stay very still. If you have to move, nod a little, maybe blink, but that's it.

3 Tell yourself that you won't die. You may feel like your brain is about to explode, what with the pounding and all,

but chances are it won't. Even if it does, you'll be
dead so at least you won't have to deal with this situation.
If the worst that could happen right now is you die, you're
doing OK.

4 Make the first thing that comes out of your mouth
something about how glad you are that they trusted you
enough to come talk to you about this issue blah de blah
de blah.

5 Resume breathing.

Sometimes the best face to present is a poker face, because just
about anything else will probably lead to trouble. Of all the steps,
though, probably the last one is the only one which is mandatory. If
you omit that last one, there's not much point finishing this book.

16

the p-word

Some years ago now I met a young man who'd been in trouble with the law. He limped into my room with his arm all bandaged up and looking very sorry for himself. It turned out him and a mate (the dropkick variety, not the good kind) had stolen a car and then been chased for an hour through the scenic countryside by the police. He was not a bad boy, and he was from a good family, nice people, but he'd been out with this dropkick mate and, for all the reasons we've talked about so far, he made some pretty stupid decisions.

They were chased quite a long way before they lost control of their vehicle, crashed through a fence into a field and got stuck. At this point he'd jumped out of the car just in time to see the police dog-handler loose the beast which then bounded across the field towards him.

He screamed, and tried to run. Not smart.

The dog grabbed him by the arm and dragged him to the ground, holding him in a writhing, whimpering mess until the police arrived. When they did get to him, they were, he alleged, less than kind. In fact in his words he got a 'solid booffing' from the cops.

As I listened to him, all I could imagine was the number of people who had come close to serious injury or death as this young idiot had driven at speed pursued by the police down country roads. In such moments I can't help but imagine my own family being hit head-on by someone like him, seeing my children lying in the twisted wreckage as a result of his thoughtless, reckless, teenage display of macho crap.

Now, in that moment I didn't know if it was true that he'd had a 'solid booffing' from the police when they finally got to him, but because I drive my own family on the same roads I hoped it was. That notwithstanding, because people like me aren't supposed to think like that, and we're certainly not supposed to admit that we do, I remained a professional. 'Gosh, young person,' I said, 'what did you think when they set the dog on you and then ran over and gave you a booffing?'

I expected to hear the usual whiney, poor-me protests. Instead he looked at me and said, very matter-of-factly: 'It made me think I'm never going to steal another car again.'

I almost hugged him.

'What was the moment you made that decision?' I asked.

He frowned: 'When I saw that big fucking dog coming towards me.'

'And what would you have thought if they'd come over and put a blanket over you and then reassured you that they'd call your mum and dad after they'd taken you back to the station for a hot chocolate and a bit of counselling?'

He didn't even stop to think. 'I'd have thought that was probably good fun and I'd have done it again.'

I knew two things in that moment. The first was that there was a very good chance that this young man would never steal another car again, and that he would go on to become a decent, upstanding member of society; and the second was that our attempts to protect our children from harm have become so ridiculously politically correct we have utterly and completely lost our way.

No Yang without Yin

It is a good and useful thing to praise young people, indeed to praise all people. Reinforcement and reward are powerful motivating factors that can produce much behaviour change. These things are an essential component of parenting, and without them children wither and die, psychologically, emotionally, and ultimately physically as well. Without those acts of kindness and concern, we live lives that are emptier, unhappier, and ultimately shorter as well.

Now having said all that, where things have all gone a bit doo-lally is that we've essentially removed 'punishment' from the modern vocabulary. It's still in the dictionary right now, but probably not for too much longer. One day soon you will open your dictionary and in between 'pungent' and 'punk', there will simply be a space.

Why has this happened?

Well, that's another whole book in itself, but let's just say that Ronald Reagan, Margaret Thatcher, and a small group of economists have a lot to answer for. Forget who shot JFK, you should be more interested in who stole parenting and why. Now, I know the answers to all that, but you'll have to wait for the next book to find out. For now, all we need to know is that in a single generation there has been a huge change in how we view parenting and children, and, whilst some of that has been good, not all of it has.

One of the worst things that's happened is that we've lost our will to impose punishments on kids. This is because the modern view of children is that they are inherently fragile and our job as parents is to protect them from any kind of bad feeling. At all costs they must feel good about themselves, even when they've done something shitty.

Especially when they've done something shitty.

In fact, if they've done something shitty then it is probably because they have LOW SELF-ESTEEM, and so we must make them feel better about themselves. If you smash all the windows in an old lady's car, then you must have LOW SELF-ESTEEM. We shouldn't punish you, because this will only make you have LOWER SELF-ESTEEM.

Above all else, do not use the word *punishment* in front of the young people. This will cause them deep emotional trauma and put harmful creases in their SELF-ESTEEM in such a way as to require counselling and lemonade and poetry.

Instead, we should use the c-word: *consequences*.

Consequences are safe, wholesome, and gluten-free. No one was ever hurt by consequences, which is nice. As long as we use the word *consequences*, then everyone will be safe, tears will not be shed, and the chickens in the barn will continue to lay warm, brown, gluten-free eggs.

Well, maybe.

You see, there are two ways to teach a monkey to sit on a blue seat. The first is to give him a banana every time he sits on the blue seat, and the second is to give him an electric shock whenever he's anywhere *but* the blue seat. Both of these strategies work.

Am I saying that's it's alright to give a monkey electric shocks?

Of course not — unless the monkey is very annoying, in which case it's fine. Even the other monkeys would probably thank you for that.

Like it or not, punishment is an effective way to change behaviour. Oddly, it is the fear of punishment that keeps many of *us* in line. As I said before, most of us slow down when we see a police car. And why do we do that? Is it because we suddenly think about the safety issues of speeding, or is it because we immediately think about getting a ticket?

Now, don't get me wrong, I'm not saying we should lock them in cages filled with rotting fish, or send them off to some form of adolescent gulag, but is punishment really that bad?

My view would be that life is a bell-shaped curve, that all things in moderation is probably the safest bet. Reward and praise are good, but if we're going to have that Yang, then we also need a little Yin. A little Yin never hurt anyone. In fact sometimes a little Yin is just what a person might need to help them to evaluate the wisdom of their actions.

They need a reason not to be bad

Recently I was talking to the manager of an organization that works with young offenders. He wanted my opinion about a case. The young person in question was 14 and had committed a string of burglaries. This young man's key worker had come up with a plan. Because he'd expressed an interest in getting fit, and in playing the guitar, the plan which had been proposed included a gym membership, $700 worth of new gym gear, a new amp for his guitar, and being taken to a couple of rock concerts.

'Is it just me, or is this a really stupid plan?' he asked me.

I understood how he felt. Sometimes people say things to you, and it is so stunningly, nakedly stupid, you wonder if you've misunderstood. It's so dumb you need to ask someone else just in case the stupidity is actually a cover for something very clever hidden underneath.

'Nope,' I said. 'This plan is so utterly stupid it makes my head hurt.'

I wasn't lying. The message inherent in this plan was that if you break into people's houses and steal their stuff, we'll give you some really cool things. I understand the intention, which was clearly to inspire this young man into a life of music, physical fitness, and pro-social behaviour, but there's a world of difference between what we intend and what actually happens.

This plan was all Yang.

There wasn't an ounce of Yin in sight.

We both stood there and shook our heads at how far the world seems to have lost the plot when it comes to dealing with wayward young men and women. Then my colleague said something so simple and profound, something which so elegantly summed up everything that was wrong with the world, that I made a promise to myself that I would steal it and pretend it was my own.

'The problem,' he said, 'is that it isn't enough just to give them a reason to be good, we also need to give them a reason not to be bad.'

And there it was. He'd just summed up my whole philosophy about how to deal with teenage behaviour problems in one sentence. Usually it took me at least a paragraph, and even then it wasn't as simple or as clear as that.

That manager is completely right. We need to give them a reason to be good, for sure, no argument from me there, but we also need to give them a reason not to be bad.

It was so brilliant it should have been on a T-shirt.

The two types of punishment

Broadly speaking, there are two ways to punish: the first is taking away something nice, and the second is introducing something not nice.

If we return to our annoying monkey for a moment, I can illustrate how that might work.

In the first instance, if he won't stop annoying the other monkeys we can take away something he likes — his bananas, for example. Monkeys like bananas, and so he will learn that annoying other monkeys results in the loss of bananas. It will hurt him to lose those bananas, and he will want them back. Next time he has some bananas he will be more likely to observe good monkey etiquette. If not, then we take his bananas again.

As long as he really likes bananas, he'll get the point. The more he likes the bananas, the more quickly he'll get the point. If he doesn't get the point, then he either doesn't like bananas enough, or he's a really stupid monkey.

The second type of punishment is where we introduce something not nice, something aversive. If, for example, we wait until our annoying monkey starts bugging his little simian friends, and then briefly introduce a leopard, this will scare the shit out of him. Literally. We don't want the leopard to eat him, but we do want him to get that impression. You're only going to need to introduce the leopard once or twice for little monkey-boy to get the point. If you introduce something the monkey does not like whenever he does something bad, he will do the maths and stop doing that bad thing.

This is how we do it with people as well: either take away their bananas, or introduce a leopard.

Taking away the bananas

☆ Reducing their curfew.

☆ Grounding.

☆ Loss of allowance.

☆ Taking away cellphones, computers, etc.

☆ Restricting television time.

☆ Restricting access to friends.

☆ Not having access to the family car.

Introducing leopards

☆ Extra tedious jobs at home (cleaning bathroom, vacuuming, sweeping drives, cleaning windows, etc). Just remember the key thing is not that the job is done to an impeccably high standard; the key factor here is the inconvenience and the tedium.

☆ Mowing lawns, weeding, general garden tedium.

☆ Shifting piles of stuff from one place to another.

☆ Having to listen to your music in the car instead of theirs for a set period of time.

☆ Having you drop them off at the door of their class if they are misbehaving in school.

☆ Having to go with you to visit your friends if they can't be trusted to be left at home by themselves.

☆ Having to call home every two hours when out to prove they are capable of following curfew times.

Be IT savvy

If you don't already know that IT stands for Information Technology, then it's a safe bet you're a long way from being IT savvy. Luckily you don't need to know a lot about computers, mobile phones and the like to utilize gadgets to your advantage. Indeed, all you really need to know is which bits of these various gadgets are the essential bits. What particular parts are the ones that are essential for the gadget to operate?

If you know this, then you know which bits to confiscate.

Taking a whole computer away is time-consuming and involves much lifting. Taking the keyboard is very simple. Resetting the password to log on to the computer is a little more hi-tech, but also involves less lifting. Taking power cables is a doddle. Taking just the essential pieces also has the added advantage that they get to look at the computer, or the Playstation, or Xbox, or whatever, and be tortured by the fact that they can see it, but they can't make it go.

Transport

Even though the strategic value of transport — or rather the lack of it — is somewhat obvious, there are some hooks and barbs in here. It's pretty easy for most parents to withhold outward-bound transport, but it can be a little harder to withhold the return fare. Once they're out there in the world, what we want is for them to return safely home. When your daughter rings up at 2.00am it can be hard to say no, and unless there are completely extraordinary circumstances I would suggest that you don't say no.

As a general rule, regardless of the circumstances, if they ring up in the wee small hours and say they want to come home, then my advice is go get them. This doesn't mean you have to be a doormat and be a free taxi. You can deal with the issues when you get them home, but best get them home in once piece first.

If it's something more benign, such as storming off to a mate's place in the middle of the day and then demanding a ride home, that's a different story. A little walk, or even a moderately long one, never hurt anyone.

It's just a word

You might well ask the question why have a whole chapter on punishment, and not even a tiny little insert textbox on rewards?

Good question.

In answer I would say only this: would you have been so surprised if it had been the other way around? If I'd had a whole chapter on rewards and nothing on punishment, you probably wouldn't have even noticed. The reason for that is that this is the status quo, that's how things are usually done. We spend an awful lot of time thinking about how to give our children reasons to be good, but bugger-all time thinking about how to give them reasons not to be bad.

Give them reasons to be good, by all means, but don't forget the other half of the pie. We must love them, and praise them, and tell them that they're special to us — all this is good.

And we must *also* give them a reason not to be bad.

The p-word

★ The word 'punishment' has become very unfashionable in recent times.

★ Despite that, punishment still remains an effective way to change behaviour.

★ Effective punishments are fair and reasonable, not punitive.

★ Punishment helps teenagers make the connection between their behaviours and the consequences of those behaviours.

★ Just as we need to reinforce the behaviours we want so they have a reason to be good, we also need to give them a reason not to be bad.

17

the ladder of certain doom

'I'm so sick of screaming and yelling all the time,' said Alice.

I believed her.

Her son Toby was 14 and was being a complete shite. She'd separated from Toby's dad seven years before and had largely been raising their son by herself. Toby's dad had started a new family somewhere else.

Nice.

In the past few years things had got harder and harder. Once Toby hit his teenage years, he metamorphosed overnight from a nice-enough wee boy to a fully grown 'shitbag', as Alice described him. He was rude, disrespectful, and seemed angry all the time. What's more, he seemed to take a perverse joy in winding his mother up. As she got more out of control, he seemed to enjoy it more and more.

Alice in the meantime was slumping into a sinkhole of despair and inadequacy. Once a psychologist called Harry Stack Sullivan had theorized that if he put a monkey in a cage and gave it random electric shocks the monkey would get depressed. Amazingly, it did. Who would have thought that random, uncontrollable electric shocks would make a monkey depressed?

Harry Stack Sullivan, that's who.

I reckoned Harry's monkey and Toby's mother had a lot in common.

'What have you tried?' I asked her.

She shrugged. 'Screaming, grounding him, taking away his stuff, not giving him money, more screaming. Nothing works.'

I looked over at Toby. He was still just a boy. He was 14, but the typical coltish 14. He was five-foot-four and bulletproof. He thought he should be free to run his life the way he saw fit, free of nagging mothers and the ghosts of absent fathers — but that would have been the worst thing that could have happened. If you put a 14-year-old in charge of the ship, he's going to crank it up to full throttle and start playing chicken with icebergs.

'What do *you* want, Toby?' I asked him.

He simply shrugged in that surly, childish, Rambo kind of way that boys his age do.

Toby didn't really know what he wanted — or rather, more correctly, he didn't know what he needed. He thought he did, but he was wrong.

I felt for Alice. She was in a tough spot. Raising her son by herself when the dear little man he'd once been had been replaced by this thuggish, rude, ungrateful toddler in a man-skin.

'Toby,' I asked him, 'what time is it?'

He looked at me for a moment, grumpy, then glanced at his watch. 'Half-three,' he said.

I smiled. 'Good. You can read the time, that's all I needed to know. I need to kick you out now so I can talk to your mum about how she can punish you a little better when you're rude. You wanna go outside and make a pipe bomb, or rob a bank or something while we talk?'

Toby looked like he was uncertain if he should be angry, offended, or amused, but he got up and left anyway.

'Right, Alice,' I said. 'Let's plot a little. I have this thing that I call The Ladder of Certain Doom, and I've found it can be useful as a tool for managing kids' behaviour. Shall I explain how it works?'

She nodded, but I could see it was one of those here-we-go-again type of nods. She'd heard it all before.

I was pretty sure she hadn't.

So what is this ladder thing?

The Ladder of Certain Doom (LoCD) is a tool I first developed many years ago, working with much younger children. It worked so well with this younger age group that a 10-year-old recently sent me a poem about how much she hated me because her mother was now using the LoCD at home. You know you're on to something when 10-year-olds are sending you hate poetry.

The success of the LoCD with younger children led me to ponder how it might work with teenagers. With a little adjusting it turns out that it works pretty darned fine.

Essentially, it's a progressive punishment system where you lose something (such as bedtime, computer time, curfew time) in graduating steps until you do what's been asked, or stop doing what you've been told not to do. The trick is the simplicity of the system, and the way in which it is applied.

How does it work?

1   All good systems need a simple structure, and the LoCD is no different. You can set this one up as a virtual ladder in a spreadsheet, write it down on a piece of paper, or just keep it in your head. I favour paper, because I think it's best for kids to see very clearly where things stand. Structures should be clear and visible. If we use curfew time as the current example, the ladder starts at the latest limit of the curfew and then comes back in half-hour steps as shown below:

Curfew time
11.30pm
11.00pm
10.30pm
10.00pm
9.30pm
9.00pm

8.30pm

8.00pm

7.30pm

7.00pm

6.30pm

6.00pm

5.30pm

5.00pm

2   If you have gone the pen and paper route, put it somewhere where everyone can see it. Fridges are very good.

3   Place a fridge magnet at the very top of the chart. The magnet now becomes the 'flag' that tells them what time they've got to be home.

4   Every day starts with the flag at the top of the ladder: 11.30pm in the example above.

5   If there is bad behaviour, then the flag moves down a rung. If the bad behaviour doesn't stop in a given period of time, then the flag moves down another a rung.

6   Similarly, if you ask your teenager to do a task within a set period of time (best measured with the microwave timer) and it isn't done, the flag moves down a rung.

7   The flag keeps moving down until your request is complied with.

8   **This next bit is very important:** if your teenager has *lost* time off their curfew, they can *earn* their way back *up* the rungs by doing a *payback job* (see below).

9   In this way, their curfew decreases with bad behaviour and increases with good behaviour.

Payback jobs

Payback jobs are fundamentally important to how the LoCD works. Payback jobs are the vehicle for getting out of negative cycles and back into positive ones. The purpose of the payback job is to encourage your teenager to enter into positive behaviour. Some examples of payback jobs are given below:

☆ sweeping the drive

☆ emptying the dishwasher

☆ hanging out the washing

☆ tidying up the room

☆ vacuuming.

It is important that you understand that it's their decision whether or not they do a payback job, and then which payback job they choose. It is a fundamental psychological principle that choice increases the chance of compliance.

That said, it's also important that you have a written job description for each task. The best way to do that is to have a small box of cards that your teen can choose from, each with a separate payback job on it and the steps that each job entails. An example is shown below:

Drying the dishes
1. Dry each item thoroughly using a tea towel.
2. Make sure it is dry.
3. Put each item away in the right place.
4. Dry the dish rack and put it away in the correct cupboard.
5. Wipe away any water on the bench.
6. Fold tea towel and put it away in correct place.

This might seem a bit pedantic, but if you don't you can end up in a debate about whether or not the job is finished. With the card, all you have to do is look at the card, look at what they've done, and then the answer is clear. If there is still water on the bench, you simply say: 'That's good but you forgot step five. Tell me when it's done and I'll let you move the flag up'.

Obviously some jobs are bigger than others, and so they may get to go up two rungs (one hour) for cleaning their room, and only one rung (half an hour) for sweeping the drive. On completion of the payback job, they get back the agreed-on amount of time.

Alternatives to curfew time

It might be that curfew time doesn't do it for your kid, but don't worry — you have a number of options. The following are suggestions only, and I'm sure if you put your mind to it you will come up lots of your own:

- ✩ bedtime (works with younger teens)
- ✩ time on the telephone
- ✩ time allowed to text message
- ✩ time on the computer/internet
- ✩ time playing video games
- ✩ time allowed to watch television
- ✩ time listening to music
- ✩ time with friends
- ✩ miles you are prepared to transport them each day.

Essentially, anything that they like or value that you can remove in incremental steps will work fine.

Key ingredient for success: robotic disengagement

When the robots eventually do take over the planet and kill us all — and let's face it, this is not a matter of *if*, but *when* — you can bet they won't feel bad about it. They won't go on about it either. They'll just exterminate us all, apart from the small group they'll keep around as slaves to use in gladiatorial death matches because they're curious about why humans are so hung-up about dying.

They might feel curious, but they won't feel bad.

Similarly, when the last remnants of humankind form resistance groups and destroy the odd robot here and there, you can bet the other robots won't feel mad about that either. They will simply approach the problem logically. I can't help feeling that somewhere in this steadfast reliance on logic lies the secret to how we will eventually defeat them and take back the planet, but we may have to wait for the sequel to find out just how.

In any case, we can learn much from killer robots. Principally, the big thing is robotic disengagement. Teenagers are always looking for a way to knock us off-balance, and getting you all wound up is the best way to do it. Teenagers are always looking for a debate. They'll argue just for the hell of it sometimes; and the more you argue, the more chance they have of getting what they want, as we talked about in Chapter 5 where we looked at teenage WMDs.

If you simply apply the LoCD in a removed and dispassionate way, there is nothing for them to argue with. Essentially, you make the problem between them and the LoCD, not them and you. Your only involvement is to move the flag up and down, the rest of it is over to them.

Why does it work?

I think that the primary reason why this tool is so effective with kids of all ages is that it places the responsibility for that behaviour back where it belongs: on them. It isn't my job to make sure my son speaks respectfully to his mother; that's his job. By the same token, it's his problem if he chooses not to speak respectfully because the hammer will fall on him and him alone.

When used properly, the LoCD can be a very useful tool for

teaching kids to manage their own emotions, and to stop and think. If the parent isn't getting all wound-up but simply keeps moving the line down, then the teenager is unable to use their parent's anger as a focus or a justification. If there is no emotion, they are left to deal solely with the cold logic of their ever-decreasing time.

The real strength of the LoCD is that it provides us with a mechanism to disengage from all the yelling, and fighting, and negative emotions. The cooler we are, the more rock-like we are, the better things are likely to go.

You have effectively defused all of their WMDs.

The other really nice thing about the LoCD is that it provides teenagers with a mechanism to get back into a positive cycle. They don't have to do a payback job, no one is forcing them, or nagging them, but if they do then they get back some more time. No one wants grumpy, rude, teenagers hanging around . . . but quiet, polite ones doing jobs?

Who wouldn't want that?

'Yes, but my kids won't listen . . .'

If you were thinking this, then you have some serious leadership issues to address. If you don't have much faith that your kids are going to listen, this means you aren't in charge — they are.

This will probably be no news to you, and I wouldn't be at all surprised if you were thinking 'Yeah, yeah, smart guy. Easy to say, but what am I supposed to do about it? Huh?'

Regaining control is important, but it's also not a small job. It's doable, but it'll take a little more space than we have in this chapter. In Part IV, 'Putting it all together', I'm going to talk about how you can do that. For now, though, if you're thinking that you couldn't get your kids to listen to you, just tuck the LoCD away somewhere handy, because you'll need it once you've got things back under control again.

Oddly enough, this was exactly what Alice said when I explained the LoCD to her.

'He'll never listen,' she said. 'I mean, it sounds all very nice, but he'll just tell me to fuck off.'

I looked at my watch. Our time was nearly up. 'Alice, I have to go to Chapter 18 next and talk about party planning, but can you come back a little later in Chapter 28 and I can show you how to get back control of things at home again?'

She nodded, and we made a date to meet again in 94 pages' time.

18

party planning
made simple-ish

Parties are often the highlight of their young, carefree lives, and
the bane of our old, worn-down, worry-laden ones. All they want
to do is go to as many parties as they can, and all we see on the
television are story after story of how parties have gone terribly
wrong.

So, what can we do?

Well, there are a few things you can do to make sure your kids
are safer out there, and I'm going to give you my tips gleaned
from teens, parents, social workers, cops, shrinks, teachers, and
a multitude of other people over the years. None of these are fool-
proof by any means, because you can never anticipate everything
that could possibly go wrong, but these are a good start.

When your teen is going out to parties

1 **Establish bottom lines.**   You need to know where the
party will be, who is organizing it, whether or not there
will be adult supervision, whether there will be alcohol,
what time your teenager is going to get there, who they are
going with, and what time they will be leaving the party.
You have every right to know all this, and if they won't tell
you then they shouldn't go.

2 Get clear about alcohol. Age is a big factor here. Obviously zero alcohol is best, but you have to be realistic about this. Most of us probably spent our teenage years going to parties as well, so we know what they will get up to. If there's a party, then will be alcohol, and probably drugs. Whatever you decide or negotiate between you and your teen with regards to alcohol, make sure that it is clearly understood, and make sure you follow through if the agreement is broken.

3 Get clear about drugs. You should have a zero-tolerance limit with drugs. That alone won't stop them from experimenting if they want, but they need to know that your start position on drugs is zero. I talk more about this in Chapter 24.

4 Harden the target. The better-informed teenagers are, the safer they will be. Talk to them about the kinds of risks they might come up against at parties, and help them figure out strategies to deal with those situations. When there is something on television about parties that have gone wrong, try to engage them in a discussion about what they would have done in that situation, and how they can watch out for that in the future.

5 Buddy up. Teach your teenagers the value of buddying up, of watching each others' backs. Just as it's good to have a designated driver, it's also good to have a designated buddy. If you're by yourself, you're far more vulnerable than if you have a mate there watching out for you. Teach this, and reward responsible behaviour whenever you see it.

6 Arrange an SOS signal. Sometimes, through no fault of their own, your kids might end up in a situation they won't have been able to anticipate and one they have no control over. If that's the case and they need an escape route, you should have a prearranged phrase or code they can use which means they want you to come get them. It can be hard for teens to back down in front of their friends, but if they can call you to 'check in' and then slip you the secret signal, they can then blame you for having to leave. This lets them save face, and lets you save them. Everybody wins.

7 **Getting them out at the end.**   One of the best police youth services officers I've ever met told me about the strategy he used with his own teenage children. Once he was satisfied that the party was above-board, he would agree to a time to meet his kids at the end of the night. When he came to pick them up, he would park down the block and around the corner so his kids didn't have to get in the car in front of all their friends. If his kids didn't turn up at the car at the agreed time, he would drive up to the front of the house, march in the front door, and take them out in front of everyone. Simple and clear.

When the party is at your place

1 **Establish bottom lines.**   You need to establish at the outset who will be coming, what time the party will begin and end, and establish some crystal-clear rules about alcohol and drugs. Also be clear about the behaviour you will and will not tolerate.

2 **Have plenty of food and non-alcoholic drinks available.** It's pretty obvious that the more of this stuff you have available, the better things are likely to go.

3 **Have reinforcements available.**   Parties can quickly get out of hand. In the age of text messaging, if you text two people, and then they each text two people, who each text two people . . . before you know it you can have 500

kids at your house. You need to have people available so that if you need more help you can get it.

4 **Be vigilant.**   Obviously you don't want to be constantly hovering about spoiling everyone's fun, but you do need to be aware of what's going on. Be on the lookout for people getting intoxicated, and for conflict, fights, and general shiftiness. A stitch in time saves hours at the hospital and police station.

5 **Consider hiring security people.**   This might seem a little over-the-top, but if it's going to be a sizable party think about the benefits of spending a couple of hundred bucks on professional security guards for the night versus the cost of a trashed house if things get out of hand. It also sends a strong message to all the kids who do come that there will be no nonsense.

6 **If all else fails, call the police.**   If things escalate and you want to shut the party down (say a car-load of older, drunken idiots turn up unannounced), call the police and ask for help. That's what they're there for, and the police would generally far rather come out early and close things down than have to come out a few hours later once there are cars burning in the streets.

It's just about being sensible

It's important that kids go to parties, because that's all part of the fun of being young. Besides, if you never let them go, eventually they will climb out a window and go anyway. Better we all do it above-board with some safety mechanisms in place. The major thing for parents to remember is that you have both the right and the responsibility to ensure that your kids follow a few reasonable guidelines.

Oddly, even though most kids protest about their parents

putting in place rules around this stuff, most of them actually want that. Just as little kids feel happier with boundaries, so do the big ones. They are entering into a world which will at times seem quite scary, so it can be a great comfort for them to know that they don't have the option of going somewhere that feels a little out of their depth because their pain-in-the-arse parents have said they need to be home before midnight.

So instead they stomp home sulkily, and harrumph down into their nice warm bed, safe and sound.

19

if they hate you,
be a stealth bomber

Way back in 1977 I watched *Star Wars* like most of my generation with a mixture of awe, excitement, and ice cream. I particularly remember thinking Luke's hovercar was completely brilliant. He scooted across the desert landscape of Tatooine in this very cool machine and I knew I just had to have one. More than that, I knew that one day very soon I *would* have one. My friends and I were convinced hovercars would be rolling off the assembly line in next to no time.

Sadly, no.

I'm not driving a hovercar. In fact I drive a Nissan. A nice sensible, utterly terrestrial, Nissan. It does have a button for climate control, which all sounds very *Star Wars*, but even that's just a big fat lie because, even though I turn the temperature way up, it still keeps raining.

I think it will be one of the great regrets of my life that I will never own a hovercar; that and never getting the opportunity to fire an assault rifle. Still, that's a whole other story.

Perhaps the one thing that has helped me bear the pain of not having a hovercar is the B-2 Spirit Stealth Bomber. I don't own one of these either — and given they cost about $1.2 billion am unlikely to any time in the foreseeable future — but I have seen them on the telly, and just knowing such a thing exists is enough. If you put aside (albeit briefly) the whole moral thing about blowing people up, you have to admit that B-2s are way cool.

Why, you might wonder, would the US Airforce spend such a lot of money on a plane? Despite all the hoo-hah about payload delivery, I rather suspect that it really comes down to the fact that there was a bunch of engineers sitting around feeling pissed about the fact that they couldn't figure out the technology to make cars hover. As a way to compensate for that dismal failure, they decided to build the coolest-looking plane the world has ever seen, and what's more the sneakiest plane that the world has ever seen as well. Using complicated materials and dizzyingly complex physics, they have built a plane which is virtually invisible to radar.

Not a hovercar, but not bad all the same.

What does all this have to do with me, I hear you ask?

Well. The B-2 was designed to go in fast, and quiet, and then to 'deliver its payload' (ie, bomb the shit out of) the target (ie, the baddies). There may well be some 'collateral damage' (ie, little pieces of old people and children), but that is OK because we're simply striking a blow for freedom (ie, looking after the interests of Big Business who put us in the Whitehouse to begin with). Now you might think that all this has no relevance to you and your kids, but it does.

Go in fast, then drop and run. Let me explain by way of example.

Danny was a tangled young man. His life was a thorny mess he wore draped about his shoulders like a perimeter fence. He was messed up in just about every way imaginable, which was the inevitable consequence of growing up with a mother who was equally damaged. She had invited every bad man she could find into their home, and they had done every bad thing possible to him and his siblings. I could say that he was traumatized, that he had attachment issues, but the best way to describe that young man's world was that he was completely fucked-up. Not very elegant, I know, but then there was no room for elegance in the nightmare that was Danny's life.

He hated me.

Why?

Simply because I breathed.

'Morning, Danny,' I would say.

'Fuck off,' he would reply.

'How's it going?' I might ask another time.

'Fuck off.'

'Seen any good movies?' I'd try the next week.

'Fuck off.'

I held no grudges, it was my fault for breathing in the first place. The problem was that we had to build some kind of relationship if we were going to work together. Now, this is similar to the problem many parents face when their children are being horrible. Sometimes you cannot say a single thing without getting a big bucket of shit thrown at you. My theory has always been this: if the other guy has a reputation for throwing buckets of shit, then you need to get in and get out before he or she has the time to load up.

Speed is the key, hence the B-2 Spirit Stealth Bomber technique: get in quick, then drop and run. How this works in practice is that you go in under the radar, then at the last minute you drop your payload and get out. In this instance, the payload is not high explosives (the use of which on your teenagers is both dangerous and ultimately counter-productive) but rather small bursts of laser-guided flippancy.

Again, let me explain by way of example.

In Danny's case, I would walk past the room that he was sitting in, pause for a moment, then lean back around the door and say: 'Those shoes.'

He would snort 'What?' at me, heavy with disdain.

I would then nod and say simply: 'Nicely scuffed.'

Then I would be gone before he had a chance to reply.

The next time I saw him, I walked right up to him, pause, and say simply: 'Excellent staring.'

Then I would decamp the scene post-haste.

The next time I walked up to him, opened my mouth to speak, and paused as if about to speak some weighty tome: ' . . . '

He stared at me, expectantly, angry. 'What?' he finally barked.

I shook my head, as if I had something to say but the moment was not right. 'Nope,' I muttered to myself and walked off.

The next time, as soon as I saw him he walked up to me: 'What the fuck are you gonna say now?'

I stared at him for a moment, as if testing the air. 'Nope,' I said. 'The vibe isn't fully formed yet.' And then off I would walk.

This went on, and on, and on, and little by little, a tiny green shoot appeared in the stony ground. The beginnings of a relationship of sorts. It was tiny, inconsequential, but no less a miracle for it. The moral of this story is of course that flippancy, and a little compassionate silliness, can bring life out of even the most barren soil.

If your kids say they hate you, and seem to have not a kind word for you, remember the B-2. Get in quick, then drop and run. The devil is in the details of course, because you can't overplay this one. If you go too far it will all backfire and end in tears. But if you're careful, and apply just the right amount of flippancy, at just the right time, you might be surprised. They probably won't say anything about it at the time, but when they've grown older, and become people again, it will make for wonderful stories.

The B-2 drop and run

★ Pick your moment, usually when they're distracted with telly or buttering toast.

★ Sidle up beside them.

★ Compliment them on some completely silly thing:

> 'Those jeans . . . nice holes'
>
> 'Nice buttering.'
>
> 'Good hair.'
>
> 'Laces. Untied. Fab.'
>
> 'Nice slouching.'

★ Mean what you say. There is no room for sarcasm here, just heartfelt silliness.

★ Get out quick.

★ Seriously: don't dilly dally in the hope of some conversation — just get out.

★ Keep 'em guessing about when you're next going to hit, and where.

part IV

putting it all together

So now we've got our bombproof frameworks to understand what makes them tick, we've got our basic principles to guide our actions, and we've got a tidy little structure for making simple plans.

All that remains now is to have a look at these things in action so it's crystal-clear how the pieces all fit together.

As I've said, it's not my intent to give you a one-size-fits-all solution, because there is no such thing. What I will do, though, is show you how you can use these three elements (frameworks, principles, plans) to build specific solutions to any problem you encounter.

How we'll do this is we'll start at the shallow end of the pool first and get our feet wet on some problems that are less complex, and then we'll progressively wade out deeper and deeper into the more complicated stuff that tends to fill most parents' nightmares.

We'll finish up by talking about hairy women.

Simple or complex, it doesn't really matter, because my

intention here is to show you that, regardless of what you're faced with, you use the same frameworks, principles, and simple plans to figure out what to do.

20

you are your own family therapist

There are good reasons why I tend to include a lot of stories about real families in my books. The first is that they're just more interesting to read. Our lives are not bullet points, they are stories. Bullet points have their place, and you'll certainly find a number of them in the pages that follow, but our lives are far more than a series of neat summaries. Just like stories, we all have a beginning, a middle, and an end. I think this is why stories are so helpful when it comes to understanding ideas. They work just like we do.

The other reason I include real stories is that I want to encourage you to think a little like I do, like someone who does family therapy for a living. This does not mean I want you to wear cardigans and say 'uh-huh' a lot. Most of all I do *not* want you to go around asking everyone how they 'feel about that'.

This is likely to make people want to avoid you, or shoot you.

I *do* want to encourage you to think about families as systems, as a series of interconnecting parts. If you adjust one wheel, you're adjusting the whole system. A tweak here and a twiddle there can change the course of history. All you need to do is figure out which piece to adjust, and then watch the changes that flow on. As an example, you cannot directly change what your teenager thinks inside their head, because that is entirely within their control, but what you *can* change is your response to what they think. Your behaviour, words, and actions are entirely within your control. If you do that, for good or ill, then you will get a different response from *them*. For every action, there is a reaction — it may not be the neat and tidy equal-and-opposite reaction of classical physics, but there will be a reaction just the same. All you need to do to change the system is to change what one person does: what *you* do.

All good family therapists understand this basic fact.

Now, you might have no interest in being a family therapist, but, trust me, if you live in a family, then you *are* a family therapist. Every single day you will be involved in analysing 'family dynamics' and trying to work out how to keep the whole thing on track. You will be mediating conflict and trying to negotiate solutions. You will be assisting family members with various trials and traumas. You will be trying to figure out how to get the train back on the rails when it periodically comes off.

When I have problems with my own kids — and, yes, I have just as many problems as anyone else — the only way I am able to work out what to do is by taking a step back from it all. I don't think about my family as if it was *my* family; instead, I think about it like any other family I'm working with. I have to step back from being a dad, and get my head into a different space. When things are getting rough, it's far more useful for me to think like a family therapist than a parent.

The same will be true for you as well.

The reason for this is that, if you're being a family therapist, you're thinking about things, you're not simply reacting emotionally to things. Thinking is good, very good in fact, and most of us don't do nearly enough of it. Reacting to things is unavoidable at times, but you will need to do more than simply react if you're going to get through their teenage years.

The big thing about working with families is that you have to be able to see how all the pieces interconnect, you need to see how one thing leads on to another. Once you understand that, then you know where the pressure points are, which bits need adjusting, and where a little drop of oil should be applied.

In all of the cases that follow, I would encourage you to think about them not as a parent, but as a family therapist. The better you become at this, the more confident you will feel with your own family. My hope is also that this will make it easier to notice how the frameworks, principles, and simple plans make themselves obvious in each case.

In my experience, even though we're all different and unique and all that nicey nicey blah de blah, there are some basic themes which are common to us all. Flowing on from that, there are some fundamental solutions that I believe are also common. In all of the cases that follow, I think it should be fairly easy to see that the better we are at communicating, the better things generally appear to go. A very wise family therapist called Steve de Shazer once said: 'Messages are not sent, they are only received.'

If I've learned nothing else over all these years of working with all these families, I have learned that de Shazer was right. The only messages that count are the ones people actually receive. It doesn't matter what your intention was, the only thing that matters is how that intention was *perceived*.

So in that vein, let me send you a message of my own: always remember that you are the best, cheapest, most committed family therapist that your family could possibly have.

I hope you get it.

21

the generation
gap(ing abyss)

teenage culture, generational differences,
parental fears

REFERRAL INFORMATION

Family details	Peter and Gail (parents), and Amy (13)
Presenting problem	Peter and Gail are concerned about Amy's mental health, and in particular about the impact of some of the music she listens to.

I thought it might be best to start with one of the more interesting requests that have ever been put to me. It was so interesting, in fact, that I was left entirely speechless — something not easily done.

Amy was dressed all in black, looking more grunge than goth. She was 13, apparently very sullen in nature, and had a deep and abiding passion for death metal. For those of you unfamiliar with death metal, it is an interesting variant on heavy metal whereby the band members simply scream at each other whilst making as much noise as possible. There is no discernable melody, beat, or pretty much anything which sounds even vaguely musical. It is like a wall of distortion. If you took Beethoven, covered him in metal bolts, fed him into a jet engine, and then revved the whole thing up, you would get some idea of how death metal sounds.

I am not a fan of it myself.

Amy was.

Her parents, on the other hand, were not. In fact, her dad hated death metal with about the same passion that his daughter loved it. I assumed that her parents wanted to talk about the conflict that all the musical differences caused them, to see if they could find some common ground, or at the very least a negotiated peace.

I was wrong.

Very wrong.

'How can I help?' I asked.

'I want you to get her to stop listening to that . . . that *stuff* she listens to, and get her listening to something better,' said Peter.

I raised my eyebrows, a little taken aback. 'Such as?' I asked.

'Pan flutes.'

This is the point where I lost the gift of speech. I looked at him to see if he was joking. Clearly, he wasn't. I tried to find words, but there were none. They had all fallen off the back of my head and were laughing their arses off somewhere.

'Huh?' was all I could manage.

'I want you to get her to listen to the pan flutes like I do. They're very nice. They'd certainly be a lot better for her than the stuff she currently listens to.'

At this point, thankfully, my words composed themselves and got back to work. 'Peter,' I said politely, 'if you made this poor girl listen to pan flutes I'd have to report you to the police for child abuse.'

Amy guffawed, which from the look of her was not something I guessed she did very much.

'It's not that bad,' said Peter, defensively.

'Oh, it is,' I said. 'Pan flute collections are the atmosphere music they play in the lifts that take you to Hell.'

This time Amy laughed.

I looked at Gail: 'Don't tell me you listen to pan flutes as well?'

She smiled self-consciously, 'Actually I'm more into country music.'

I winced. 'Tell me it's just Johnny Cash?'

'More Tammy Wynette, Dolly Parton, that kind of thing.'

I looked at Amy with genuine sympathy. 'You poor child,' I said.

Unperturbed, Peter pushed on: 'Lately, we seem to argue all the time,' he said. 'We used to be able to talk about stuff, but now all she does is stay in her room and put on that . . . that . . .'

'It's *music*, Dad,' Amy said in exasperation. 'Just because *you* don't like it doesn't mean it isn't music.'

For the first and only time in my life I found myself defending death metal as a valid form of musical expression. 'She's got a point,' I said.

'Yeah, well that's all very well, but I can't see how that music is going to do anything other than make you get completely depressed and want to jump off a bridge.'

I shrugged. 'To be honest, whilst her music might give me a headache, pan flutes would be one of the few types of music that would make me feel like jumping off a bridge.'

More guffawing.

'Well, what else has made you suddenly stop talking to us?' Peter demanded. 'Ever since you've been listening to that *stuff* it's like you can't stand being around us.'

And there it was: the real nub of this generational clash. This wasn't about music, this was about fear.

Where did it all go pear-shaped?

There were a couple of things going on here, and most of it came down to Peter and Gail not having any way of understanding what was going on. They weren't seeing this in terms of frameworks, such as the weirdness of puberty or the bitchy physics of the Girl-niverse, and they also weren't employing much in the way of systems thinking. All they saw was that the daughter, with whom they had previously had a very good relationship, had become sullen and withdrawn. Instead of trying to understand what this meant from within some kind of useful framework, they blamed it on the music.

It was the oldest trick in the world and one that had probably been playing out over the course of human history. Every generation swears they will never lose touch with the music of 'today'. They know all the Top 50 and tell themselves they always will. They vow that when they have children they will not roll their eyes and play sad old tunes on their record player.

And that is exactly what they end up doing. It is the task of every generation to reinvent itself, to find its own identity and culture. No matter how much you might try, it is almost impossible to remain hip. Only a very small number of people can manage this, and they are mostly incredibly rich rock stars. Staying hip requires more money and time than most of us will ever have.

This all went wrong when Peter and Gail — although I actually suspected it was more the former than the latter — reacted without thinking.

What would be better than this?

'I just don't want to fight all the time,' said Peter.

'That's what I'd like,' said Gail. 'Just living in a less angry house would be nice.'

'Well, I just want them to stop going on about my music all the time,' said Amy.

All this was good stuff, but not specific enough for me. 'What do you mean when you say you don't want to fight all the time?' I asked Peter. 'How much of the time do you want to fight?'

'None of the time.'

I smiled. 'And when you're actually being realistic, what would be better than this?'

He shrugged. 'It would be nice if we could at least have one conversation in the day where we didn't argue.'

'You'd agree with that, Gail?'

She nodded.

'Good. That's easily doable. And you, Amy?'

She shrugged. 'I dunno.'

'You said you don't want your dad to hassle you all the time about your music. Are you saying that you want him to like your music, or that you just want him to not like it more quietly?'

'Yeah,' she said. 'More quietly.'

'Great,' I said. 'All of this is doable.'

What needs to happen to get there?

There are some incredibly simple things that need to happen. First, Peter and Gail need to get their heads around some of the developmental frameworks we talked about in Part I. They need to understand that it's normal for their daughter to experiment with things that seem quite alien to them. Music is one way teenagers carve out their own place in the world. It is one of the more common ways they start to build their own identity away from us.

Rather than resent them for it, we should thank God this happens, or we would never have moved away from pan flutes in the first place.

They also need to understand that withdrawal is completely normal. There is no cause for alarm here. Instead, they need to get their head around the fact that they are raising a teenager who lives in the Girl-niverse, and in the Girl-niverse death metal is sometimes the soundtrack *de jour*.

Then they need to get their head around some of the parenting principles we talked about in Part II:

1 $R^3 - F$.

2 Remember Mad Uncle Jack.

3 Don't be a Big Jessie.

4 Not too loose, not too tight.

5 Find points of contact.

6 Punctuation is everything.

7 Be the rock, not the sea.

8 Don't make their problem your problem.

9 Keep making decisions.

10 Life is suffering.

And this is where the real benefit of the basic principles can be found, because once we start thinking about them it becomes easier to see where Peter and Gail have started to lose balance. The primary benefit of the basic principles is that they provide direction, they give you a pointer about which way to go. I'll probably repeat this a few times as we trundle along, but only because I think it's worth repeating.

In that vein, let's think about some directions that might be helpful for Amy's mum and dad. They need to remember that it's all about relationship, not friendship. It's not about being Amy's best buddy and talking death metal trivia, but by the same token they don't want to dig themselves into opposing foxholes. They might also find it helpful to remind themselves that Mad Uncle Jack has come to stay for a while, and so they need to be patient. What's more, they need to make sure that the rules at home are not too tight (and not too loose), and find points of contact with their daughter. If it were me, I'd look for those points of contact through the music. I'd engage in discussions about it and — despite the fact that I don't like the stuff myself — I'd genuinely try to understand what it's all about. If that didn't work, I'd try something else; and if that didn't work, I'd try something else; and I'd keep trying until something finally worked, or she grew out of it. Whichever came first. Fighting over whose music is the most crap will achieve absolutely nothing. Besides, Amy clearly had the moral high ground as far as music was concerned in this family.

So the first simple step they can take to avoid many of the

arguments is simply to shut up, give the girl some space, and stop criticizing her choice in music. Just that alone will start to make things a little better. If they simply give her some room to breathe, they will also likely find there is room for conversation.

Fixing stuff

'You just have to shut up about it,' I said to Peter and Gail after I'd sent Amy out of the room.

'But I really hate it,' said Peter. 'And I think this stuff leads kids into drugs, and depression and God knows what else.'

'Which I'm sure you know is all the stuff they said about Elvis, and the Beatles, and probably pan flutes as well.'

He shrugged, unwilling to concede the point.

'Believe me, I understand,' I continued, 'but you can't stop her from liking it, and in fact the more you say you hate it the more likely she is to play it. If you say it sucks, then she has to play it just on principle.'

Peter nodded. 'I know,' he said, 'but I just worry that we're drifting apart. She doesn't seem to like anything about me these days.'

'Of course she doesn't. That's her job.'

Peter laughed. 'You say that like it really *is* her job.'

'It is.'

'Oh.'

I then spent some time explaining some things to Peter and Gail — all that stuff about puberty, and developing brains, and basic principles. At the end they seemed in a better space, which was not surprising because now they had a more realistic way of understanding what was happening with their daughter. It wasn't bad, it was simply growing up.

'So we just let her be with that awful music?' asked Gail.

I nodded. 'Yup.'

'I still really hate it,' said Peter.

'Well, there is maybe *one* thing you could do,' I said.

'What?'

'Pick the one album you really *really* hate, and then start to listen to it yourself. Maybe in the morning when she's there ask her if she could put that one on, then in the car as well. Act like you're starting to enjoy it. If you love it, she might not think it's so cool any more.'

Gail laughed.

'Nice,' said Peter.

'It's worth a try,' I said.

Low and behold, things improved for Peter, Gail, and Amy. They gave Amy some space, and she started to cut them some slack. They established some basic rules about the volume of music in the house and then left her to it. The nice thing was that the more they left her to it, the less they argued, and the more they ended up talking again. Little by little, small bright yellow patches of conversation began to appear in their home.

Interestingly, Peter did try the trick of pretending to like the album he hated the most, and much to his surprise Amy began to like it less and less. It's a funny old world.

Lessons from the road

★ Their music might sound like shit, but the kids are OK.

★ Youth culture might look a bit alien to us, but it's supposed to. If we wore baggy jeans with our underpants showing and baseball caps facing the wrong way, they'd all be wearing three-piece suits.

★ It's their job to find stuff we don't like, that's how they make their own place in the world.

★ Don't try to fight youth culture. You'll lose.

★ Instead, embrace young people's fundamental right to find their own identity.

★ Whatever they discover out there, it can't be any worse than pan flutes.

22

grunt city

*angry boys, mums and sons,
lack of communication*

Referral Information

Family details	Carol and John (parents), and David (15)
Presenting problem	Lots and lots and lots and lots and lots and lots and lots and lots and lots of arguments.

Anger is like bird flu without the birds: if you don't quarantine it pretty quickly, then before you know it the End Times are here.

Carol and John were in the early stages of a global pandemic. Their son, David, was 15 and generally a very pleasant boy. At school he was no problem, he had nice friends, and was a very polite young man when visiting at their homes. His extended family knew about the troubles at home, but never saw that behaviour when he was with them. I had no doubt that if he saw an old lady who needed help crossing the road he would immediately oblige. Yet their home was a disaster.

They all looked angry just walking into the room. When I asked them where was a good place to start, Carol launched into a passionate oratory on the evils of David. I listened glumly, John listened resignedly, and David didn't listen at all. She had a lot to say, and, even though she could have been bang on the money with everything she was saying, I found myself wanting her to stop talking. It was like a verbal avalanche.

After a while I held up my hand. 'OK,' I said. 'I give in: this is all David's fault.'

David, for his part, slumped further in his chair.

'You have something to say?' I asked him.

He looked at me, angry. 'No.'

'Come on, you must have something to say.'

He shook his head. 'Nothing.'

'See?' said Carol. 'See what I have to deal with?'

I turned to John. 'What's your take on all this?'

He shrugged this time. 'I don't know, I really don't.'

But there was something in his tone which suggested that he did. 'Something in your tone suggests that you do,' I said.

He glanced at his wife, then back at his son. 'I get caught in the middle of these two,' he said. 'Whatever I do, it's wrong.'

'How so?'

'There are constant arguments, and I just end up getting caught in the middle of the whole thing. If I defend him, then Carol gets annoyed; and if I defend her, then he gets annoyed.'

'No I don't—' Carol began, but I cut her off with an expertly raised hand.

'Let's let John let out his side of things,' I said, counting on my excessive use of the word 'let' to distract her. It worked.

'Sometimes I can hear an argument starting up,' he said. 'It's in her tone. Carol starts to get annoyed and then climbs into David. If I step in and say something, then I get it in the head as well. If I don't, then David starts mouthing off at his mother and then I have to get involved anyway. I didn't start the argument, but suddenly I'm the one in the middle of it all, trying to keep everyone in their corners.'

The relative quiet of Carol and David suggested to me that,

although they might not necessarily like what John was saying, they didn't disagree with the substance of it.

'So, why has all the arguing got worse all of a sudden?' I asked.

John answered straight away. 'I'm sick of being the referee and getting punished for it. I just gave up. If they want to fight all the time, then let them. I'm tired of being everyone's punching bag.'

Carol shot John a look, the kind of look husbands instantly recognize.

'What was that about?' I asked her.

'What?'

'That look.'

'What look?'

'The one you just gave John.'

'I didn't give him a look.'

I laughed. 'I'm married. I know that look. That's the *just-you-wait-till-we-get-home* look.'

John laughed, and so did Carol, albeit a little self-consciously.

'Do you feel that he undermines you?' I asked her.

She was quiet for a moment. 'Sometimes, yes.'

'Because?'

'Because sometimes he sticks up for David rather than backing me up.'

'Why does he do that, do you think?'

'I don't know,' she said.

David harrumphed.

'Did you just harrumph?' I asked him.

David said nothing. He just stared at the floor, simmering away like a pot of instant noodles with too little water and too much time.

'Come on,' I said, 'out with it, man.'

'Nothing.'

'Nothing is what Hitler said when Neville Chamberlain asked him what he was thinking when he caught Hitler looking at Czechoslovakia with a strange gleam in his eye. Spit it out.'

'I just wish she'd leave me the fuck alone,' he spat.

Fair enough. I did ask.

John jumped straight in, coming out of retirement more from reflex than intent: 'Don't talk to your mother like that.'

'Fuck this,' David said, leaping to his feet with the kind of wounded sense of indignation only a 15-year-old can pull off. 'I'm fucking sick of this shit. I'm gonna wait in the car.' He walked to his father. 'Can I have the keys?'

'Not until you apologize to your mother.'

'Can I have the keys?'

'Not until you apologize to your—'

'Fuck it, then,' David said, stomping from the room.

We listened to the front door slam, and then sat there in silence for a moment.

'Well,' I said finally. 'That seemed to go well.'

Where does it all go pear-shaped?

This very same argument plays out in homes all around the country, and many other countries as well, every single day. Once again it comes back to having bombproof frameworks to help understand what is going on. All these arguments are built around a very basic pattern that will probably continue to play out until the end of human civilization:

1 Teenage boy becomes Neanderthal and retreats to cave.

2 Mother finds this behaviour hard to understand and so positions herself outside his cave and talks/cajoles/ threatens.

3 Cave boy comes out and grumbles at mother.

4 Mother uses many, many words to explain to cave boy that she doesn't like his tone.

5 Cave boy loses his rag and yells at mother.

6 Father, who has been listening in quiet frustration, hoping mother will just get to the point and stop talking, is now forced to wade in and defend actions of mother that — in his heart — he knows were always going to end in this fight.

7 Cave boy stomps back into cave, muttering under his breath.

8 Mother continues to lecture cave boy as he retreats.

9 Father tentatively suggests to mother that maybe she should try to be a little more direct and use fewer words.

10 Mother feels undermined and snaps at father.

11 Father realizes there is no solution. Father stops talking. Father dreams of his own boyhood cave.

I have seen variations of this pattern play out more times than I've had the hiccups. The shape and form change from family to family, but the song remains the same.

Now, it might appear to the mums reading this that I'm simply playing the old blame-the-mother card, but I'm not. Well, actually, I am, but not completely. This pattern of communicating is simply what happens when you put boys and girls under the same roof. We think differently, we process information differently, and we talk about things very differently. The reason this pattern of conflict replays so frequently is because mums and adolescent boys speak quite different languages. One uses words whilst the other mostly grunts; and, because of this mismatch, conflict finds rich and fertile ground.

The way that I see it, you can either insist he learns your language or learn to speak his. My advice would be that he has no more interest in learning your language than you do in learning Swahili. This isn't to say that there is anything inherently wrong with Swahili, it's just that for most of us it has no immediate relevance and so we are unlikely to sign up for the course.

What would be better than this?

'All I want is for him to stop being grumpy and rude,' said Carol.

'And you?' I asked John.

'I just want everyone to be happier. I'm tired of all the fighting and the arguing.'

'I don't think we can stop him being grumpy,' I said to Carol, 'but we can definitely make some progress on the rudeness. Can you live with that?'

She nodded.

Good.

'Wait here,' I said to them both, and then went out to find David. He was sitting on a fence by their car. 'What would be better than this?' I asked him.

'A proper seat.'

Bless his little concrete thinking.

'No, I mean in your family. What would be better than how things are at the moment?'

He thought for a moment. 'Just for everyone to get on,' he finally said.

'All the time?' I asked, one eyebrow raised.

'Nah, no one ever gets on all the time. I mean, you know, just more than we do now.'

His pre-frontal cortex may have been in disarray, his corpus callosum may have been only partially complete, and his amygdala may have been working overtime, but he was not without wisdom.

'Can I ask you something?'

'Sure.'

'Are your parents mean people?'

'No.'

'And you know they love you?'

'Of course.'

'You guys just bitch at each other all the time?'

'Yeah.'

'So basically they're reasonable people, it's just that everyone gets angry and loses the plot.'

He nodded. 'Yeah.'

You would be surprised how many teenagers have said that to me, even from the depths of the worst kind of conflicts. If I was to ask yours the same question, I'd lay money on the fact that I'd get the same answer.

What needs to happen to get there?

So, if we start with our basic principles we can get some sense of which direction things need to be going in. Now, even though all of them apply, what do you think your top three would be?

1   $R^3 - F$.

2   Remember Mad Uncle Jack.

3   Don't be a Big Jessie.

4   Not too loose, not too tight.

5   Find points of contact.

6   Punctuation is everything.

7   Be the rock, not the sea.

8   Don't make their problem your problem.

9   Keep making decisions.

10   Life is suffering.

I'd go for 6, 2, and 7.

This all hangs on punctuation, getting David's behaviour in perspective, and not chasing him for conversation. His parents should just be still and wait for him to come to them.

Usually, there are two approaches to deal with uncommunicative teenage boys: force and diplomacy. Force involves compelling him to communicate with you, and then taking a solely behavioural focus on the rudeness which will inevitably occur if you back him into a corner. This means you will have to punish him. Essentially, you go to war with him over his lack of words, and you fight with all you've got until he surrenders and starts talking.

That might work, but I wouldn't recommend it.

Even if you win that way, you will have lost. To win with that strategy you have to crush his resistance, and there is a cost that comes with that. You can do it, but only if you're willing to sacrifice a large part of the goodwill that is the basis of your relationship with him. Goodwill is the only thing that will keep him coming back to visit once he leaves home.

For that reason, I favour diplomacy in situations like this one. I always think that, wherever possible, it's better to come to an amicable solution than one driven at the sharp end of a stick. Sometimes you have to go to war, sometimes you have no choice; but where you do have a choice, you'd be wise to exercise it. There are a few simple steps which can really help people caught in this destructive pattern attain a little more peace:

- ☆ Learn how Neanderthals think (ie, Chapter 7). They don't like to talk about everything, they like their caves, they are pragmatic to their very core, and need to know what's in it for them.

- ☆ Remember that you need to be a rock, not the sea. Don't chase after him begging/nagging/threatening him to try to get a conversation. Just sit and wait.

- ☆ Don't be a Big Jessie. The idea is not to negotiate like some weak-kneed apologetic sop, but to be clear about what you expect, and what the benefits are to everyone. You don't want to give way, you want to lead the way.

- ☆ Whatever the cause of the rudeness, you must punish it when it happens. Do all that you can to avoid putting him in a position where rudeness is likely, but if you see it you have to deal with it. Do not under any circumstances give him the message that you will tolerate rudeness, because you have rights, too.

- ☆ Establish your bottom-lines around his behaviour, the important rules like respect for each other, and then leave him alone.

- ☆ Above all, remember the supreme value of punctuation with teenage boys. Apply the full-stop the first chance you get. The more words you use, the more chance there is of it all going wrong.

Fixing stuff

Over the course of the next few months, Carol and John worked really hard to change the pattern of conflict in their home. Carol was a great mum who loved her son dearly, and because of that she was able to stand back and take a good, honest look at what had been happening. With the benefit of the Neanderthal framework, she was able to take a whole new approach to dealing with David's surliness. In particular, Carol found it easier to be the rock, because she could understand why David was the way he was, and how she would actually be building their relationship by not hounding him to talk to her.

The flow-on effects of this for the rest of the family were huge. Because John was able to see Carol making a real effort to change the way she communicated with their son, he was able to really step up and parent as a team. They were both on the same page at last, and that made a big difference. Carol no longer felt undermined, because John no longer undermined her.

They established their bottom-lines about behaviour in the home — for everyone — and did a pretty good job at sticking to them. They started using the LoCD tied to his curfew to punish David for his rudeness rather than yelling at him. Because the way they used it was fair, David responded in kind. He still got grumpy, but he was way less rude.

There were still the occasional flare-ups, but occasional was a lot better than inevitable. David was still about three to four years away from being able to openly say that he enjoyed his mother's company, but he was able to grudgingly acknowledge that it wasn't the wost thing in the world being around her.

Occasionally, he even gave her a hug.

Lessons from the road

★ Conflict comes from poor frameworks (he's just a rude person versus he's a Neanderthal) and unhelpful principles (I'm right, you're wrong).

★ The way out is through a combination of using our bombproof frameworks to understand what is going on, basic principles to help set our direction, and a simple plan to get there.

★ You don't have to change him to change him. All you need to do is change the way *you* do things and that will flow on down the line.

23

the girl who wanted to be a tarot card reader

angry girls, school problems, inappropriate jokes, wanting different things

Referral Information	
Family details	Melinda and Brian (parents), with Grace (13)
Presenting problem	Grace was previously a good student, but in the past year or so she has stopped trying and is now chronically underachieving.

Grace had always been a handful. At 3 she had been tricky; at 13 she was apparently diabolical.

'She's diabolical,' said Melinda. 'Isn't she, Brian?'

Brian nodded his agreement.

Grace, who at that moment was sitting slumped in her chair looking more depressed than diabolical, sighed heavily. My first instinct was to feel sorry for her; I didn't know why just yet, but I knew I needed to find out.

'When you say diabolical,' I said, 'do you mean diabolical as in spinning heads, vomiting green bile, and speaking in Aramaic, or diabolical as in very badly behaved?'

Grace giggled. She got the *Exorcist* reference which told me she was either a cinema buff, a goth, or much older than she looked.

Brian's face never changed.

Melinda looked disapproving.

Now I knew why I felt sorry for Grace: I suspected her parents had no sense of humour. Humourless people make life hard for us all, but especially hard for their children. 'So, what is it that's brought you all along, then?' I asked.

Melinda may have disapproved of my sense of humour, but she made it abundantly clear that she appreciated her daughter's life choices even less.

'She's such an intelligent girl,' Melinda said, 'but she makes no effort to apply herself in school. It's as if she doesn't care about her education.'

'I don't,' muttered Grace.

'You don't?' I asked her.

'No.'

'Uh-huh.' See, here was the thing: there was something about the way she said it that made me want to take her seriously. She didn't spit the words out like stones to throw at her parents, and they didn't float out on a vacuum of adolescent girly nonsense. Instead, she said it with a calm certainty I couldn't fail to be impressed with.

'You see what I mean,' said Melinda.

I did, but I was not sure we were all looking at the same thing.

'So, what do you want to do?' I asked her.

She didn't even pause for breath. 'I want to be a tarot reader in a gypsy fair.'

If it had been a different context, I might have laughed out loud.

Her mother sighed and looked at me as if to say *Typical.*

I was intrigued by Grace, and over the years I've learned to follow that particular white rabbit whenever I see his little cotton tail.

'Can I spend some time with Grace?' I asked.

Her parents were only too pleased to exit the room and let me get on with the real business of fixing her.

When they'd gone, I returned to the business of tarot reading. 'Interesting career choice,' I said.

She shrugged, although now her parents were gone a little of the edge had dropped away. She looked kind of sad. She was a smart kid, of that I was sure, but she was also a sad kid.

'So, I'm going to take a punt and guess that tarot reading isn't your burning life's ambition.'

She looked at me. 'No,' she finally said.

'You say that just to annoy them?'

She nodded.

'You've tried talking to them about what you really want to do, but they either didn't hear or they didn't care. So, what is it?'

'They don't hear.'

I waved my hand dismissively. 'Not that, what is it you *really* want to do?'

She laughed. 'I want to be a pianist.'

I nodded. 'An artist, very cool. Classical?'

She smiled. 'Jazz.'

'How long have you been playing?'

'Since I was six.'

We talked for a while, and it became apparent that she was indeed a passionate musician. She was less passionate about English, maths, science and geography. As a result, she had been less than diligent in applying herself to her studies.

'What do your parents say about all this?'

'They say it's a hobby and I need to study hard so I can get a real job, like being a lawyer or something.'

'And you don't want to be a lawyer or something?'

'Nope.'

'What happens when you get in trouble at school for not doing anything?'

'I get the usual big lecture and then they take away my piano time.'

'How does that work?'

'The piano used to be in my room, but they've had it shifted into the living room and then they ban me from it if I've got in trouble.'

'Are you banned at the moment?'

She nodded.

'How long?'

'It's about a month now.'

'So how do you cope?'

'I go to my friend's house. Her brother has a keyboard and I play that.'

Smart. 'So the tarot reading thing is just to wind them up?'

'Yup.'

'And it works because they want you to go be a lawyer or something?'

'Yup.'

'What do you call 300 lawyers at the bottom of the ocean?' I asked her.

'I dunno.'

'A good start.'

Where does it all go pear-shaped?

Now, I'm sure there are lots of people reading this who would gladly swap Grace's interest in piano for whatever it is your son or daughter might be interested in. In the broad scheme of things, piano playing might seem pretty benign compared to racing cars or playing video games. What you have to step away from here is the details and see the big picture, because this case is a classic example of parents thinking they know what's best for their kids.

You might when they're six, but it gets a little more complicated as they get older.

Grace's parents wanted the best for her, as most of us do for our kids, but there is a huge difference between *wanting* what's best and *knowing* what's best. I can understand they would be concerned when their daughter says she wants to be a pianist, given the fact that there aren't many people who make a living doing that. If she'd been a good scholar as well, I'm sure they would have been much more relaxed, but she was not a good scholar. To make things worse, she was also clearly a very intelligent girl with lashings of potential and the ability to be anything she wanted to be. She should have been scooping prizes, but instead she was under-achieving on a grand scale.

Yet none of this is where it truly started to go pear-shaped. The thing which had finally tipped the balance was when her parents let their anxiety take the steering wheel. When that happened, they became increasingly desperate and started taking away the one positive thing she had going on in her life: her music. Remember from Chapter 16 where we talked about punishments and I said that effective punishments make you stop and do the maths? Well, all that Melinda and Brian were achieving was breeding more resistance.

In some ways, it was similar to when the Luftwaffe bombed London during World War II. The intention was to crush the British spirit, but instead all they succeeded in doing was creating an iron determination not to be broken.

What would be better than this?

At face value this was easy: Brian and Melinda wanted Grace to work harder in school, and Grace just wanted her piano back. It took a little bit more digging to establish that their real goals were slightly different: mum and dad wanted their daughter to be happy and secure, and Grace wanted space to be her own person.

All of this was good and healthy stuff, but it would take a little fine-tuning.

What needs to happen to get there?

So, bearing that in mind, what would be your big three for Melinda and Brian to keep in mind from the following list?

1 $R^3 - F$.

2 Remember Mad Uncle Jack.

3 Don't be a Big Jessie.

4 Not too loose, not too tight.

5 Find points of contact.

6 Punctuation is everything.

7 Be the rock, not the sea.

8 Don't make their problem your problem.

9 Keep making decisions.

10 Life is suffering.

Again, the primary value of the basic principles is that they help to establish a direction, a where-to-next. Once you start thinking about principles, you can't help but think about what to do.

In this case, mum and dad need to understand that they can't know what's best for Grace. They can want the best, but they can't *know* what's best. Only Grace can know that. Now, let me be clear, this does not mean you have to blindly accept any behaviours from your kids. They may, for instance, tell you that what they want to do is smoke dope and play video games all day, but that doesn't mean that's a great idea.

What I *do* think is that we should encourage passions and strengths in our kids as much as we can. Having a passion for something is fantastic. Passion is the common thread that drives our most successful artists, business people and leaders. Passion is the fire in the belly which makes the steam which gets the engine going. If your kid has a passion for something, then you should feed it as much as you can. Be warned, though: passion is a fragile thing. It is easily killed by over-zealous parents. If your kid has a passion for tennis and you have them out practising every hour of the night and day, it will likely die. If they have a passion for the flute and you hound them to practise that, it too will die.

Passion comes from inside, it cannot be forced upon someone, and it is easily smothered. Treat it with reverence, because it's as close to magic as most of us will ever come.

Problems often set in when parents see their children's passions as the enemy rather than a welcome guest. In Grace's case, her passion for piano was the doorway back into school. Rather than withholding this from her, Melinda and Brian should have been encouraging it for all it's worth. Learning is learning is learning. Most of *all*, what they should want Grace to learn is that learning is fun.

I suggested that they give her back her piano that very day, and not use it as a bargaining tool. I had a tremendous amount of faith in Grace, and I suggested they probably did, too — it was just buried under all that worry. Rather than fight her, they should believe in her ability to figure things out for herself. Instead of threatening her over schoolwork, they should provide rewards for certain milestones, and if these could be based around her interest in music, all the better.

I thought that if they could just let go of their anxiety and let Grace find her own way, things would turn out OK. I thought that any kid with that much brains, passion, and sense of purpose was going to end up somewhere good.

Just by the bye, my big three of the basic principles for Grace's mum and dad were 5, 1, and 4.

Fixing stuff

It took me quite a while to sell the idea, but eventually Melinda and Brian agreed to giving the plan a try. Grace got her piano back, and they agreed to put that off-limits as a punishment. They also came up with a very good idea of their own. If Grace could show an improvement in four out of five subjects by the end of the term, they would pay for her to go to a live-in music school over the summer holidays.

That proved to be the master stroke.

Grace showed an improvement in all five subjects. Not earth-shattering, but a definite improvement. What's more, when she got to the summer music school she was mixing with a whole bunch of talented, driven, similarly passionate kids, most of whom understood how important an education was to their future musical dreams. Grace came back a changed woman. With very little fuss, she set about excelling in everything except maths, which she still did OK in. She hated maths and likely always would. Still, who can blame her for that?

When I asked her what had made her stop fighting her parents and buckle down in school, her answer was illuminating and typically adolescent: 'Because they were trying, I thought I would too.'

Nice.

When everyone is locked in conflict, sometimes the smart thing to do is for one side to blink first. After all, a little blinking never hurt anyone. In this case, Melinda and Brian blinked first, and the end result was an outbreak of blinking all round.

'I think we're all getting along better now because we're giving Grace credit for knowing what she wants,' said Melinda, 'and she's showing us she understands what we were trying to tell her.'

'That education is important?' I asked.

'Yes, exactly.'

'And you're not so hung-up on her becoming a lawyer anymore?'

'We'd still like her to end up in some kind of professional degree, like law or accountancy, but we respect the fact that it's her choice.'

Again, nice.

'Hey,' I said, 'what do you call 300 lawyers at the bottom of the sea?'

Melinda's face tightened slightly. 'What?'

'A good start.'

Grace laughed her arse off, even more than the first time I'd told the joke. Melinda looked the least amused I'd ever seen her.

'What?' I asked Grace, who looked like she was going to pop.

'Mum's a—' she burst off into another peal of giggles, 'Mum's a lawyer.'

Bugger.

Lessons from the road

★ Ultimately we don't know what's best for our kids; only they can know that.

★ We have to trust their judgement, not all the time obviously, but the only way they'll learn to trust their own judgement is if they see us trusting it first.

★ We have to have faith that they will eventually find their own way in the world. It might take a while, but they'll get there eventually, even if they turn 50 first.

★ Our job as parents is to help them discover their passions, and then to help grow those passions. Life is a twisty turny thing, and you never know where those passions might lead.

24

mr blobby

lazy kids, lack of direction,
drug use

REFERRAL INFORMATION

Family details	Graeme (dad) and Sandy (stepmum), and Steven (17)
Presenting problem	Graeme is concerned because Steven does not appear to have any focus or direction. His life seems to be going nowhere.

There was something about Steven that irritated me from the moment I first saw him. He was 17 and had been brought in by his father, Graeme, and Graeme's new wife, Sandy. They seemed nice enough people, but Steven just plain grated on me. He sauntered in as if the whole thing was some tremendous imposition. He was a busy man with nothing to do, and he'd rather have been busying himself with nothing than exerting the massive amounts of energy it took him to slump on my couch.

'So,' I said, 'what's brought you along today?'

'Steven has some motivational issues,' said his father.

I looked at the boy, and thought to myself that I was not in the least bit surprised. 'Tell me more,' I said.

It turned out that Steven had never been much of a student. He'd turned up, but that was about all that could be said for him. It wasn't as if he was stupid, because he'd demonstrated a number of times that he wasn't. He just didn't seem very interested.

'Are you interested in anything?' I asked him.

Steven looked up, mid-slump and mumbled, 'Just my music.'

'Your what?' I asked. 'Did you say you feel sick?'

'No, I said my music.'

'Oh, right. Do you play?'

'DJ.'

Now, ordinarily when kids talk about being into music I get excited, because that means there's at least a little life in them, but I didn't feel any of that with Steven. The way he said it made me think of those sad buggers who chat girls up in pubs telling them stories of their time in 'the Regiment', when the closest they've ever gotten to the SAS is reading an Andy McNab novel.

'That's why when he came to me at the end of Year 11 and said he wanted to take a year off school to work on his music I thought it could be a good idea,' said Graeme. 'So we set him up in the basement with his own studio — you know, all really good gear — on the agreement that he'd pay us back once he started getting some money from DJ-ing.'

'And how has that gone?' I asked Steven.

'OK.'

I turned back to Graeme. 'Would you agree?'

'Not really.'

'How would you say that the year has gone?'

'Well, it's been about a year and a half now and we haven't seen anything much come of it.'

'What have you seen?' I asked him.

'Mostly what he seems to do is smoke cannabis and play playstation.'

Steven looked at his father and sneered. 'No.'

'Well, that's how it looks to me, mate,' said Graeme.

'I don't do drugs in the house anymore,' he said with an indignant, petulant tone.

'I could smell it down there last night.'

'No, that was incense.'

I laughed. 'You're kidding, right?'

He turned to me. 'No.'

'So, how does he support himself?' I asked Graeme.

'I give him $50 a week for an allowance.'

'And what does he have to do for that?'

'Nothing, really. Just help out around the place.'

'Help out how?'

'Does his laundry, a bit of cleaning. Stuff like that.'

Sandy, who until now had been sitting quietly in her seat, could clearly contain herself no longer. 'Oh, come on, Graeme,' she said. 'When was the last time he did anything about the house?'

'I can't remember, but he does help out.'

'Doing what?' she demanded.

He shrugged, dejectedly. 'Oh, I don't know. He probably doesn't do very much.'

'He does nothing,' she said.

'Can I make a wild guess and then ask you one simple question?' I said to them both. They nodded. 'I'd guess that this is a source of quite a lot of conflict between the two of you, because you,' I said pointing to Sandy, 'probably think Graeme is too soft. And you,' I said, this time pointing to Graeme, 'probably think she's right, but you end up defending Steven anyway.'

They both nodded again.

'Now,' I said, 'I only have one question.'

'What is it?' asked Graeme.

'Well, given that he gets to live there rent-free, he never has to do any work around the house, he gets paid 50 bucks a week which he spends on dope and junk food, and all he does is lie around all day playing video games . . . I was wondering if you wanted to adopt *me*?'

Where does it all go pear-shaped?

If you haven't figured this one out by now, you probably should abandon all hope of being able to successfully raise your own children. I'm sure you'd agree that it seems a little obvious that the real issue here is that Steven is living the fat life without having to do a single thing in return. His father wanted the best for his son, but had unfortunately done the very worst thing you can for a lazy child — he'd given him a free ticket.

Lazy kids do not need free tickets.

Now, it might seem less than kind to call poor Steven lazy. In these modern child-centred times it is more normal to frame this up as low self-esteem, or a crisis of self-confidence. I tend to think that we should call things how they are, and Steven was most definitely lazy.

Of course, the fact that his dad appeared to be indirectly supporting him in smoking vast amounts of cannabis would also not be helping things much.

Drugs

Drugs are bad. Hardly a revelation is it? Of course, the thing which we're only just beginning to understand is that drugs are particularly bad for teenagers. As we talked about in Chapter 4, teenagers are more likely to become addicted, and are more prone to the effects of drugs as well. What is bad for us is even worse for them. To make matters worse, there are a lot more drugs around than when we were their age, and a lot worse drugs to boot. The scourge of methamphetamine is but one high-profile example. I am not going to go through and list all the effects of all the various drugs, because all that stuff is on the internet in buckets. Again, if you go to my website, www.goldfishwisdom.co.nz, I'll direct you to some sites that I think are helpful. Just for now, though, let's stick with the fact that drugs are bad.

Talking to your kids about drugs

This is something you should do, and you should do as early as possible, because I've come across kids as young as seven who have been stoned at school. We have always talked with our kids about drugs, and in fact my younger son decided at four years of age that he didn't like Jimi Hendrix because he took drugs. I like Hendrix, but I'm glad my son doesn't.

So here are some tips to get you started:

☆ Make the most of opportunities that present themselves to talk about drugs (eg, TV, movies, newspapers).

☆ Don't preach, but do tell them about your values and beliefs in relation to drugs.

☆ Give them accurate information.

☆ If they ask you if you've used drugs, be honest. Tell them why you did, and why you don't anymore.

If you do still use drugs, stop hounding your kids, sort your own shit out, and continue the discussion then. It is beyond stupid to expect your kids to 'say no to drugs' if you're stoned all the time, or even some of the time. You have to lead by example, so you can't expect them to take you seriously if they see you using drugs or getting drunk.

☆ Ask them about their values and beliefs when it comes to drugs.

☆ If they do admit to using drugs, then keep calm and talk it through with them.

☆ Talk to them about peer pressure, and give them strategies to deal with this stuff — for example, they can say things like 'I can't, because my parents drug-test me.'

☆ Also talk to them about the risks they expose themselves to if they are stoned and/or drunk.

☆ Make sure they understand that, whatever happens, they can come to you for calm, reasoned help and advice.

☆ All of this applies just the same to alcohol as well.

How can I tell if my kid is on drugs?

There are a number of signs and symptoms of drug use that may alert you to a problem. These are some of the more common indicators:

☆ You find drugs or drug paraphernalia on them, or in their room. If you don't know what this stuff looks like, use Google Image Search and get familiar with it.

☆ You smell it on them. A sneaky thing to do is give them a hug when they get home after a party, although remember they may have been around drugs but not using them — not spying, just being vigilant.

☆ Bloodshot eyes, although some teenagers use eyedrops to keep their eyes clear.

☆ Staggering, difficulty focusing, and/or slurred speech.

☆ Sudden change in mood or behaviour.

☆ Loss of interest in activities they had previously enjoyed.

☆ Suddenly changing friends.

☆ School performance deteriorates.

☆ Secretive phone calls.

☆ Money or other items going missing at home.

☆ They fail a home drug test. These are now available over the internet, so that parents can test their kids to see if they are telling the truth.

What can I do if my teenager is using drugs?

☆ Don't panic.

☆ Don't go in with all guns blazing. If you do this, they'll just get defensive and put the walls up.

☆ Choose your moment carefully. You want a calm, peaceful moment, because you need them to engage in a conversation with you.

☆ Be direct about your concerns without being accusatory.
> *Good opener:* 'I'm feeling concerned because I know that you have been using marijuana.'
> *Not-so-good opener:* 'I know you've been getting stoned, so don't lie to me.'

☆ Listen to what they have to say — don't just pretend to listen when all you're really doing is waiting for a gap to start lecturing again.

☆ Remember that you have rights, too, and that includes the right not to have drugs in your house.

☆ If they deny there is a problem, and you remain convinced there is, then you should get some outside help.
There are a number of agencies in most communities that can help you figure out what to do next if the problem is serious. Pick up the phone and call them, because you are probably going to need expert advice and assistance.

The big message with drugs is the same as everything else: it all comes down to you building a relationship with your kids whereby they feel OK about coming to talk to you about this stuff. If you've got teenagers who have opted out of the communication loop — as some of them clearly do — then you need to make a stand and get involved. It is not OK to let them continue using drugs unopposed. You have rights, too, and that includes the right to have a home that is drug-free. Wanting a drug-free home is not being a fuddy-duddy, it's being a responsible parent.

So what would be better than this?

Not surprisingly, perhaps, when I asked Steven what would be better than this he just shrugged his shoulders. 'I don't see what the problem is,' he mumbled. Indeed.

Graeme said he wanted his son to start doing something with his life. He wanted to see some evidence he was starting to get himself sorted out. When we got really specific about what that meant, Graeme said he'd like to see Steven either working or back in the formal education system. He didn't care which; he just didn't want Steven sitting around all day.

What needs to happen to get there?

So, how do you get Mr Blobby up off the couch? The upside of lazy is that it is fairly easily fixed. If you want to get Mr Blobby off his chuff, then bang a few nails through the seat.

Let's review our basic principles from Part II and start thinking about where to go:

1   $R^3 - F$.

2   Remember Mad Uncle Jack.

3   Don't be a Big Jessie.

4   Not too loose, not too tight.

5   Find points of contact.

6   Punctuation is everything.

7   Be the rock, not the sea.

8   Don't make their problem your problem.

9   Keep making decisions.

10   Life is suffering.

Specifically, I'd be thinking about the need for relationship but not friendship, the principle of not too loose but not too tight, and the need for Graeme to make it Steven's problem rather than his. Most of all, I'd be thinking about the fact that Graeme needs to stop acting like a Big Jessie and get in there and make some decisions. In that light, the 'fix' in this case requires a bit of metal.

I suggested a stepped plan as follows:

1   No more dope in the house. Break the rule: you get kicked out of the house.

2   In addition, if Steven wants to stay at home then he has to agree to random home drug-testing. If he doesn't like that or feels it's an invasion of his privacy, he is always welcome to leave and get his own place.

3   Steven is given a time limit in which he either has to get a job or get back into school.

4   If he hasn't got a job or got back into school, then his dad needs to kick him out of the house.

5   If he gets a job and still elects to stay at home, then he needs to contribute board and help with specific tasks around the house.

6   If he goes back to some form of education, then he needs to help around the house plus get holiday jobs to pay for his tuition fees.

7   The studio equipment is sold to pay for his father's expenses to date. At dad's discretion, this money could be used towards tuition fees.

8   Whatever happens, the days of Steven having his meals cooked, his room cleaned, and his laundry done are over.

This might seem a little hard, but hard is what was needed here. Steven was living on Easy Street and he wasn't about to move voluntarily. Instead, Easy Street needed to be demolished to make way for a major redevelopment called 'The Real World'.

Kicking your kid out on the street definitely seems harsh, and it is, but in my view if you continue to protect your children from the consequences of their actions you are doing them immeasurable harm. One day you will be dead, and so if they haven't learned to clean up their own messes, then shortly after your funeral they will be completely screwed.

Fixing stuff

Sadly, it never happened; at least I don't think it ever did.

Before we left that session, I discussed my proposed plan with Graeme and Sandy. He was a little hesitant, but seemed to get on-board with the idea. As they were leaving, Sandy turned to me and whispered: 'He'll never do it.'

The week before we were supposed to meet to review things, Graeme left a message on my phone to say that he would have to cancel our session and would call me as soon as he could to make another appointment.

That was about a decade or so ago.

I hope things worked out OK for them, but I have a nagging feeling that somewhere out there is a dad with his 30-something son still living in the basement, still smoking pot, still doing nothing, and still playing video games.

What's more, I'm sure it will be a PS3 by now as well.

Lessons from the road

★ There are two ways to get Mr Blobby up off the couch. The first is to plead with him, and the second is to bang some nails through the couch.

★ I'd go with nails every time.

★ You do your kids no favours by sheltering them from the hardness of the world.

★ If you suspect there are drugs involved, or you know that, then you need to take a stand.

★ Don't panic, and don't come in with your guns blazing.

★ Keep the lines of communication open as much as you can.

★ If the lines of communication close, get some outside help.

★ One day you won't be there to protect them, and when that day comes you want them to have some experience behind the wheel.

25

bitchytown

*girls on the rampage, rudeness,
parents feeling helpless, lack of direction*

James and Kelly were triple-blessed. There was Jane, aged 10, Kate, aged 12, and Milly, aged 14. They were also triple-cursed. There was Jane, aged 10, Kate, aged 12, and Milly, aged 14.

'After the third girl, we decided that we'd stop trying for a boy,' said Kelly as we sat in their lounge, talking.

'Oh, great,' said Jane, with a level of displeasure you might have expected from her oldest sister, 'so I'm supposed to be a *boy?*' rolling her eyes with a degree of prepubescent bitchiness that spoke volumes of the suffering her parents were enduring. 'So, you didn't even *want* me. Great.'

Kate and Milly just sat there, each texting furiously on pink mobile phones which occasionally *ting-tonged* in reply.

Kelly looked as if she was going to speak, but then looked at me and sighed as only a mum can. She didn't have to say. I knew.

'Actually,' James said, 'I wanted a dog, but your sister was allergic.'

Jane looked at her father and sneered.

I laughed, instantly deciding I liked James a great deal. He was like the 101st airborne division at Bastogne, in World War II. He was completely surrounded by the other side, outnumbered, undersupplied, and exhausted, but he still managed to keep his sense of humour.

'So, where are things up to?' I asked them.

Kelly began by telling me what wonderful kids they were, really great kids. Most of the time. Well, some of the time. Actually, lately not much of the time at all. I could tell from the way she was talking that she was a great mum. You can just tell. But I could also tell she was really struggling with everything that was going on.

'You've no idea,' she said. 'Some days I just feel like packing a suitcase and leaving. They spark up at the smallest thing and then it's like getting sucked into a black hole. The neighbours must think we're killing the girls with all the screaming that goes on at our house sometimes.'

I smiled. 'The only people who know how crazy you really are, are your partner and your neighbours.'

'True,' she said.

All the while, Kate and Milly sat there texting away on their phones as if it were as natural as breathing. They were blonde-haired, blue-eyed, angelic-looking girls. They were girly girls, pink and frilly. So sweet that butter wouldn't melt.

'So, Milly,' I said, 'you're the oldest, right?'

She deigned to give me a very controlled, slightly patronizing glance, and then went back to her texting.

Interesting. 'It's just I was wondering something.'

'What?' she said, without looking up.

'Do you ever worry about the fact you're going to end up with the thumb of a Russian woman weightlifter?'

She stopped texting and looked up, giving me a scornful glare. 'What?'

'Oh, yeah, I've seen it before. All that texting you do, you're going to end up with the kind of thumb you see on those enormous Russian woman weightlifters on steroids. You know, the kind who look like guys from WWF.'

She frowned at me.

'You're gonna have this big, old, muscle-woman thumb for sure. Heck, you'll probably have to shave it.'

(My theory is that you need to get their attention. How I do that is I pick the thing that jumps out at me first — in this case, the excessive texting, which is only their slightly subtle way of saying 'fuck you' to me — and then pound on that for a bit. What's more, if you do it in a good-natured way they're never sure whether they should laugh or be offended.)

Milly's little sister, Kate, was sniggering at her, which meant it was her turn next.

'Don't you laugh,' I said to Kate. 'You're starting even younger than she is, which means by the time you get to Milly's age you'll be known simply as the girl with the freakishly large thumb. "Who's that girl with the freakishly large thumb?" people will ask when you walk past. "I don't know, but you should see her little sister, Jane, she's been texting since she was 10 and now the whole right-hand side of her body is one huge button-pushing muscle. She has to be fed through a garden hose — it's gross." '

Jane's prepubescent bitchy sneer tracked left and locked on me.

'So all this gets pretty bad?' I asked Kelly.

'It's like sharks having a feeding frenzy sometimes. As soon as one starts, they're all in.'

'What do you make of all this?' I asked James.

He shrugged, and it was the classic shrug of the bewildered father. 'I don't know what sets it off, and then I don't know how to slow it down. Kate might take a CD that belongs to Milly, who then starts screaming at Kate. Then in the middle of trying to sort all that out, in wades Jane. It's like a complete mental asylum in our house some days.'

I could well see that living in a house with three teenage girls would be a little asylum-like at times.

'Just as an example, the other morning,' continued James, 'I walked into the kitchen and Milly was making some toast. I swear to God all I said was good morning, and she picked up the pot of jam, threw it into the sink, smashing it, and stormed out.'

'Did *not*,' muttered Milly, her face turning a deep crimson, and her tone suggesting that she perhaps did.

Kate's phone went *ting tong* as she received another text message from the cosmos. She set about replying to it as if smashing pots of jam was a perfectly acceptable morning greeting.

In the laws of the Girl-niverse, it was.

'And so, what do you do when their behaviour starts to escalate? How do you manage that?'

James shrugged and looked at his wife, which I rather suspected was a bit of a metaphor for how this family worked.

Kelly, for her part, gave me a completely helpless look. 'We just don't know what to do anymore,' she said, and her tone was that of someone who feels the battle is already lost.

Now, I need to point out here that Kelly was a woman who had carved out a very successful business career for herself. On top of bringing up the three girls, she ran her own company, a cracking little venture that employed a number of people. She wasn't an absent mum, either: she was in there with boots on, and had been their whole lives. She worked hard, but her daughters had always come first.

Yet still, this intelligent, successful, driven woman was flummoxed by her own daughters, and all dad could do was shrug his shoulders.

Ting tong went one little pink mobile phone.

Ting tong went the other.

Where does it all go pear-shaped?

One could argue that in this case it all went pear-shaped once the number of girls reached a critical mass, and here I mean critical in every sense of the word. There is nothing wrong with girls, at least not until you get them in a group. In this house, the girls outnumbered the parents 3:2, which is tough.

The parents had no frameworks to understand what was happening around them, so when puberty and the bitchy physics of the Girl-niverse descended upon them, they were quickly overwhelmed. Consumed with doubt over what was the right thing to do, they had done nothing. They had surrendered their authority to their three lovely girls about seven years too soon.

Uncle Jack was mad, except there were three of him, and what's more he was a she. Their lovely girls were also adept in the use of WMDs (see Chapter 5), such as Confusion, Deflection, Distraction, Exhaustion, and Splitting. The parents were outnumbered and outgunned, so they had simply surrendered. They had become the parenting equivalent of the United Nations: weak, and without resolve or direction.

This is something that happens in a lot of homes. Faced with seemingly convincing displays of the desire for autonomy, many parents simply give way. They let their children quickly assume control of the ship and become reduced to the status of helpless passengers. Then all they can do is stare in horror as the iceberg gets closer.

What would be better than this?

'Anything,' said James.

I wasn't about to let James get away with that. Whilst mums may struggle with punctuation, the classic dad trick is to stand around looking a bit lost until mum sweeps in and sorts everything out. I do it myself from time to time. Luckily, however, my behaviour wasn't the one in the spotlight.

'You'll need to be a bit more specific than that,' I said. '"Anything" is a little broad. "Anything" could include military boarding school, trading them for camels, taxidermy . . .'

James thought for a moment. 'I'd like them to show us a little respect,' he said, 'and to listen when we say no.'

I nodded. Good. 'And you, Kelly?'

'The same,' she said. 'If they would show us some respect and listen when we say no, then I'd be a very happy woman.'

All this was good stuff. There was a goal, it was achievable, and it was realistic.

What needs to happen to get there?

In situations where the root cause is too much control, it's usually best not to introduce more; but in situations like this where the issue is that the girls have been running the ship, then the opposite applies. The waters have become muddy because there is a lot of chaos and yelling. What's badly needed here is a little structure. Remember that having things not too loose is just as important as having things not too tight.

Essentially, this is a three-bullet-point situation:

✰ James and Kelly need to understand some more about the brains of teenage girls, and how this flows on through to the Girl-niverse.

✰ They need to readjust their attitude and take back control of the ship. To achieve this they're going to need to follow some of the basic principles we talked about in Part II:

1 $R^3 - F$.

2 Remember Mad Uncle Jack.

3 Don't be a Big Jessie.

4 Not too loose, not too tight.

5 Find points of contact.

6   Punctuation is everything.

7   Be the rock, not the sea.

8   Don't make their problem your problem.

9   Keep making decisions.

10   Life is suffering.

✧ They will need to introduce a clear structure where the rules are clear, as are the consequences for breaking them. In this situation, a tool like The Ladder of Certain Doom is usually helpful.

Fixing stuff

After kicking the girls out, I had a long talk with James and Kelly about what I thought. It wasn't a hard sell.

'OK,' said Kelly, 'so what do we do?'

We talked for a little while about applying the principles from Part II. Specifically, we talked about Mad Uncle Jack, that they needed to be more rock-like, to watch their punctuation, and, most of all, that they needed to make the rudeness their girls' problem rather than their problem. As well as that, I gave them my tips for setting rules (see page 165) and also for negotiation (see page 164).

'But how do we make it their problem?' asked Kelly.

I asked them what they could take away from the girls that would really hurt.

Without thinking, they both said together 'their phones'.

Great minds.

Then I explained the LoCD to them. James liked it. He was a guy, and guys like tools. Guys like to be able to do stuff. Kelly was also keen. Mums like just about anything that works.

Then we made a date to meet in a month's time.

What a difference 28 days makes. Things weren't completely turned around, but they were certainly markedly different. They had implemented the LoCD, and it had proved a winner. The big hook was that texting was like oxygen to their girls. Without it, they began to wilt. Once the girls got the basic idea that good behaviour equals mobile phone time, they began to get themselves in control fairly quickly. There were still times when one of the girls simply lost the plot, as you'd expect given their ages, but not as many as before. What's more, the plot-loser seemed more motivated to find said plot again much more quickly than they ever had been before.

'The main change is us,' Kelly said.

'How so?'

'We feel better, don't we, James?'

He nodded. 'Absolutely.'

'So what's different?' I asked them.

'I think we've just got more determined to take charge of things,' she said, 'to not accept some of the crappy behaviour we used to.'

'Such as?'

'The bad language, the disrespect. I mean, don't get me wrong, the girls still have their moments, but now we feel we're able to deal with it much better than before.'

'I think what we've found is that we're back in the driver's seat again. Even when it gets really loud, we keep focused on the fact that we're the ones in charge.'

'What helped you the most to do that?' I asked. I always ask this stuff, because I want to know so I can tell the next parents I meet.

'For me it was two things,' said Kelly. 'The first was getting some structure back into our home, which was the rules and the Ladder of Certain Doom; and the second was getting the image of that rock in my head. I just decided I wasn't going to be pushed around anymore.'

'It's the same for me,' said James. 'A bit of structure and the rock thing made all the difference.'

'And do the girls hate you now that you've introduced all these rules and stuff?'

James laughed. 'Some of the time, for sure, but that's the nice thing about being a bit more rock-like: rocks don't tend to lose sleep over stuff.'

Never has a truer word been spoken.

Lessons from the road

★ The Girl-niverse is a strange and chaotic place. It works to laws that none of us understand. In the Girl-niverse, you say good morning by breaking jam jars.

★ The worst thing you can do in the face of the dark forces that sweep out of the Girl-niverse is surrender. That way lays chaos.

★ Instead, go back to basics: structure, principles, and action. Don't talk about what you're going to do, just do it.

★ If you find the things that are important to them, and you can make them understand that those things are a privilege and not a right, then you will start to gain some ground.

★ As long as whatever you do is fair, they won't hate you.

26

tim the destroyer

going completely off the rails,
getting in trouble with the police,
threats of violence, major conflict at home

Referral Information

Family details	Ian and Mary (parents), with Jennifer (9), Sam (11) and Tim (14)
Presenting problem	Having major problems with Tim. Has been getting in trouble all over the place, huge rows at home, disappearing for hours on end. He seems to hate everything and everybody.

If Big Bird had been in my consulting room the day Ian and Mary brought their family in to see me, he wouldn't have been able to resist singing the 'Which one of these is not like the other?' song.

I almost started humming it myself.

Ian was in a suit, smart-looking. Mary was similarly dressed, not a suit, but stylish. Then there was Jennifer, the youngest, looking very much the nice girl in pinks and pastel blues. Sam was the middle child, and he had a kind of upmarket-skater-thing going on, tastefully faded jeans and yellow T-shirt.

Then there was Tim.

Tim was dressed all in black, and he looked filthy. His jeans hadn't seen a washing machine in a long time, and greasy strands of hair poked out from underneath a paint-splattered black beanie. Everyone else looked kind of fresh, but he looked as if he'd just crawled out from under a bridge. Actually, it turned out that it wasn't a bridge he'd just crawled out of, but the police cells. Tim was facing charges of wilful damage after he'd got drunk and kicked in a fence the night before when he was out with his friends. When the police had shown up, he'd decided to get lippy, which, funnily enough, didn't get him any further than a cosy, little cell.

'Did the fence say something which pissed you off?' I asked him.

No response, which was not all that surprising.

'So where's a good place to start?' I asked his parents.

'We just don't know what to do anymore,' said Mary. 'It doesn't seem to matter what we say to Tim, he either ignores us or he's incredibly rude.'

Tim rolled his eyes and slumped down further in his chair.

I could see the pain that Tim's behaviour was causing Mary and Ian. 'What was he like when he was little?' I asked.

'He was lovely,' said Mary. 'He was a very cuddly little boy. He was very affectionate and very sensitive.'

Now, whenever people use the word 'sensitive' I always prick up my ears. In boys, 'sensitive' usually also means 'intense' and 'highly strung'. These types of boys are usually hyper-attuned to perceived rejection and have skin so thin you can almost see through it. They are easily hurt, and when hurt their predominant response is to get angry, which in turn makes them want to hurt people — usually emotionally, but sometimes physically as well. They are usually fairly stubborn souls.

'Was he a stubborn wee bloke?' I asked.

'Absolutely,' said Ian. 'Nothing was ever easy with Tim when he was little. He could never just do something, there would always have to be some kind of performance first.'

'But nothing like we get now,' said Mary. 'He would have tantrums and things like that, but nothing like the kinds of behaviours we see now.'

'When did the trouble start?' I asked them.

'What kind of trouble are you talking about?' asked Ian. 'We've had it all: school, home, the police, drugs, everything.'

'I guess the point when you felt the wobbles first set in.'

Ian thought for a moment. 'I think it was when he went to middle school,' he said, 'from about 11 on. He got new friends and we started to have more serious problems happening at school. Don't you think, Mary?'

She nodded. 'Yeah, I'd say it was about then.'

I turned to Tim: 'Would you agree with that, Tim?'

He looked at me and snarled. 'With what?'

I smiled, unaffected by his venom, and quite clear about the fact that Tim was determined to be a shit. 'With your parents' suggestion that you're to blame for global warming?'

'What?'

'Well, your parents have just been saying that you've been contributing more than your fair share of greenhouse gases to the atmosphere for quite a while now.'

Sam giggled, and Tim rounded on him instantly: 'Shut the fuck up, *faggot!*'

'Tim,' his father said. 'That's *enough*.'

I could hear the anger in his father's voice, but underneath that was also generous helpings of sadness and fear as well. This was a man who loved his son more than life itself, yet he couldn't understand why this wasn't enough.

At that point, I stepped in and sent the children out, to separate, supervised parts of the building, and continued the discussion with Tim's parents.

'So,' I said, 'tell me all the worst stuff.'

It turned out there wasn't much that Tim's mum and dad hadn't had to suffer through. It was pretty much a train-wreck across the board. Tim hadn't been kicked out of school yet, but he was on the cliff edge. Even when he was there, which was less and less often, he didn't do anything except smoke cigarettes and wind up the teachers. At home, he was rude to everyone, and ruthlessly mean to his little brother and sister. They were both scared of him, although to date he was mostly more bark than bite. He did nothing around the house, and regularly took off without telling anyone where he was going. Then he'd come home hours later smelling of alcohol and/or drugs. Mary had recently found a small bag of marijuana in his room, and when she'd challenged him about it he'd simply laughed at her and walked away. The crimes of the previous evening were a recent addition, and it was this that scared his parents most of all, because he was starting to mix with older, more serious thugs who were already well known to the police.

His parents were terrified, stressed out, frustrated, angry, hurt, and just about every other thing as well.

'Sounds like Tim's a bit of a train-wreck at the moment,' I said.

'Can you help us?' asked Mary.

'Well,' I said, 'I can't change Tim's behaviour, because that's pretty much entirely in his control, but I can give you guys some ideas about how you might be able to change some of the things that you're doing. The nice thing is that, because you're all part of the same system, if we change gear in one place, then everything else is affected as well.'

Next, I told them I would have a talk with Tim by himself for a while.

He dragged himself into the room once his parents had left, and slumped down into a chair, clearly displeased about having to be there, and clearly unwilling to talk to me.

Now, this is the moment when you don't want to be a Big Jessie and start begging the disgruntled young person to share their thoughts and feelings with you. As soon as you do that, they've won the game because all they have to do is say nothing.

Never put yourself in the position of begging them to talk to you, because then his silence is *your* problem. You want to make his silence *his* problem.

'You know what annoys me?' I said, pausing only very slightly, as if I didn't even want to give him an option of responding. 'People in bakeries who stand too far back from the counter. I hate them. It does my bloody head in. You walk in and they're standing about three feet from the counter, and why? Why would a person do that? What kind of immoral, illogical, unreasonable person would behave like that? Because you know what happens, then? It isn't obvious if you're actually in a queue, or you're simply standing waiting for some unspecified thing. Then it all gets confused, because the next person walks in and they cut in front, and then you just know that . . .'

And on I merrily went for another 10 minutes without pausing.

Tim looked bored, then irritated, then ultimately confused. 'What the fuck are you talking about?' he finally said.

I looked at him as if he was an idiot: 'Bakeries. What did you think I was talking about?'

He scowled. 'Why?'

'Why what?'

'Why are you talking about bakeries?'

'I wasn't.'

'Yes, you were.'

'No, I was talking about *people* in bakeries who don't know how to *queue* properly, and wondering what it is about them which draws so many of them to bakeries at lunchtime.'

'But you were still talking about bakeries.'

'Indirectly, true, but the main thrust of the conversation was about queuing.'

What was interesting was that at that precise moment Tim seemed to catch himself in the process of becoming engaged in our conversation, and instantly slipped back into his alter ego of Tim the Destroyer.

'You're fucked-up,' he said, as snotty as a recently used paper tissue in the bin at a doctor's surgery in the middle of winter.

I shrugged. 'Maybe I am, but I'm not the one digging myself so deep into a mountain of shit that I can't get out by myself even if I wanted to.'

'What?'

'You heard me, shovel boy.'

He frowned, and slumped deeper in his chair.

'I'll tell you what I see,' I said. 'I see a guy who isn't really a bad person, but who's got himself locked into doing all these shitty things because he's too stubborn to say he took a wrong turn. I see a guy who knows his parents love him, who also loves them in return, and yet still keeps saying and doing all these shitty things to them because he doesn't know how to turn the ship around. I see someone who doesn't like who he's becoming, but who doesn't know how to admit he was wrong. Not even to himself. I see someone who, despite the fact that he's out carrying on like some big man, actually feels like the whole thing is spinning out of control and he forgot where the brake is. That's what *I* see.'

He looked at me for a long moment, and it was hard to tell what he was thinking.

Then he turned away. 'Yeah, well who the fuck cares what you think,' he said.

'I could tell you the answer to that question,' I said, 'but then I'd have to kill you.'

He sneered again, for old times' sake, and with that we were done.

Where does it all go pear-shaped?

It's clear that this family has quite a bit going on. This is where I find it helpful to have some basic frameworks to process all this information through, so I can start to untangle what appears to be an impenetrable wall of teenage nastiness.

☆ **Breathing = Hope.** First off, we need to remember that

there is still plenty of room for hope here. Everyone is still breathing, so anything is still possible

☆ **The weirdness of puberty.** Tim is right smack-dab in the middle of the trip. He's overrun with hormones that are making him look bigger, and that are rewiring his body from top to bottom. He's not a grown-up yet, though, and my bet is that a lot of the time he's going to feel like his life is out of control, which is going to make him unhappy.

☆ **Remember Mad Uncle Jack.** Ian and Mary need to remember that Tim is not right in the head. This is not who he really is; this is simply Mad Uncle Jack. They must treat his unkindness as simply the ravings of someone who is temporarily unhinged.

☆ **Not the whole walnut.** It's pretty obvious that Tim is doing a number of things that don't seem all that rational. His reasoning appears a little clouded, he frequently explodes, and he appears to generally have trouble managing his emotions. Risk is not something that he considers, short-, medium-, or long-term.

☆ **A tank will always be a tank.** Personality-wise, we can see that Tim is a smart, stubborn, sensitive boy. He has been from the start and always will be. Our job is to teach him how to drive the personality he's got so he doesn't hurt himself or anyone else. The fact that he's stubborn will bring special challenges, because if we lay down some laws he will test them to the very limit of his ability.

☆ **WMDs.** Tim appears to rely mainly on Fear and Tactical Hatred, with lashings of emotional Exhaustion. There are early signs that he is already gearing up towards the use of actual physical Violence, but at present he's still at the threat stage.

☆ **The rise of the Neanderthal.** He's 14 and clearly thinks he's bulletproof. He also has all of the signs of a boy at the early stage of the adolescent ride trying on the 'tough guy' persona. He's a rebel without a cause, and also without much reason.

⭐ **Systems thinking.** At this point, I'm thinking there have probably been some fairly loud 'discussions' in Tim's house. I know that he's done some yelling, but I'm pretty sure his mum and dad would have done some yelling back as well. Frustration and fear can make ogres out of even the most reasonable parents. I'm guessing that by this stage all kinds of things have been said, and this history will mean that both Tim and his parents are fairly well dug in.

When you combine all of these factors, it's easy to see how you can end up with a Tim-load of trouble. This is a young man who is smart, sensitive, and stubborn. It's as if he's been given the keys to a very powerful car long before he had any idea how to drive. Now all he does is crash into stuff all the time. His mum and dad jump in the way to try to get him to slow down, but he just runs them over without blinking. Even when he knows where the brakes are, the pride and stubbornness and general teenage craziness make him unable to slow down just on principle. This is a boy who wouldn't stop at cutting off his nose to spite his face — he'd take off his whole head.

What would be better than this?

'We could sell him on the internet,' said Ian, largely joking.

'Who would buy him?' Mary asked.

'Rich Americans who needed spare parts?' I suggested.

We sat there for a moment, reflecting silently on how unjust it was that we cannot sell our wayward children to rich Americans who want to harvest their organs.

'But, seriously,' I said, 'what would be better than this?'

'I just want him to be decent,' said Mary.

'Define "decent" for me.'

'I suppose I'd like him to be not mixing with those thugs, not doing drugs, and be nicer at home.'

'Thugs, drugs, and hugs?'

She smiled. 'I guess so.'

'And you, Ian?'

'I'd just like to have my son back, because I don't know who this guy is.'

Language is an interesting thing, because the words we use to describe things don't simply describe reality, they actively create reality. Whenever parents say things like this it troubles me, because they're building a picture of their kid as some stranger. This is simply not true, because he's the same boy he's always been, it's just that all the teenage bullshit and bluster makes it a little more difficult to see.

I shrugged. 'His name is Tim, and he's the same stubborn, sensitive, smart, gormless boy he's always been. It's all still there, it's just buried in hormones and stupidity right now. We just have to figure out how to help him 'til he can dig his own way out.'

Ian frowned, 'I just don't know anymore.'

'Well, what's one thing he could do differently that would be better than how things are now? Just one thing.'

'I'd just like to not have to worry about him so much,' said Ian.

I shook my head: 'No can do. You're both good parents, which means that, no matter how things are going for him, for good or ill, you will worry about him 'til the day you die. Let's shoot for something a little more realistic.'

Ian thought for a moment. 'I'd like for him to stop making our family life such a misery.'

'By doing what specifically?'

'By leaving his younger brother and sister alone, and not being so horrible to Mary and me.'

Nice. That we could work with. Now it was time to come back to Mary.

'You said that you wanted fewer thugs and drugs, and more hugs,' I said.

'Well, I'm not sure that we'll get more hugs from him any time soon, but I'd like to try to get rid of the thugs and the drugs at least.'

'So would I,' said Ian.

'How much do you want that, Mary?'

She looked at me without blinking. 'More than you can imagine.'

'Are you prepared to go to war if you have to?'

She nodded, resolute. 'Yes.'

'And you, Ian, are you prepared to go to war if that's what it takes?'

He nodded. 'Just show me the button.'

'Alright then,' I said, 'time to lock and load.'

What needs to happen to get there?

Make no mistake that the stakes are high here. Tim is messing with drugs, alcohol, stupid thuggish mates, and crime. Most dangerous of all, Tim is under the mistaken belief that he's some kind of gangsta when in reality he's just white bread from the suburbs. He's mixing with kids who *are* gangstas, though, and that is going to be putting him in harm's way. If he doesn't get himself in all kinds of trouble with the police, it's entirely possible a real gangsta will do him some serious harm.

On top of that, his family is being torn apart. His parents love him but are feeling powerless to do anything about it, because nothing they do is having any kind of impact.

The reason I asked them whether or not they'd be prepared to go to war is that this is exactly where they must go. Tim is beyond negotiating at this point. He's a closed book, and the chance of him engaging in any kind of constructive dialogue with his parents is so slim it would make a rice cracker feel like dieting.

Some people might think it's unhelpful to think about this family's problems in terms of conflict. Some would say that we need to be thinking about peace and reconciliation. My view would be that there's no point trying to hug a tree if it's trying to bite you. First deal with the teeth, then let the hugs come next spring.

Recall if you will the basic principles from Part II, and ponder for a minute on where Ian and Mary should head first. If you were to prioritize this list and pick the three that you think Ian and Mary most need right this moment, what would they be?

1   $R^3 - F$.

2   Remember Mad Uncle Jack.

3   Don't be a big Jessie.

4   Not too loose, not too tight.

5   Find points of contact.

6   Punctuation is everything.

7   Be the rock, not the sea.

8   Don't make their problem your problem.

9   Keep making decisions.

10   Life is suffering.

I'm sure you'd agree that *all* of them apply here. The nice thing is that as soon as you start thinking about this list of principles you get some forward momentum going. Without direction, you just go round in circles, which is where Ian and Mary were at. Once you start ticking through the list of basic principles, a plan will start to form all by itself. You will start to get ideas — they may not be perfect in the detail, but just the act of reading through each principle sends your thoughts off in a specific direction.

I'd pick 3, 5, and 8, in that order.

Why?

I think the first thing is that they need to be the complete opposite of a Big Jessie. They need to make a clear and unambiguous stand.

They must show determined leadership and absolute strength of will. They must get their head into the right space, which in this case is the absolute belief that they will not abandon Tim to his bad behaviour at any cost. The second thing is that they must find points of contact. This might surprise you, given all they have going on, but I would predict that things are going to get rough, and so they must look actively and constantly for the little moments when they can show Tim that they love him and that they are still here for him. Thirdly, they must make this problem Tim's and not theirs. At the moment, he is sitting on a set of railway tracks and pretending he can't feel the low vibration in the rails. He thinks the approaching train is everyone else's problem, which is obviously not a good starting point when you're the only guy on the tracks.

All of the rest of the principles apply as well, and Ian and Mary will need to remember *all* of them if they're going to help Tim, but those would be my top three for right that moment.

So, where to from here?

Simple — we go to war.

Fixing stuff

After I'd outlined the plan that I was proposing to them, they sat there in silence for a few moments. It was Mary who finally spoke: 'And this will work?'

I shrugged, not dismissively, but genuinely: 'I don't know. No one can know these things. What I *can* tell you is this: if he was my son, this is what I would do. I'm not able to give you any guarantees that this will keep him from harm, but it's what I would do if he were my boy.'

This was true. I wouldn't ask anyone else to do something I wouldn't be prepared to do with my own children.

'Shall we get him back in?' I asked them. 'I think it's important that you tell him about the new rules, not me.'

Mary nodded; so did Ian.

And in Tim came.

'Tim,' said his father, 'we've been talking together while you were out of the room. Your mum and I have decided that there are going to be some big changes at home. We love you, and we want you to be part of our family, but we understand that we can't force you to be a part of our family. That's actually your choice.'

Tim just sat there, brooding, as pissy as a public toilet on New Year's Eve.

'For a start, there will be no more drugs at home. If we find them in the house, we will contact the police. There will be no more yelling and disrespect at home. If you yell at anyone, or abuse them, then you'll be grounded for the weekend. If you want to walk out of the house, then you can do that, but we won't be letting you back. You'll have to find somewhere else to stay that night. You also need to go to school. If you don't, then you need to be out of the house by the time everyone else leaves and you can explain that to the school yourself. The bottom-line is that the abuse and the disrespect at home have to stop, and you have to get your act together. If it doesn't, then you will be punished.'

'Fuck you,' said Tim. 'I'm not gonna fucking stay. I'll just walk out.'

I'd prepared them for this inevitability.

'That's your choice,' said Mary, 'but you're only 14 years old, so you aren't allowed to be out in the world on your own. If you decide not to follow our rules, then you can leave but we will have to contact social workers and have you placed in a foster home.'

This was the king hit, the final line in the sand. Sometimes teenagers need to be confronted with the fact that if they keep trying to get away from home, they will. The flipside is that they will end up in someone else's home. This is an extreme step, but sometimes extreme circumstances require a proportionate response. I have worked with many very good parents who have been left with no choice but to have their teenager temporarily placed in care. It's never easy, but sometimes you have to call their bluff.

Tim shot her a filthy look: 'I don't give a shit if you do,' he snapped.

Mary held his gaze.

'We're going to write all this down for you, Tim,' said his father, 'to make sure you understand it all, but that's how it's going to be from here on. OK?'

'Fuck you,' Tim snapped. 'You just want any fucking excuse to get rid of me.'

'Tim—' his mother started, but he cut her off.

'Just fuck up,' he said.

And right at that moment Ian stepped up and took the game: 'You know what, Tim? Fuck *you*. You're *not* going to talk to your mother or me like that *anymore*, and if you do then you're getting *punished*. Right now you're *grounded*. Understand?'

Tim gave his dad the filthiest of looks and opened his mouth as if he was about to say something else.

'Enough, Tim. You're my son, and I love you more than life itself, but I'm not going to let you continue to shit all over us. We love you and we're going to do everything we can to stop you from fucking up your life. And if that means you have to hate us, then fucking hate us, but right now just put your shit back in the drawer and fucking *shut it*.'

OK, now technically Ian had just told his son to shut the fuck up which, in most people's eyes, might seem like less than ideal father–son communication. I thought it was reasoned, and passionate, and honest.

I thought it was a thing of beauty.

Points of contact aren't always pretty, but they *always* hum, and this baby hummed like a big drunken bird.

Tim stared at his dad for a few moments, dumbstruck, then he recovered his composure, hauled himself out of his chair, and stomped out of the room.

I looked at them both, and I knew instinctively that the steel I'd just seen exercised in front of me meant that if anyone could save Tim from himself, it was them.

The road to adulthood is sometimes paved with tears, sometimes paved with broken glass, and occasionally with both.

They went home from that session and all was quiet for about an hour or so, then Tim came out of his room and said he was going out. His parents said he wasn't because he was grounded.

Out he walked, despite them.

Tim returned home later that night around midnight to find the front door locked. He banged on the door to no avail. Ian and Mary lay in their bed, feeling terrible, but pretending as hard as they could to be rocks.

Then Tim picked up a rock of his own and hurled it through the window. Even though it was the hardest thing, they had ever done, they called the police. When the officers turned up, they restrained Tim and asked his parents what they wanted to do. Ian did the right thing, the hard thing, and told the police that they weren't prepared to have Tim in their home. These are the magic words — because if his parents won't have him, then the system gets him by default. Tim was taken into care, then and there.

Ian and Mary later told me that that night was the bleakest, blackest, most terrifying night of their lives.

It did Tim no favours that he'd just been in Youth Court the day before, and the system decided he would be best to have a spell away from home. This was very hard for Ian and Mary to agree to, because it felt as if they were abandoning their son. I met with them and tried to reassure them that in fact the opposite was true. If they'd tried to shield Tim from the consequences of his behaviour, they would have been teaching him that he can treat people any way he likes and nothing bad would happen to him. This way, they were teaching him an important lesson: actions have consequences.

It would be a full 18 months before life settled back to something approaching normal for Tim and his family. He was in a foster home for three months before he finally got the message that his parents weren't giving in. From that point on, he started to try to work with them. Often this is how it happens: if the parents hold the line, the wayward teen eventually does the maths and things start to change. In Tim's case, he transitioned home with increasingly longer visits that were contingent on his following a few simple rules. He also had to go and get help with his alcohol and drug use, and to get himself back into the formal education system. These latter two conditions were non-negotiable.

Gradually, over time, relationships healed, and Tim began to loosen up. In my view, this was as much about the passage of time as it was about him making choices. He got older, his brain matured, and new options opened up to him.

Most importantly of all, though, his parents held the line. They did not buckle or abandon him to the world, they kept making decisions. They drew a line in the sand, and they held that line. It was a long and difficult journey, but then, like Buddha says, life is suffering.

The last time I saw them, Tim was back living at home, and going to tech where he was taking a course in diesel mechanics. Things were still not perfect, but then nothing ever is. The nice thing is that they were all back under the same roof, and, even though there were still tense moments, they felt like a family again.

When I asked them what they thought had been the most important thing, they both agreed that it was changing their attitude.

'We just decided that we weren't going to give up,' said Mary. 'Even when we gave him up, we didn't give up. We knew the real Tim was in there somewhere and all that stuff was just Mad Uncle Jack. We just decided we weren't going to tolerate any more of his shitty behaviour, and we weren't going to let go of him.'

Ian nodded. 'And we drank a lot of wine,' he said. 'A *lot* of wine.'

Whatever gets you through the night, right?

Lessons from the road

★ The most important thing that you can do when faced with an avalanche of nastiness is to not let yourself turn into a Big Jessie.

★ Stop, assess your bottom-lines, and make your stand.

★ If you have to go to war, then go to war.

★ Find every chance you can to tell your teen you love them, but that doesn't mean you will tolerate their behaviour.

★ Being part of the family isn't optional, but staying in the family home is. If they won't stick with your bottom-lines and their behaviour is placing themselves and/or others at risk, then you need to get help: call the police or social services. A spell in foster care might seem extreme, but it's better than a spell in jail or hospital.

★ Returning home, or staying at home in the first place, is contingent upon them meeting your bottom-lines.

★ All this works exactly the same for the Tinas of this world, just as it does for the Tims.

★ Remember Mad Uncle Jack — and don't drink too much wine.

27

depression, suicide, and paper cuts

depression, suicidal thoughts, self-harm

Family details	Theresa and Bob (parents), with Chloe (15)
Presenting problem	Chloe's friend committed suicide six months ago. Since then, Chloe has been depressed and withdrawn. Recently, her mother found a journal where Chloe talked about not wanting to live. She has also been cutting herself. Was assessed by Adolescent Mental Heath Services and placed on antidepressants.

Parenting is as much about learning to live with fear as it is about raising kids. From the moment they're born, our happiness is inextricably bound to their happiness. If they suffer, we suffer. Yet one of the great truths of being a parent is that we cannot protect them, not really.

Shit, as the saying goes, happens.

Sometimes the worst kind of shit.

Chloe's best friend, Helen, was a nice girl. Everyone liked her; she was intelligent, attractive, and a gifted athlete. She had everything going for her, and for reasons that no one could quite understand she went out to her garage one afternoon and hung herself.

After Helen's death, it transpired that there were some things swirling around no one had known about. She'd been having an ongoing feud with some other girls at school, who were circulating rumours about her that she found upsetting. She had been feeling increasing pressure to maintain her marks at school, yet at the same time felt school was increasingly pointless. The afternoon that she hung herself, she had had an argument with a boy she liked.

There were none of the usual warnings, no signs, nothing which could have suggested that Helen was thinking of killing herself. In hindsight, it was possible to see a path, but hindsight is always the cruellest view.

All this was why Theresa and Bob were so worried about Chloe. They looked absolutely terrified, which I could completely understand. I would have been, too.

Chloe just looked glum.

'Do you understand why your mum and dad are so worried about you?' I asked her.

She just shrugged. 'Kind of.'

And that is where kids are so scary — because to us grown-ups it looks as though they take death a little too flippantly. They haven't been around long enough to understand what a gift life is, so to throw it away on some teenage whim appears to be no big deal to them.

'What specifically has made you feel so concerned?' I asked them.

'Well, after . . . after Helen . . . you know . . . died . . . Chloe just seemed to change,' said Theresa. 'It's like her batteries just went flat. She used to be such a bubbly happy kid, but now . . . Well now she seems sad all the time.'

Chloe might as well have been carved from stone. None of this seemed to reach her.

'And there was the journal,' said Theresa.

Chloe rolled her eyes and slumped deeper in her chair.

'Would you like to see it?' asked Theresa, taking a small black book from her bag.

Now, I hate it when parents do that to me, because the risk assessor in me does want to look, but the clinician knows I can't go traipsing about in a kid's private writings unless I'm invited by the rightful owner.

'No, thanks,' I said. 'I don't need to see that stuff. Perhaps you could just tell me what it was about it that you found concerning.'

Theresa opened it to a page she had bookmarked and read aloud: 'I hate everything and everyone. Life sucks. Helen is the lucky one.'

Fuck, I thought. *Fuck, fuckity, fuck.*

Chloe said nothing. She slumped in her chair like a robot with no batteries.

'Plus she's been cutting herself as well,' said Theresa, talking too fast. 'We try and talk to her, but she won't tell us what's going on. She just withdraws into her room for hours and hours and hours.'

By this stage, Theresa was nearly in tears. Bob just fidgeted with his coat and looked completely lost.

'What help have you all had so far?' I asked.

'Chloe has been seen by the doctor at the Child and Family Unit, and he gave her some antidepressants,' said Theresa. 'Plus she has counselling there every week as well.'

'Is that helping, Chloe?'

She just shrugged again.

At this point, I sent her parents out of the room so I could talk to Chloe alone.

'Your mum says you've been cutting yourself,' I said.

'No.'

'She said she's seen the marks.'

'No, she didn't.'

'So what were the marks then?'

She gave me the old Chloe shrug again. 'Paper cuts.'

I looked at her for a moment. 'Paper cuts?'

'Yup.'

'What do they make your paper out of? Recycled Ninja death stars?'

She laughed, which was the nicest thing I'd heard all day.

'You know, most people don't understand the reason why people cut themselves,' I said. 'Most people think people cut themselves because they like pain, but the opposite is true, isn't it? People cut themselves so they *don't* have to feel pain. Cutting means you just have to focus on what you're doing, and not on the stuff that really makes you feel bad, right?'

She shrugged, but it was more of a nod-kind-of-shrug this time.

Actually, there are a number of reasons why people cut themselves: some use the pain as a way to punish themselves, some use it as a display to get attention, and some kids do it because it's cool. I thought Chloe was doing it to stop herself from hurting.

We sat there in silence for a while.

'You and Helen were good friends, huh?'

She nodded, but it was a very small nod, dampened by great pain.

'And you've been talking to a counsellor about all that stuff?'

Again with the nod.

'And that's helping?'

'Kind of.'

'Good.'

A little more silence, and why not? It is golden after all.

'You know your mum and dad are worried about you doing the same thing, don't you?'

She sighed. 'I just wish they'd chill out about everything. They're all intense and worried all the time. It makes me want to scream. I just wish they'd leave me alone.'

'Do you ever think about doing it?'

She sat there a moment. 'Sometimes.'

'How often?'

'Just sometimes.'

'When was the last time you thought about it?'

'I dunno, a week ago or so.'

'Have you thought about how you'd do it?'

She shook her head. 'No.'

This was good, if she was being honest, because the presence of a plan greatly increases the risk an attempt.

'Have you thought about how your mum and dad would be affected if you did?'

'I guess they'd be a bit bummed out for a while.'

She was a lovely kid, but when she said that I just wanted to slap her. 'You think?'

She nodded. 'I just get sick of them always poking around in my stuff,' she said. 'I really hate it, and now they feel like they have a right to do whatever they want.'

'Do you want your privacy back?' I asked her.

She nodded. 'Yeah.'

'They're very worried about you. They're actually terrified. Can you understand why they feel that way?'

She nodded.

'OK, so would you want to see if we can work together so that you are *all* feeling a bit more normal?'

She shrugged, 'I guess so.'

Good enough.

Where did things go pear-shaped?

Fear is a dangerous emotion. It can be useful up until a certain point — because a little fear is sometimes very helpful in maintaining focus — but, like most things in life, if you have too much then it's not good for you at all. Theresa and Bob were good people and very worried about their daughter. They had good reason to be. They'd been at Helen's funeral as well.

Chloe was clinically depressed, which was bad; but she was taking antidepressants under close supervision from a child psychiatrist, which was good. She was getting individual help from an experienced clinician who was helping her to develop stronger coping mechanisms, which was also very good. The last thing she needed was touchy-feely stuff where she was encouraged to wallow in her feelings. What she needed most were strategies to get her up and engaged in the world.

At this point, there are a few frameworks we need to remember when we're trying to figure out where Chloe is at. The most important is the fact that breathing = hope, and it has never been more true than it is here. Mixed in with all the usual swirling stuff is the fact that she's grieving for a dead friend, and is clearly feeling overwhelmed at times, hence the cutting.

The problem now was that Theresa and Bob's fear — albeit completely justified — was driving a wedge between them and Chloe. They had become so fearful and hyper-vigilant about it that they were pushing her away just at the time they needed to be drawing her closer.

In such dire circumstances, where does a parent draw the line between prudent concern and destructive intrusiveness?

What would be better than this?

At one level, it was easy. Chloe just wanted everyone to leave her alone, and her parents wanted to know she was safe. The only problem with that was that both things were impossible. No parent in their right mind would leave Chloe alone, and rightly so. Leaving her alone would be about the worst thing that you could do.

By the same token, there is no way for her parents to know she is safe other than to have her admitted to hospital under 24-hour observation. Even if they did that, and the available information wouldn't support such a drastic course of action, eventually she's going to get out.

In the end, after we'd talked it through a bit more everybody settled for something a little greyer. Chloe wanted a little more of her privacy back, and her parents wanted at least some kind of reassurance that she was OK.

My goal was a little clearer: stepped progression back to a more 'normal' family life, and that would be contingent on a number of factors we'll talk about a bit further on. Before we do that, though, first I'd like to run over some of the important things all parents should know about this issue.

Age and suicide

In the majority of developed nations, youth suicide is usually the second or third highest cause of deaths in young people between the ages of 15 and 24. Suicides under the age of 15 are very rare. They still happen, but they're rare. The majority of deaths are in the 18 and older age bracket. The good news is that youth suicide rates have been declining over the past 10 years. In some countries, including New Zealand and Australia, the rate has reduced quite markedly.

The gender paradox

The 'gender paradox' refers to the fact that, whilst girls make more suicide attempts than boys, they are less likely to die than boys. Girls tend to make more attempts because they are more prone to the kinds of depressive and anxiety disorders which place them at higher risk. Boys are more likely to die because, even though they make fewer attempts, they tend to use more lethal methods, such as carbon monoxide poisoning from vehicle exhaust, hanging or shooting themselves. Girls tend to choose drug overdose as a method, which is far less likely to be lethal.

Risk factors

✩ **Psychiatric illness** — approximately 90% of young people who die or make a serious attempt have an underlying psychiatric illness such as depression.

✩ **Substance abuse** — alcohol is a depressant and lowers inhibitions, just as substance abuse or dependence creates similar problems.

✩ **Family dysfunction** — things like poor relationships with parents, family history of suicide, abuse and/or neglect increase the risk.

✩ **Stressful life events** — often attempts are preceded by particularly stressful events, such as relationship breakdowns.

✩ **Stressful life circumstances** — this could include things like trouble at school, sexual-orientation issues, feeling isolated from their peers, or illnesses.

✩ **Access to methods** — pretty obvious really, but if you have access to the materials you've got a better chance of succeeding.

Warning signs

If you are concerned about the risk of suicide, there are a number of warning signs that you should look out for. It's important to remember, though, that these are not definitive or definite signs. The golden rule is that, if you are in any doubt, get some professional help.

✩ Talks or writes about committing suicide.

✧ Changes in eating or sleeping patterns.

✧ Significant change in behaviour.

✧ A sudden 'improvement' in depressed mood.

✧ Losing interest in previously enjoyable activities.

✧ Withdrawing from friends and family.

✧ Making a will and/or giving away prized possessions.

✧ Stressful life events, such as relationship break-ups.

✧ Increased alcohol and/or drug use.

✧ Apologizing for past behaviour.

What should you do?

There are a number of things that you can and should do if you are concerned.

✧ Talk about your concerns with them. Be direct and talk about suicide. Say the s-word.

✧ Listen to what they say, and make sure you use your poker face, because if you look like you're freaking out they'll clam up. Be calm, or at least convincingly portray calmness.

✧ Don't try to brush over the stuff that is upsetting them, but don't wallow in it either. Instead, try to understand it.

✧ Don't lecture them, because if you do that they won't come to you again.

✧ Make sure they know you're there, and that you want to do whatever you can to help them.

✧ Make the immediate environment as safe as you can. Get rid of ropes, guns, hoses, and any pills. Do it subtly.

☆ Get help. Talk to them about this first, but if you're worried then you need to get some professional help. There are many agencies around, and even if you ring the wrong one they will give you the direct number to the right one. It doesn't matter who, just ring someone.

What needs to happen to get there for Chloe and her family?

Theresa and Bob had done all the right things, and they were getting expert help and advice about the suicide risk and the underlying issues. They already had all the information I've just covered, so we had to focus more on how to get things a little more normal for their family.

Recall again the basic principles from Part II:

1 $R^3 - F$.
2 Remember Mad Uncle Jack.
3 Don't be a Big Jessie.
4 Not too loose, not too tight.
5 Find points of contact.
6 Punctuation is everything.
7 Be the rock, not the sea.
8 Don't make their problem your problem.
9 Keep making decisions.
10 Life is suffering.

What we need here are generous helpings of 1, 3, 4, 5, 6, 7, 9, and 10.

They need to focus on building their relationship with Chloe and in finding points of contact. They need to continue to monitor her (not too loose), but not crowd her (not too tight). So that they could work out what that would look like, we would need to negotiate where the line should be drawn between monitoring and intruding.

Most of all they needed to give her their time and attention without swamping her. Shopping with mum, coffees with dad. Not all the time, just enough for them all to know they were all still there.

Points of contact.

There needed to be some flow of information between Chloe, her parents, and the people working with them, which both respected Chloe's right to privacy and her parents' right to know she was doing OK.

Fixing stuff

It was a slow road back to normality for this family, but day by day they plugged on. In truth, I don't think the spectre of suicide would ever be gone from her parents' minds, but they were all doing OK.

As each day passed, together with the specialized help she was getting, Chloe seemed to get a little happier. Her parents made a real effort not to hover, and she made a reciprocal effort to let them know something about what was going on for her.

I think the greatest change was that Theresa and Bob learned how to live with the constant background fear that Chloe might kill herself. It never went away, but it learned to sit quietly at the back door. Instead, they focused their efforts on really connecting with their daughter, on trying to get to know her on her own terms.

Breathing = Hope.

Lessons from the road

★ Be vigilant.

★ Knowledge is power — know the warning signs.

★ Talk about it. Be direct. Use the s-word, and use your poker face.

★ Take action if you're concerned. Take whatever steps are necessary to make them safe.

★ Support, monitor, but don't crowd.

★ Get help.

★ Just be there; be there as much and as little as they need.

★ Be there as if their life depended on it.

★ Just do it quietly.

28

toby and the tribe
of hairy women

angry boys, single mums,
non-compliance, taking a stand

REFERRAL INFORMATION

Family details	Alice (mother), with Toby (14)
Presenting problem	Toby is rude and non-compliant. Won't do simple tasks around home. Ignores his mother whenever she asks him to help out. When he isn't ignoring her, he's rude and sulky. She feels powerless and doesn't know what to do.

You'll recall from our earlier session with Toby and his mum in Chapter 17 that this young man seemed to take considerable pleasure from winding his mum up. His dad had been gone for many years and played virtually no role in his life. Toby had become a Neanderthal, and Alice was trying to get him through his teenage years flying solo.

When I'd initially met with Alice, I suggested she put the Ladder of Certain Doom in place and, while she liked the idea, she was worried that he wouldn't listen to her. This time, she's come alone so we could talk more about how she could get some changes going at home.

'I could tell him that he was going to be losing time off his curfew, but I don't think he'd listen,' she said.

This is a common concern of parents: that their teenage children simply won't listen to any consequences they put in place. The fear that they will be ignored leaves many parents feeling powerless and frustrated; not a good place to be when you've got an outbreak of adolescence at your home.

'Can you give me a typical example of a time in your house when it gets ugly?' I asked Alice.

'Just this morning, before I left. I told him he needed to get up to go to school, but he just lay in his bed and said nothing. I give him five minutes and he's still not up, so I go back and start yelling at him 'til he finally gets up and stomps off to the bathroom. He takes ages in there, then he says he just wants toast for breakfast and we have another argument about that. When he finally stomps out of the house, he's already 20 minutes late for school.' She sighed — the frustrated, exhausted, angry variation of the common sigh. 'It doesn't seem to matter what I say, or how many time I say it, he just does whatever he likes.'

'And you think that if you gave him an early curfew he wouldn't listen?'

She nodded. 'Yup.'

'What is he into?'

'Nothing.'

'Nothing at all?'

'Nope. He just likes watching television, playing on his Playstation, and walking the streets with his mates.'

'And you said before that his friends' parents say he's a lovely boy?'

'Yeah, I can't understand it. They say he's polite, and helpful, and never a problem. Yet all I get at home is this shitty behaviour.'

'So his friends' parents say he's a nice boy, but you just get shittyness?'

'Yup.'

'Do you have the internet at home?'

She shook her head. 'No, that's one of the things he's constantly complaining about.'

'Do you have any friends who do?'

'My neighbour does.'

I smiled. 'Great. I'm going to introduce you to the wonders of YouTube.'

'What's that?' she asked.

'It's a website with lots of videos that all kinds of people send in. It's fantastic, a bit like cocaine in a computer.'

'Is that good?'

I shrugged. 'No . . . and yes, but we're not going to get hung up on all that. I just want you to go look at some videos of silverbacks.'

'Silver-what?' she frowned.

'Silverbacks. Let me explain . . .'

Where does it all go pear-shaped?

It is perhaps one of the great themes of modern parenting that mums and dads everywhere are having a crisis of confidence. We are faced with all kinds of problems and with kids who seem older and more sophisticated than we ever were. Increasing numbers of us seem to be throwing up our hands in despair. We don't know what the right thing to do is, and so we do nothing.

All of which is why parenting is definitely easier if it's a team sport. The best parenting teams work like tag wrestlers: first one has a crack, and then tags their partner in when they need a break.

Tag wrestling by yourself doesn't work. If you're single, then you're playing a whole different game. Stamina is the goal when you're doing it alone, because there's no one waiting to take over when you get tired.

In Alice's case, she's raising a boy all by herself, and struggling with all the guilt that single mums feel about not having a male role model for their boys. What's more, Toby is a stubborn wee soul who knows exactly how to push his mum's buttons.

If we hark back to the bombproof frameworks from Part I, it's clear that there are a number of things going on. Uncle Jack is quite mad, his brain is not seeing the same world that Alice is. Toby is emotional, and sullen, and generally grumpy. He is a tank, and always has been. He's also employing a number of WMDs, including Fear, Guilt, Exhaustion, and Tactical Hatred. More than anything else, he is a Neanderthal, with all that this brings.

Toby also believes — wrongly — that there is nothing his mother can really do. That in itself isn't the problem; instead, the real issue is that Alice also believes there's nothing she can do.

It is true that when children are younger it's easier to deal with bad behaviour, because we can just pick them up and put them in time out, or some such thing. There comes a point, though, where the power balance begins to shift, where kids start to wonder what their parents really can do, and that is where it *really* starts to get interesting.

Alice had made that most common of mistakes: thinking that limited options means no options. It doesn't. It just means you have to be more focused, and be smarter than them. You must be determined and resolute.

And hairy — but more of that in a moment . . .

What would be better than this?

'I don't know if anything is possible,' Alice had said when I'd asked her.

'How about his following some basic rules that you both negotiate and agree to?'

'I'd like that, but I don't think he'd ever do it.'

'That's OK, we can figure all that out. But would that be better?'

She nodded: 'Yes.'

Yes would do just fine.

What needs to happen to get there?

We've already talked about the LoCD, but now we need to work out how Alice can apply it effectively. Not surprisingly, our first stop is having a look at some basic principles:

1 $R^3 - F$.

2 Remember Mad Uncle Jack.

3 Don't be a Big Jessie.

4 Not too loose, not too tight.

5 Find points of contact.

6 Punctuation is everything.

7 Be the rock, not the sea.

8 Don't make their problem your problem.

9 Keep making decisions.

10 Life is suffering.

Again, as you look at this list it's a little obvious where Alice may have been losing her way. All you need to do is start orienting yourself to these principles and courses of action start to emerge all by themselves. If you remember Mad Uncle Jack, this changes how you react to what your teen says. If you think about the principle of 'not too loose, not too tight', then you start thinking about where it might be too loose, and where it might be too tight. If you start thinking about the importance of punctuation, then it changes what you say and how you say it.

This is the reason I'm such a big fan of having some basic principles to operate under, because they act like a compass when you're not sure which way to go.

So what we need to do here is tighten things up a little, and find a way to make this *Toby's* problem and not his mother's. To do this, I suggested Alice take the following steps:

1   Get the family rules sorted (see page 165) so that the expectations are clear.

2   Negotiate these with Toby so that he feels involved and not simply dictated to (see page 164).

3   Explain the LoCD as described in Chapter 17.

4   Use curfew time as the leverage, because 'roaming the streets with his mates' is what he likes.

5   If he ignores a reduced curfew time, then go into his room every 15 minutes past his curfew time until he comes home and take something precious away.

6   Start with his television, then the Playstation power cable, then anything that isn't nailed down.

7   If you have to, take *everything* — his clothes, shoes, everything.

8   Leave only a mattress and a blanket.

9   If you think he'd just take his stuff back, arrange to stash it at the neighbour's.

10   He gets his stuff back only when he gets home on time for his next curfew. For each night he gets home on time, he can have five things back. (This is individual items, not classes of items. For example, if he says he wants his underpants back, then he gets only one pair, not all of them.)

11   You are allowed to give him fresh clothes each day, but only one change of clothes and you get to choose what it is, not him.

Draconian?

Depends who you ask.

You see Alice is by herself and she's being ignored. She needs to act decisively if she's going to make Toby understand that she's actually the boss. He gets a say, but she's the boss. Toby thinks he can run the show any way he wants, and so he needs to get a clear and unambiguous message that he isn't in charge, his mother is. As we discussed back in Chapter 16, effective punishments are fair, contingent on behaviour, and make kids do the maths. Effective punishments give kids a reason not to be bad.

To achieve the attitude change that was necessary for Alice to do this, we would first have to go on a YouTube safari.

Single mums, sons, and the tribe of hairy women

Many mums raising boys by themselves worry desperately about the need to provide their sons with good male role models. We hear a lot about this stuff, which inevitably puts yet another burden on the shoulders of good mums going it alone.

Of course it goes without saying that it is a good thing if boys have access to positive male role models. A good bloke brings with him man-wisdom, and man-wisdom is good for boys. Man-wisdom is about understanding that sometimes words get in the way of communication. Man-wisdom is about the value of humour, and loyalty, and not making a fuss about stuff. Man-wisdom is knowing that you lead by what you do. Man-wisdom is about watching over the clan. Man-wisdom is about knowing that the world won't end if the toilet seat is left up.

The problem is that, for many mums, there simply are no male role models. Sometimes there is no sports coach, no neighbour, no uncle, or stepdad.

Sometimes the vacancy remains empty.

So what do you do if there really is no male role model?

Well, the first thing is not to get too stressed about it. Do what you can, by all means; but if there's no one there, then there's no one there.

Life will go on.

In the hierarchy of needs, there are other things that are far more important: food, water, shelter, and the love of a concerned adult are *all* more important.

These are also *all* things that are in your control.

Male role models are good for boys, and they're important, but not so important that you see the United Nations arranging airdrops of male role models in times of disaster. Usually they drop off stuff like water, rice, tents, blankets and medicine. You'd be pretty pissed off if you were huddling cold and hungry amidst the flood-ravaged ruins of your home and the UN planes dropped a lean blond-haired man named Brad who only wanted to go kick a soccer ball around with you.

If things were bad enough, you'd probably kill Brad and eat him. Actually, you'd probably kill him just on general principle.

So, apart from not getting too stressed, what else can you do?

Here's what you do: you go to YouTube and type in the word 'silverback'. What will happen next is that a whole lot of videos will come up. Some of them will be for bands, and some of them will be crazy people. Ignore those ones.

Maybe watch the crazy people ones later once the work is done.

What you're primarily interested in are the videos that come up of silverback gorillas, because if you watch them you'll get a lesson in how to be with boys. The silverback is a remarkable animal. They are quiet and dignified, and radiate strength. A silverback could crush a person with one blow, but will let the baby gorillas hang off them like little hairy lunatics because they know that this is simply what little gorillas need to do.

They are patient with the young.

And if you watch these amazing creatures, you are in no doubt that you do not want to fuck with a silverback.

In fact, the role of the silverback in gorilla families is quite complex. They lead a group of 5–30 and are the centre of the family life. They make the big decisions, they choose which direction the family is headed in, they mediate conflict, and they are responsible for the wellbeing of the group.

If necessary, they will die protecting their families.

Watch a few movies and you'll see what I mean. There is a silverback vibe that is unmistakably masculine. It has its own quiet, calm, gentle power. *That* is what you should aim for, because that's what your boys *need* you to be.

Piffle, you say. I'm a lady, that's not my thing.

Well, here's something spooky you might want to consider. In 1847, a man called Thomas Savage wrote about a new type of animal he'd discovered in Africa. He decided to call them *Troglodytes gorilla,* choosing the name from a description he'd read from a Carthaginian called Hanno the Navigator, who had explored the North African coast in 480BC. On his travels, Hanno had seen a peculiar beast that he had called 'Gorillai' from the Greek meaning 'tribe of hairy women', because that's what he thought they were.

Some 24 centuries later, when Savage first saw the animals we now know as gorillas, he recalled Hanno's writings and choose that name to describe these majestic creatures.

Gorillai.

Tribe of hairy women.

No greater compliment has ever been paid.

Fixing stuff

Alice went home and watched every silverbacks video she could find on YouTube.

She got it.

Then she went to work.

It was a fairly fraught week, that first week, but she stuck to it. She negotiated the rules, she set up the LoCD, and she took Toby's stuff when he ignored his curfew. Actually, quite a bit of stuff.

He wailed and complained.

She chewed a leaf and casually picked tics from his head.

He squealed and said rude words.

She ambled over and took some more of his stuff and hid it in the jungle.

He slammed doors.

She sat amidst the rich, tropical foliage and watched him go, replete in the knowledge that sometimes young male gorillas need to beat their chests a little.

And, little by little, things improved.

She made a stand that was hard, clear, negotiated, but fair. Toby was a nice-enough kid underneath, so he wasn't going to take it all the way to Armageddon. He wasn't about to burn the jungle down, because he had nowhere else to go, and he was too young to set up his own troop, so in the end he backed down.

In my experience, if you stack the odds right, then the vast majority of them do.

It would get easier with time for Alice, because increasingly Toby was maturing and readying himself for the moment when he would strike out on his own to find a mate and set up his own group, but not for a while. For now, he was just playing at being a silverback.

Luckily for him, Alice was the *real* deal.

Lessons from the road

✦ Don't let them make you feel like there's nothing you can do.

✦ There's always something you can do.

✦ Establish your bottom-lines and then stick to them.

✦ Find male role models for your boys if you can; but if they're not there, don't stress too much because they'll still be fine.

✦ If you're flying this one solo, simply remember the tribes of hairy women — they've been doing this stuff for centuries.

29

getting it sorted:
a step-by-step guide

At the very beginning of all this, I said that there were no paint-by-numbers solutions, no one-size-fits-all answers, and I would still stand by that. Now, having said all that, what I do want to leave you with at the end of all this is a very clear process you can use to figure out what to do if you're up against it.

What I've done below is outline each of the three steps and provide some questions you might want to ask yourself along the way.

Step 1: Where has it all gone pear-shaped?

This is where you use the basic frameworks to help you get your head around what is going on for them.

Breathing = Hope

Have I got things in perspective?

Would I rather be facing this problem or visiting them in an oncology ward?

The weirdness of puberty

How far through the journey are they?

What are the puberty-related stressors they're carrying
around?

What are the other 'teenage-specific' problems they may be
having outside of this, such as boyfriend/girlfriend problems
or popularity issues at school?

Mad Uncle Jack

Do I feel hurt when they are rude/nasty to me?

Am I taking their rudeness/nastiness personally?

Why on earth am I doing that?

The teenage brain: not the whole walnut

What evidence is there that they aren't functioning like adults?

Are they emotional? Grumpy? Impulsive? Irrational?
Unreasonable?

Do they accuse me of being angry when I'm not?

What changes have I seen in how they function in the past six
months? One year? Two years?

Weapons of Mass Disruption

Confusion

Deflection

Distraction

Fear

Guilt

Splitting

Exhaustion

Collective bargaining

The pseudo broken heart

False hope

Start high

Tactical hatred

Violence.

A tank will always be a tank

What kind of vehicle is my teenager's personality?

A tank? A Ferrari? A people-mover? A bus? A scooter? A bulldozer? A combine-harvester?

What's good about that?

What's not so good?

What skills do they need to learn to get along with the world better?

How can I teach them to do that? (Hint: Break it down into little steps and teach them one bit at a time.)

The rise of the Neanderthal

How much of a Neanderthal is he?

How does that affect how he sees the world?

What does he want from me?

What does he actually need from me?

The bitchy physics of the Girl-niverse

How far out in the Girl-niverse is she?

How does that affect how she sees the world?

What does she want from me?

What does she need from me?

Systems thinking

What are the ways in which we all influence each other in this situation?

What do they all do that makes it worse?

What do I do that makes it worse?

Extra information

Gather any specialist information that you need to help you figure out what's wrong. If you're worried about drugs, find out what you need to know about those specific drugs. If you're worried about bullying, google that, and ask your kid's school what their bullying policy is. If you're worried about depression or eating disorders, find out about that. You can get enormous amounts of information from the internet, you can talk to friends, or you can talk to a professional. There are more places you can get specialist information from than you have time to visit, so make the most of this incredible connected world that we live in and find out what you need to know.

Step 2: What would be better than this?

Remember that the aim is not to come up with a plan to make life completely perfect. That will likely be impossible. All you want to do is figure out what would make it better than what it is right now. Once you've done that, test your goal with these questions:

> Does it take into account the issues raised from the frameworks?
>
> What's in it for them?
>
> What's in it for me?
>
> Is it achievable?
>
> Is it fair?

Step 3: What needs to happen to get there?

Use the basic principles as your compass to help guide your response:

1 $R^3 - F$.

2 Remember Mad Uncle Jack.

3 Don't be a Big Jessie.

4 Not too loose, not too tight.

5 Find points of contact.

6 Punctuation is everything.

7 Be the rock, not the sea.

8 Don't make their problem your problem.

9 Keep making decisions.

10 Life is suffering.

Set rules
All kids need structure, and they need to know where the limits are. Define your bottom-lines.

Negotiate
It's never good to simply impose things on teenagers. If you involve them in negotiating the rules and limits, they are more likely to follow them.

Remember, too, that they need a reason to be good *and* a reason not to be bad

Evaluate
Once you've made some changes to how things operate in your family, continue to evaluate how helpful the new regime is. There's nothing wrong with a bad idea, but there's a lot wrong with holding onto it when it's clearly not helping. Evaluate, and if necessary change course.

If you need outside help, get some
There is no shame in asking for help. Many parents are periodically faced with issues that are bigger than what they can deal with themselves. Keep going until you get the help that you need.

part V

the end
times

The real test for any system is the End Times.

If you can survive that, you can survive anything. We've talked about frameworks, and principles, and simple plans — but just how robust are they?

Would they, just for instance, still be effective in managing teenagers' behaviour when the human race is teetering on the brink of extinction because a genetically-engineered virus has turned almost the entire population of the world into rabid vampire-like mutants intent on eating anyone not infected?

Would all this stuff still work then?

Yup.

29

principles and
popcorn

So you want irony?

I'll give you irony.

And vampires.

It's a Wednesday night and I'm at the movies — not just any movie, though: I'm watching Will Smith in *I am Legend*, which is a fantastically scary movie. In a nutshell, he's the last person left alive in New York, possibly the world, after a plan to use a genetically-engineered variant of the measles virus to cure cancer has gone completely pear-shaped. The virus has killed 90% of us and turned just about everyone else who is left into incredibly scary, rabid vampire mutants. During the day, they retreat into groups called 'hives', huddling in the basements of abandoned buildings and panting in unison in a particularly scary way. At night, they come out *en masse* and spend the hours of darkness running around screaming and howling, looking for people to eat.

Looking very hard.

Just that day, I had typed the last full-stop of this book — apart from this last chapter, of course — and the movie was my treat for getting it finished. Because I'm a bloke, I use bloke time-management, which is leave it until the last possible minute and then work incredibly hard to get the job done. I'd spent the past eight weeks living and breathing teenagers, and behaviour, and all the things you've just been reading about. Which is where the irony comes in, because, after eight weeks of living, breathing, and writing teenagers, this was my first night away from them. This was the first night my thoughts wouldn't have to be consumed with the endless whims and vagaries of teenagers.

So off I went to the movies to see a film I'd been looking forward to seeing ever since I'd seen the very first trailer. Yet that particular night, of the 20 or so people in the theatre, 17 were under the age of 17. They gathered in their own little adolescent hives and proceeded to giggle and chatter their way through the movie. These hives weren't scary; just very bloody annoying.

I'm pretty sure that going to a movie on the first night off from writing about teenagers I'd had in eight weeks and then ending up surrounded by annoying teenagers qualified as ironic.

There was a particularly hilarious ongoing gag amongst the young people, whereby someone would go 'ssshhhhhh', which would be answered by someone else going 'ssshhhhhh', and so on, and so on, and so on.

It was just terrifically amusing.

I tried to be a good sport about the whole thing at first. I tried to tell myself that they were just kids being kids, out having a good time with their mates.

Come on, I chided myself, *you of all people should be understanding about this stuff. You just wrote a whole book about them for gosh-diddly-darned sake. They're young, so how about you just cut the kids a break, huh?*

Except the thing was that all I actually wanted to do was watch my movie in peace and quiet.

There was one particular group down the front who were the loudest and most irritating. Three girls and four boys, none of them over 15. I noted with some intellectual curiosity that during a couple of the very sad scenes they all giggled.

Unripe amygdalas and shoddy pre-frontal cortexes, I muttered to myself.

Yet even these intellectual observations could not suppress the growing sense of utter bloody annoyance that was mounting. I sat there stewing.

Then it hit me.

I'd just spent all this time writing about teenagers. I *should* know what to do. It was just a matter of running through the steps.

So where was it going pear-shaped?

Well, I was making their problem my problem.

What would be better than this?

If they were to shut-the-hell-up so I could enjoy my bloody movie.

What needs to happen to get there?

Simple.

'It's not just me, is it?' I whispered to my wife. 'Are they bloody noisy?'

She nodded. 'Yes, they are.'

'Right,' I said, leaping to me feet.

She made a grab for my arm, sensing quite correctly my intentions, but luckily she missed.

I walked with the purposeful gait of a man on a mission, a man who carries with him not so much as even a single ounce of Big Jessie. I approached the group from behind, electing to loom over them from the second row judging that this would be more of a surprise and lend me a generally more menacing air.

I picked the middle of their giggly little hive to make my entrance: 'Look,' I said, using the tone I usually reserve for teen hoods, 'I didn't pay 25 bucks to listen to *you* guys, so can you *shut up.*'

No question mark was needed because it wasn't a question. Having now said my piece, I went back to my seat and enjoyed the rest of the movie.

In silence.

Not too loose, not too tight.

Mostly not too loose.